MISERICORDE

BOOK ONE OF THE MERCY SERIES

CYNTHIA A. MORGAN

With special thanks and appreciation to:

My Beloved

And

Jennifer Hughes- for your valuable support and
feedback, even during your own challenges.

———

I am Blessed and Truly Thankful for all the Mercy that
has touched my life.

PREFACE

The Mercy Series is a Post-Apocalyptic Fantasy Romance that takes place in the future of our own planet. It is the year 2446. The first three Horsemen of Revelation's Apocalypse have ridden. Pestilence, War and Famine have shifted world-wide cultures and governments from technologically advanced civilizations to dictatorships that are ruled with an iron-fist and where commoners have very few rights. Liberty is a distant memory.

Many of the references you come across will be familiar, but some of the names I've created 'out of thin air'. This brief lexicon is provided in the hope of creating a less frustrating and more dynamic reading experience.

PHONETIC PRONUNCIATIONS:

Miséricorde – Miss air ee cord- Which means Mercy
in French
Tzadkiel - T zad key el
Le Châtelet – Leh Shat elay
Lévesque – Leh ves kuw
Marçais – Marsay
Phillippe – Fill eep
Delacour – Del a core
Hashmallim – Hash Mall eem
Brigyda – Bri gee da
Madam Ornaly – Madam Or nall ee
Ghislain – Gis lain (Soft G as in give)
Privoweth, shunar rivway – Prih vow eth shu nawr
rihv way
Chambon – Sham bohn
Sauvage – Saw vawg (soft G sound like in the word en-
tourage)
Keervath uneeya braven – Keer vawth ooneeva
brahven
Jshunamir – Zshoo naw meer
Chevalier – Sheh volley aye
Sra loothath – Sraw lee thawth
Cerise – Share ees
Binow quiron? Vroth cara mixtok – Bih now keeron?
Vrawth cara mix tock
Travere – Tra Vayre
Daigrepont – Day greh pon
Dai – Day

She was only a scullery maid.
Nothing.
No one.

She was as unimportant as the scraps she cleaned up and just as forgettable. She had been inconsequential since the moment she arrived at The Bastion of Resolution and nothing would ever change that. She knew it and she expected nothing. Ever since she was twelve years old, she understood that those around her were far better than she. Growing up in the presence of others far above her station, she had learned her life was trivial and meaningless; in comparison to those who made The Bastion their home she was nothing and she accepted this as fact.

As the long and tedious years passed, she grew into a young woman and her gangly, childish body matured into rounded curves and blushing tones. Although her heart longed for a connection with another, she understood that no one would ever turn their head to look at her. It was a heavy weight to bear, but she also realized it was much better that way. Her features were undeniably lovely, but with her chestnut-red hair pulled up tightly under her servant's cap, her body cloaked in dull gray, wrinkled servant's garments that were stained from over-use, and her hands cracked and reddened from exposure and hard labor she garnered no interest from those around her. No one looked closely enough to notice her and she had learned not to gaze wonderingly at anyone else. It was safer to go unnoticed.

Day in and day out she went about her tasks, toiling with heavy buckets of wash-water, scraping leavings from delicate china, scouring pots and pans, peeling countless vegetables, trimming succulent cuts of meat she would never taste, and crying from more than the onions she chopped, but she was only a scullery maid.

Nothing.

No one.

She was simply one of many who lived and breathed beneath the notice of those around them. Her betters were interesting, beautiful, wealthy, and above all, powerful. When they spoke, others rushed to serve. Where they wished to go, others made way. They were inaccessible and inescapable. Those who made the Bastion their home were the officers of the ruling faction, The Eminent Protectorate, and their families who outranked even the nobles of the land. No one questioned them. Ever. Those of the Eminent Protectorate were the elite of society and, in a world where poverty was common-place and where being healthy was a rare distinction among the masses, serving was a privilege most commoners could only dream of experiencing.

Year 2446.
The 96th Year of the 4th Era after the Great Cataclysm
Le Bastion de la Résolution, - Marçais, New France

Nearly every night for the past year she heard the screams. When they first began, she'd cried herself to sleep for many nights, desperately trying not to hear them. After several nights of being forced to listen to them, she found herself leaning from her small window in the servant's tower trying to locate their source, but the stone walls of The Bastion of Resolution, an ancient fortress the Eminent Protectorate had claimed as their headquarters, sent echoes scattering in all directions. Screams were not uncommon in this place, but these stole her sleep and broke her heart. She could not quite fathom why they should be more terrible than the many others she had heard throughout the years of her residence there, but they were far worse, somehow. Each night she sought their source and when she could not find it, she offered a soft prayer for the one who suffered.

Now, after nearly a year of hearing them, she'd grown horrifyingly accustomed to the sound. It was not because they no longer tore at her heart, because they did, each night, every time. Now, however, she accepted them, just as she accepted her own plight. She knew there was nothing she could do for the one who suffered. She could not change their situation any more than she could change her own. Both of them had little choice other than to endure their predicament. Life at the hands of The Protectorate was, by its very nature, precarious. The Protectorate was above scrutiny and at liberty to do as they wished. They would not be questioned about screams of torture any more than they would be interrogated for their merciless governing policies or ruthlessness. Whoever the poor soul was who bore such brutal torment, they were doomed to continue suffering without any more hope of rescue than she might wish for.

Less.

Climbing the ten flights of circling stairs that led upward to her tiny tower chamber as she had done every night since she had been taken on by the Eminent Protectorate nearly ten years earlier, Lourdes nibbled on an apple she had found on the dining room floor after the officers and their families had finished their evening meal and retired. The food that touched the tables of the Eminent Protectorate was off limits, but servants were permitted to scavenge any of the day's leavings after the end of their shift, which was typically around ten o'clock at night. The only meals provided for servants were a small breakfast each morning at five and a meager supper twelve hours later, so, although scraps were just that, scraps, they were also a necessity.

Weary in body and numb of mind, she trudged up the slowly circling stairs in a haze of exhaustion. Her days were all the same, filled with labor and drudgery in an endless routine that had grown boring years ago, but she had no options. She was alone in the world; an orphan of no consequence who was suitable only for service. She had been fortunate to be given the chance to prove herself when she turned up at The Bastion. She was only twelve years old at the time and had no reference papers or identification of any kind, but they gave her a position as a scullery maid. It wasn't ideal, but she had very few choices, then or now. The Protectorate was her best option. Although a life of service was taxing, often in the extreme, things could be far worse. She could have been relegated to the life of a regimental whore, doomed to a brief and painful existence.

It was something she didn't like to think about.

Turning the handle of her chamber door, she clenched the apple between her teeth as she stepped inside and paused to light the candle waiting on a wooden crate placed beside the door for just such a purpose. When it glimmered dimly, she continued inward with the candleholder in one hand and the remnants of the apple in her other. The room was exceptionally dark. No moonlight shone through her small window from the cloud-filled sky above and she squinted into the darkness to find her way. Setting the candle down upon her table, which was little more than a few boards tied together with old twine supported by four logs she had managed to acquire before they were split for kindling, she took another bite of the apple and moved toward the window. It was a humid, summer night; sultry with little air moving, but any breath of breeze would help cool her and make her small room more comfortable for sleeping. Pushing the ancient shutters of The Bastion window further open to receive whatever air the night had to offer, she stood for a moment with closed eyes, listening.

Quiet.

"That's odd," she murmured and then she nearly choked. Quiet because there were no screams. "Oh, God!" She knew what silence meant and, despite the fact that she had never met, nor even seen the one for whom she quietly mourned, she bowed her head briefly. There was so little love left in the world, only hatred and fear, avarice and ambition. Although she didn't know anything about the one who was so unexpectedly silent, she offered a wordless thought of peace for them before she turned from the window to gaze around her room. Though her world was humble, it was at least secure. No one ever came to hammer on her door to force their way inward. No one ever demanded anything other than what her duties as a scullery maid dictated and, for that, she was exceptionally thankful. Keeping her hair pulled up in a tight, unattractive knot and wearing clothes that were over-large and unkempt hid her features from curious and unwanted gazers, and ensured her safety.

Gazing around her small chambers, she realized it wasn't much of a world. Not really. All she had was one small table, a deep windowsill below a small window, a minuscule fireplace large enough for only two logs and a kettle, a rope-framed cot with a straw-filled mattress, a solitary washstand, a handful of crockery and a few uniforms. It wasn't much at all, but she realized it was far more than many enjoyed in a world where poverty was common and comfort was rare. Below, in the great halls of The Bastion, luxury and comfort abounded. Lavish carpets and ornate wall-hangings proclaimed the affluence of The Protectorate. Fine linen draperies bedecked the many broad windows; silver and crystal adorned the over-sized tables, and silks and soft linens clothed the fortunate. Clean running water was pumped through elaborate systems whenever desired; food was plentiful to fill the bellies of the privileged and safety was never questioned. Those of the Eminent Protectorate had more than enough of whatever they wanted, while she and so many like her had....

A chilling scream echoed from the bulwarks and she twisted in surprise, staring out the window with sudden trepidation. The cry hung on the thick, summer air as if the one who gave it voice was standing just outside. She listened in breathless dismay, dreading the silence she expected to follow as much as she feared another scream. Death would have been far better than the endless torture the poor soul endured. It was a harsh thought, but how they survived such torment was beyond her comprehension; it seemed impossible.

6

Several moments passed. The stillness of the dark night was consumed by the hammering of her heart while she waited. Anxiety twisted within her until she was made nearly sick by it; then, another scream pierced the blackness that was even more blood-curdling than the first.

"What are they doing to you?" Unexpected tears slipped from her distinctive, caramel-hued eyes and she moved suddenly to close the window, hoping to drown out the harrowing screams, but the weather-worn shutters barely held the elements at bay and could not silence such piercing cries. As she stood in the center of her small room, the heartless action she had taken weighed on her like a heavy millstone. She couldn't bear the sense that she'd shut out the very one who needed her compassion the most and forced them into an insolation even greater than what they already endured. After several agonizing moments, she turned back and opened the shutters once more, staring out into the darkness as she searched the ramparts, avenues, and walls with guilt-ridden desperation.

"I'm so sorry. If you can bear it, I can bear it. You're not alone." Her whispered sympathy drifted into the sultry night, but only the distant drone of machinery from the mines of Le Châtelet answered her and, after what felt like hours, she finally turned away.

"I've got to sleep. I hope you are too." Finishing the apple with a knot in her stomach that made her feel queasy rather than satisfied, she peeled off her uniform, gave it a generous powdering with scented talcum, shook it vigorously and hung it beside the window to refresh. Water was a valuable commodity and servants were only permitted to do their laundry once each week, so she had to make the best of the four uniforms and three aprons she had been provided. Blowing out her candle, she trod wearily to her cot and lay down with a heavy sigh.

Tired.

So Tired.

She wasn't sure if she had just closed her eyes or if she had been asleep for hours, but she was awakened by another shrill scream that brought tears to her eyes even before she opened them. Not just one, not this time. This time the screams continued, one after the other, until the sound was like a blade burying itself inside her. Covering her ears in a futile attempt to keep herself from hearing, she was only successful in muffling the repeated, agonized cries. Shaking her head with an inability to comprehend such cruelty and deep remorse at being unable to help in any way, she sat listening until she couldn't bear the horrifying screams another moment. Lunging up from her bed, she rushed to the window and shouted in anger.

"Stop hurting him! You horrible monsters!" The second the words flew from her lips she clamped her hands across her mouth in terror. Was she a fool? If anyone heard her outburst, she could lose her position and be flung out into the poverty of the crumbling city around The Bastion. Or worse, she could be handed over to the garrison commanders as punishment. The thought sent a shudder over her more terrifying than his screams.

Standing in appalled silence as his cries faded into hoarse wails that lingered on the heavy night air like an apparition, she felt insane with helpless desperation. Scanning the walls and battlements again, though she had searched them numerous times before, she sought the place from which his cries emanated. It wouldn't really matter if she discovered their source. There was nothing she could do for him, but she felt compelled to find him.

So many other nights when she stood in her window listening to his heartbreaking anguish, moonlight had brightened the dark stonework and no interior lights emanated from within the fortress to betray his location, but tonight no moon shone. Tonight, as his wails echoed across the ramparts, she spied a dim sliver of orange torchlight near the base of the tower that stood opposite and to the left of hers. Tonight, she looked down on the place where his voice called to her heart and she shuddered.

It was a place none were permitted to venture. Only those with the highest levels of clearance or servants with specific assignments could enter the gates and tunnels of Tower Obligar. It was a place none wished to go because it was where The Protectorate housed and tortured their prisoners. It was a place she couldn't possibly penetrate.

But she had to.

Somehow.

Year 2445.
The 95th Year of the 4th Era after the Great Cataclysm
The Coast of Calais, New France

He stood on the ocean shore, his back to what was left of a once vibrant landscape as his brilliant, violet gaze searched the empty miles of ocean before him. His essence listened for any sign of life, a heartbeat remaining among the silence of the deeps, but barely a single pulse broke the deathly hush. Humanity had caused a cataclysm entirely on its own. So much of what was once beautiful, colorful and diverse was gone.

The seas had died.

The thought pained him and he closed his eyes,

bowing his head to mourn what had been sacrificed and all that had been lost. Upon this lonely shore no terns cried on the ocean breeze and no laughing gulls sang praise to the skies; there was only the sound of the waves rushing and breaking upon the stones of the beach and the hollow moan of the wind. Without wings to dance upon it, the air itself seemed bereft and grief-stricken. In this languishing part of the world the song of the lark didn't cheer the entrance of the day and the carol of the robin didn't serenade the evening. The only songs that remained in this place, where pollutants had poisoned the waterways and decimated the once thriving eco-system, were the reverberations of count-less insects. These thrived in the predator-less environ-ment to the point of becoming their own form of pestilence and he cocked his gaze at the swarm of flying vermin dancing only a few yards from him.

The ruddy glimmer of the late day sun, slowly fading into a crimson haze behind the distant clouds, played through the layers of his shoulder-length blonde hair and sparkled across the perfection of his features. He was neither rugged nor boyish, but strikingly hand-some. His physique was tall and powerful, but not burly and his appearance was undeniably beautiful while still masculine. Black pants and a deep gray shirt accentu-ated his trim build as well as the vivid color of his eyes and he wore a gray leather harness across his back with a scabbard to carry a sword, though the weapon was currently sheathed in the scabbard at his hip. He bore no scars of any kind and wore around his neck an amethyst crystal upon a silver chain. The deep violet of the unworked stone matched the color of his eyes pre-cisely and glowed faintly as if it contained an internal light. Standing there upon the vast ocean shore, he was the most stunning sight for countless miles.

Behind him, a thunder of hooves pounded across

the beach and the coarse profanities of men accosted the quietness. He didn't turn to face them as they formed a perimeter around him, barricading him against the sea, nor did he immediately answer when they demanded to know who he was. Instead, he closed his violet eyes and sighed wearily. Nothing had changed, even after three horrendous cataclysms had shaken the foundations of the world, hatred, suspicion, and fear still ruled those who remained.

"He has a weapon, Sir!" one shouted with officious zeal.

"Shall we disarm him?" another offered eagerly.

"It's only a sword," a third supplied with obvious disinterest.

"Swords are as deadly as guns when wielded correctly."

He listened as they debated, their French accents painting their words, and his thoughts tangled in a maelstrom of compassion and exasperation. They were so tied to their militant ways they couldn't see the opportunity standing before them.

"Turn around slow and put your weapon on the ground."

The command came from one who had not yet spoken and he looked down at the scabbard of black leather and shimmering silver that hung from the belt encircling his hips, contemplating his options.

"I said, turn around."

The one addressing him had a tone of authority and impatience the others didn't. Raising his hand slowly, he reached for the hilt of his sword.

"Don't be a fool. There's a full regiment of weapons trained on you. Turn slow and drop that sword."

He drew the blade from its scabbard, the finely polished silver glittering in the late day light as he turned to face them, but he didn't immediately drop it.

Looking at each of them with a vigilant, piercing gaze, he assessed their ranks with the leisure of one thoroughly assured of his position. The one he presumed to be the captain of the regiment urged his mount forward and glared down at him, his tone growing more aggressive. "You don't really think you can take us, do you?"

Looking up at the officer with an undaunted stare, he could see clearly that his self-assurance infuriated the man. "It is not within the scope of my purpose to 'take' you." His poised reply and speech that held no distinct accent caused the captain to grind his teeth with annoyance.

Turning in his saddle, the officer shouted belligerently to those who were mere yards away. "If he makes any threatening move, shoot him."

Several bold "Aye, Sir's" answered as the officer turned back to glare down at him again. "This isn't a battle you'll likely win. Just lay that sword down and come along with us quietly."

Looking up at the man with an unreadable expression, the beautiful blond stranger studied the officer who was visibly older than the others in his unit. He had permanent creases around his eyes and mouth and deep furrows in his brow to attest to his wealth of experience, but there was hostility in his dark brown eyes. The stranger shook his head.

"Coming along with you is not my purpose either."

At his indifferent response, the officer's eyes narrowed and he glared at him silently, his anger noticeably mounting. The stranger could sense his hatred of him in the essence of what he was, even though they had never faced one another previously. Standing his ground, he said nothing more, but waited on the officer's next actions.

"What's your name, son?" Attempting to shift tactics, the officer spoke with an openly condescending tone, but he only succeeded in providing the stranger with another opportunity to annoy him.

"I am no more your son than these stones." His persistent self-control dissolved the officer's patience and he shouted with ire.

"What is your name?"

Sighing again as if the entire situation was dismally tedious, he closed his violet eyes and relented. "I am Tzadkiel."

When he heard the name, the officer's eyes widened with recognition and, without a moment's hesitation, he raised his gun and fired until he had fully discharged his weapon. He watched the stranger stagger backward and fall to his knees, but he didn't collapse, not initially, and as he gasped for breath and groaned in prodigious agony, the officer observed him with callous interest.

Daylight faded rapidly as the sun slipped behind the gray ocean, sending up a final radiant stream of scarlet vibrancy before disappearing. Soldiers milled about in small groups, waiting with palpable curiosity as the captain of the regiment and his lieutenant discussed their captive. Standing over him with calm disregard, they debated their options as he bled into the sand.

"He's still alive, Sir. Shouldn't we finish the job?" Lieutenant Delacour was a young officer just recently promoted to serve with Captain Sébastien Lévesque. He was youthfully handsome, almost to a fault, with platinum blond hair and a smattering of freckles across his fine features. He kept a day's growth of scruff on his chin and upper lip to offset his otherwise boyish good looks and had a scar across one bright blond brow that stood out in stark contrast to his fair complexion.

Looking up at Lévesque uncertainly, he waited for his anticipated, curt reply. He was not an officer to be trifled with and had a reputation for strict adherence to protocol, as well as a notoriously bad temper. As expected, he glared at his subordinate irritably.

"You suppose fifteen bullets weren't enough?" Lévesque's sarcasm caused Delacour to look down at their hostage and shake his head.

"Should have been." As soon as the remark passed his lips, he turned back to his commanding officer and apologized. "Sorry, Sir. I'm stating the obvious. What I meant was why is he still alive?"

Lévesque nodded, "Why, indeed." He walked around the fallen man, watching him bleed and listening to his labored and rasping breaths with heartless detachment. "Have you never heard the name Tzadkiel before?"

The younger man shook his head, but remained silent. Circling all the way around without once showing a hint of concern over the distress his captive suffered, Lévesque returned to his lieutenant and leaned closer to impart the information he was about to share as surreptitiously as possible. "Archangel."

Delacour's gray eyes widened with astonishment and he looked down at their hostage with a new and potent combination of hatred and fear twisting his features. "What'll we do with him?" he asked with similar caution, stepping back from the fallen Archangel as if at any moment he might leap up, entirely healed, and attack. After a moment's contemplation, Lévesque turned and began issuing orders in a loud voice for all to hear.

"Transfer the ordinance from that supply wagon to the pack horses. Attach ankle and wrist restraints to the bed of the wagon, then bring it here." Turning back to Delacour, he continued so only he could hear. "We'll take him back to The Bastion."

Delacour stepped back from the Archangel another time, his voice clearly betraying his concern. "Alive, Sir?" His anxiety was ignored.

"He won't be for long."

Long into the night the troop marched for Marçais, their prisoner lying in a pain-ridden, semi-conscious state in the back of the supply wagon, which had been converted into his prison cell. They had secured him to the wagon with leather restraints that had been hurriedly nailed into the sides of the conveyance, but they were entirely unnecessary. He could barely breathe, let alone fight to escape. Delacour had been assigned to the wagon and ordered to keep strict watch over him, either to confirm his demise when and if that actually occurred or to report on his condition when they stopped for the night. His attention was, at first, unwavering; his curiosity riveted by the creature straight out of the history books he'd studied as a child. An Archangel, a being of supposed consummate power and strength, lay at his feet.

Bleeding.

The thought was as sobering as it was astonishing. Had any of his ancestors known how easily the Archangels were injured, perhaps the catastrophes they had unleashed would not have occurred, but Delacour had never been a keen student of history or a philosophical thinker. He was a soldier, through and through, designed to obey orders and follow routines. Besides, the onset of the Great Cataclysm was nearly 400 years in the past, so as the hours dragged on and the Archangel remained motionless with the exception of the spasmodic coughs that intermittently wracked his body, Delacour's curiosity waned and his head began to nod.

When around the middle of the night the order was finally called to stop, the weary soldiers made a hasty camp and guards were posted around the perimeter. Many went straight to bed, not bothering to wait for their evening rations and unconcerned about their captive who clung to life with unprecedented tenacity despite his repeated groans of pain, rasping breaths, and blood-spattered coughing. Leaping down from the wagon after making a final inspection of his condition, Delacour hastened to give his report in the hope of being released to retire, but Captain Lévesque had other plans. Calling for torches, he ordered his exhausted lieutenant to return to the prisoner's wagon, following him in a state of mounting agitation and yanking the wagon gait down impatiently when they reached it. He stared at their hostage for several moments, silently considering his options.

Around them, the moonless night echoed with the trills and trebles of innumerable insects and Lévesque raised his head to glare into the raucous darkness with even greater irritation. Shadows infiltrated the spaces between the many fires that had been built throughout the camp and from that spectral realm a youthful messhand in a disheveled uniform and scraggly red hair peeking out from under his cap appeared like an apparition. He nodded respectfully to the officers and held out two small canvas bags that buzzed with muffled life. The captain and lieutenant looked at them, recognizing the rations of high-protein insect-replacement nourishment with similar expressions of disgust, but Delacour was hungry and took one of the pouches with a turn of his lip. Lévesque growled, his anger escalating when the subordinate held the other bag out to him. It was more than he could bear. Bounding up onto the bed of the wagon, he stalked towards his captive, glared down on him mercilessly, and snarled.

"If it weren't for your kind this world wouldn't be in the state it's in and I wouldn't be eating insects to survive!" Drawing back, he kicked his semi-conscious prisoner in the side brutally, watching with vicious satisfaction as blood spurted from his mouth and he curled in pain. Crouching down beside him, he gazed with avarice at the crystal he wore around his neck. He grasped the chain and yanked on it viciously, but despite the force he exerted the chain held. Tzadkiel looked up at him with an irritated glare.

"You cannot...have that." His voice was a deep growl that was made guttural by his injuries. Lévesque raised an incredulous eyebrow.

"Can I not?" Dubious of the fact, he yanked on it even more forcefully, but only succeeded in driving the fine metal chain into his skin. Cursing, he released the amulet and pressed his hand against Tzadkiel's throat instead, listening to his splutters for breath with satisfaction before hissing with deliberate cruelty. "It seems the reports are accurate. Your kind may be immortal, but you suffer pain just like we human's do."

Tzadkiel looked up at his captor with an alarmed stare, a wave of genuine fear washing over him for only the second time in his long life. Shaken, he listened as the captain patted his shoulder with feigned compassion and leaned in closer to convey his next words in a cold, sadistic whisper.

"Be assured, Archangel, we may not be able to kill you, but you'll wish we could before long."

2

B eyond The Bastion of Resolution, which was strictly governed by the Eminent Protectorate, an immense, disintegrating city stretched outward in all directions. Ruled by the iron-fist dictatorship of The Protectorate, the destitute municipality floundered between functionality and chaos. There were few businesses within the straggling districts because there were no profits to be made; no one had any money. Those who lived within the city's riotous neighborhoods barely had enough to survive. Everything that was not considered a necessity was negotiated through trade and necessities like food and clean water were doled out by the provisional dispensaries in severely limited quantities. Each person was allotted a daily ration that was barely enough to sustain a hard-working adult.

Little to no meat was ever provided with the daily rations, only insect proteins, which were abundant. Similarly, very few dairy products, vegetables or fruits ever made their way outside the fortress walls. These were reserved for the officers and families of the Eminent Protectorate. Commoners were provided only just enough to keep them alive, sometimes less if population control required such measures, and as a result riots and crime were a daily occurrence. Those who made the remnants of the once beautiful city their home faced corruption, starvation, and disease every day of their lives and they lived in unnatural squalor, but there were very few other places they could go.

Vast stretches of land lay outside the borders of the festering city, but they were controlled by either The Protectorate or other powerful factions. These invaluable farmlands, pastures, orchards and resource repositories were guarded through the use of viciously trained forces that would not hesitate to shoot on sight anyone they thought to be vandals. Any small villages around or near these principalities were severely exploited. Families that stood their ground against the governing dictatorships and refused to move off their own lands were forced into servitude to support the governing families and the ranks of patrolling guards. 'Free' lands not claimed by a governing party were either polluted, decimated by mining, or unfertile bogs that were useless as either a resource or residence.

Outside the boundaries of the lands surrounding The Bastion of Resolution, rival dictatorships controlled other stretches of land. Beyond those borders even other factions squabbled over less fertile lands, leaving the crumbling cities dotting the continent like infected blemishes the only choices that entire populations had on where to go to reside.

In the centuries after the Great Cataclysm, if you were not one of the powerful, you served the powerful. There was nothing in between.

Year 2446.
The 96ᵗʰ Year of the 4th Era after the Great Cataclysm
Le Bastion de la Résolution, - Marçais, New France

Lourdes opened her eyes wearily and stared at the stone ceiling of her small chambers as she tried to clear the lingering wisps of sleep from her mind. It felt as if she had only just fallen asleep, probably because it had taken so long for her to settle her thoughts after discovering the whereabouts of the one she had been hearing for so long. It wasn't as if there was a great deal she could do for him. He was locked into The Tower, a place that was entirely off limits to her. As a scullery maid, she had permission to enter the kitchens and sculleries and she could visit the dining rooms after meals were finished in order to collect dirty dishes and garbage. Anywhere else within the fortress she might wish to go required specific permission given to her by a superior. There were no exceptions, but the inexplicable pull within her to try to help the man who was The Protectorate's captive kept her awake long into the night considering possibilities. Now, as morning crept across the sky, she felt exhausted both physically and mentally.

Regardless of her fatigue, however, the brightening horizon urged her from her bed into another day with tireless insistence. Weary though she was, she knew if she wanted a sufficient breakfast that would see her through the day, she needed to arrive in the kitchen early. The hour of five was considered servant's breakfast, which provided thirty minutes for eating and thirty minutes for cleaning up before the six A.M. bell sounded, signaling the start of the day shift.

Stretching repeatedly, she moved to the small washstand situated in the corner. On its time worn surface, a basin and small pitcher of water waited, which she had filled the day before. A single towel hung from a nail she had driven into the side of the small cabinet and a bar of soap rested upon a tattered sponge. Pouring water into the basin sufficient for her needs, she washed her face and dried it with the towel before retrieving a comb from the cabinet's single drawer and using it to hastily draw her hair up into a tight knot that she covered with her servant's cap. She washed up and cleaned her teeth, as was her morning routine, then powdered herself liberally and put on the same faded gray dress she had taken off the night before. Covering it with one of three aprons that hung from hooks she had driven into the stone wall beside the cabinet, she pulled on a pair of worn shoes and exited without a second glance at herself.

If she didn't want to look at herself, no one else would either.

Descending the long, spiraling staircase that led down ten flights to the kitchens located on the ground floor above the fortress cellars, she focused her thoughts on a single challenge: how to gain access to Tower Obligar. Several other servants joined her in her descent from the heights of the servant's tower, which housed many of The Bastion's servants, but they, too, were weary and none of them spoke. As the clatter of the kitchen became perceptible and bright torchlight spilled along the otherwise shadowy corridor, several hastened by her to join the growing line of those already awaiting their morning meal, but Lourdes moved unhurriedly, lost in her contemplations.

Changing shift assignments was difficult, nearly impossible. The Head Housekeeper in charge of all indoor servant assignments didn't like to waste time crosstraining. Once a servant was considered adequate in meeting the duties of their assigned task, there was little reason to alter shifts. Several servants who were veterans to the establishment had enough training to cover any shifts left open by acute illness, which was the only reason a servant might be excused from their responsibilities on any given day, but there was no other reason to cross-train.

Persuading someone to take her assignment was not the problem. Being a scullery maid meant she had access to trimmings and leavings that kept her stomach reasonably full, a luxury most other servants didn't enjoy, but she had no other training or skills that would make her a benefit on any other assignment and she couldn't switch with someone unless she knew what they did and how they did it.

A bowl of colorless oatmeal found its way into her hands before she turned towards the table where her fellow servants sat eating in dismal silence. Without paying particular attention, she crossed the floor, sat down with her morning meal and tea. Her thoughts tumbled in conflicting directions that led her back, again and again, to the sweltering night she had just passed and the screams echoing among the battlements. They were nearly more than she could bear and she tried not to think about what he suffered. It was well known that The Protectorate could be unimaginably cruel and it was far too distressing to think about. Instead, she tried to focus on the problem at hand and how she might find a way past the Eminent Protectorate Guards that secured the entrance to The Tower, but the memory of his screams filled her mind repeatedly. Without being fully aware of their presence, tears slipped down her cheeks.

"What's wrong, Lourdes?"

A timid whisper shook her from her tortured musings and she turned to look into the eyes of one of several new housemaids that had been acquired by The Protectorate within the last few months. She smiled unconvincingly at her. Barely beyond the age of 15, the young servant she had recently befriended had an immaculate ivory complexion and pale blue eyes nearly white in hue. Her curling hair was bright blond though it was tucked beneath her servant's cap, but a few unruly strands always seemed to escape. Her pale eyes were red from crying and Lourdes wiped her own tears quickly, attempting to dismiss her curiosity.

"Just tired, Brigyda." She leaned closer to the girl and looked into her eyes more directly. "Are *you* ok?"

The girl nodded and tried to smile in return, but the tears that had welled in her eyes rimmed and flooded over and she looked down into her bowl of half-eaten oatmeal miserably. "It's my assignment…. it's so horrible!" Attempting to explain, she stuttered for a moment, then bounced to her feet and fled the room, leaving her breakfast and confused friend behind her.

Several heads rose at her unanticipated departure, but no one followed her. The food she left behind was of far greater interest and the young man who sat on the other side of her, who was devouring his breakfast like a feral beast, eyed her abandoned bowl ravenously. Although Lourdes wanted to take the food and follow after her new friend, she knew the rules of the kitchen too well. No food left the confines of the servants eating space and any food left on the table was fair game. Brigyda's breakfast hardly lasted ten seconds. Even as he stared at the bowl hungrily, an older male servant reached across the table and snatched it away.

Unsympathetic snickers answered the first's curse of disappointment before all fell into silence once more.

CYNTHIA A. MORGAN

Year 2445.
The 95th Year of the 4th Era after the Great Cataclysm
The Road to Marçais

The road to Marçais was 360 miles. With an attach-
ment of thirty soldiers, ten auxiliary personnel, two
dozen pack horses and a train of fifteen supply wagons,
including the one turned into an open-air-prison,
Lévesque knew the journey back to The Bastion would
take at least a week. When they arrived, he planned to
deliver his captive to his commanding officer, The
Marshal of the Eminent Protectorate, and he felt certain such a fortuitous and advantageous acquisition
would ensure an elevation of status for him. Provided
they were not assailed along the road by bandits or in-
surgents keen to steal the provisions they were transporting, he was sure they could traverse the distance
with relative speed. He didn't, however, anticipate the
difficulty they would face transporting the Archangel's
sword.

It appeared normal enough to the undiscerning eye;
a long-sword forged with exceptional skill, but not unusual. Upon close inspection, one could see its black
leather scabbard appeared ageless and bore no mark of
any kind upon its luxuriant surface, although it was ev-
idently older than any could comprehend. The blade
was etched with runes and indecipherable writing that
somehow shimmered with a silvery light all their own
and the edge was sharper than any ordinary steel could
ever be honed. Even more incredible was its incomprehensible weight. When Lévesque attempted to pick it
up from the beach where it had fallen, he discovered it
could barely be moved. Two men together, then three,

24

then four tried to raise the sword from the rocks and sand, but all were unsuccessful. They struggled with it for some time, ultimately devising a sling for it using a tarp they managed to slide beneath it before harnessing the sling to two draft horses.

On day two of their journey, one of the horses collapsed out of exhaustion. He was replaced by two pack horses, their goods being redistributed among the remaining animals, but halfway through the day the other draft horse needed to be spelled. The unfathomable burden the sword created required routine cycling of the horses and slowed their return to Marçais considerably. Lévesque grated irritably at the delay that would easily add several additional days to their journey, but he refused to leave the priceless trophy behind. Instead, when they came upon farmsteads with horses, they bartered for an exchange of animals. Many agreed without much argument. Those who asked were Eminent Protectorate soldiers after all, but some of those with whom they bartered were EP Guards stationed at interval checkpoints or resource repositories who required additional provisions. The loss of beetles and mealworms didn't produce any measure of dissension among Lévesque's ranks, but when the high protein food was refused, the animals they needed were simply taken by force.

Tzadkiel's recovery was monitored closely by the unit medic, a man by the name of Phillippe who was much the same age as Lévesque, his mid to late thirties. He was a man of average height and slightly higher than average weight. His dark brown, nearly black hair and similarly dark eyes were also average. In fact, there was nothing remarkable about him, except that he had a peculiar interest in the Archangel's suffering. He took extensive notes on the condition of their captive and

studied the rate of his miraculous regeneration, which
seemed contingent upon the amount of time he spent
in open sunlight, as well as his responses to varying
stimuli, all of which Phillippe reported back to
Lévesque at the end of each day when they made camp.

It took mere days for their prisoner's injuries to
heal and, although no food or drink was required to
sustain him, but when they were provided the speed of
his rejuvenation increased. Phillippe also noted that the
amulet he wore, which none of them could remove
even when they tried to cut it from around his neck
with a bolt cutter, seemed to pulse radiantly when he
was in directly sunlight. Its energizing pulsations were
less notable when it was cloudy or raining and, during
the hours of the night, it emitted a steady subtle glow.
He concluded its function was somehow tied to the
Archangel's regenerative process, but he could not
force Tzadkiel to speak about its purpose even when he
intentionally inflicted pain in order to prompt him.

Having never had the opportunity to study one of
the Archangels and curious beyond measure, Phillippe
spent every spare moment of his time with the prisoner
testing theories and analyzing results with callous im-
partiality. The Archangel's suffering was scrutinized as
closely as his improvements, but when on the fourth
day of their journey his strength and vitality returned
to such a degree as to threaten their ability to hold him,
Captain Lévesque ordered Phillippe meet with him to
discuss the situation.

Walking within the captain's tent with an armful of
notebooks and papers he had scribed over the several
days he had spent studying their prisoner, Phillippe
stopped as the tent flaps were closed behind him and
glanced around curiously, raising a hand to wipe his
brow absently. The mid-July evening was hot and
muggy and his short hair stuck to the back of his neck

and was soaked beneath his cap. His impassive, brown gaze took in the brightly lit pavilion, finding it large enough to house half a squad, though only one officer made it his lodging. It was immaculately clean and orderly, held a folding desk and chair, as well as an oversized cot with comfortable bedding, a standing washbasin with its own vessel of clean water, as well as several clean uniforms. The privileges of rank.

"What's your report?" Lévesque, who stood in the far corner where several swords and other armaments were displayed, wasted no time and Phillippe nodded sharply.

"His recovery is astonishing, Sir. Even, miraculous, one might say."

Lieutenant Delacour, who had been invited to participate in the meeting as well, looked sideward to the captain who was polishing a dagger with casual disinterest.

"Miraculous for an Archangel?" Lévesque rebuke warned his medic to share only the relevant facts and Phillippe shifted uneasily before continuing.

"I, I don't know, Sir. I've never had the chance to study one before."

"You'd like the opportunity to continue, though, wouldn't you?" Lévesque proposed without looking up and his lieutenant and the medic shared a surprised glance.

"Well, yes, Sir, I, I believe I would, if given the opportunity. There's so much we could, well, learn."

Lévesque raised his head to glare at him with disapproval. "Learn," he repeated abrasively. "Like how to keep so powerful a being under strict control?"

It was not actually a question and Phillippe stammered even more awkwardly than usual in an attempt to keep up. "Uh, well, I think, um...that is, yes, Sir."

"Learn how long it takes for him to recover and

how much he can endure on a daily basis. Learn how to keep him under control by not allowing him to recover enough to be a threat. These are the things you'd like to learn; am I right?"

Phillippe looked curiously between the two officers, who had clearly already discussed the matter, and nodded vaguely. "Yes, Sir."

"Good, because we need to know all those things. He cannot be set at liberty. The world has endured enough chaos thanks to his kind." Moving closer to the medic, Lévesque raised the dagger he was cleaning, twirling it aptly between his fingers and looking at it with a kind of affection that made Phillippe raise an incredulous brow. "You want to serve mankind, don't you Phillippe? That's why you became a physician, isn't it?"

He nodded mutely, watching the dagger vigilantly as Lévesque strolled around him with it.

"What better way to serve? How better to keep all of us safe, but by determining precisely what keeps this creature harmless; in what measures such controls need to be applied and how often. All your papers and careful computations could be put to no better use, could they?" He stopped circling and glared at the medic with an expression that sanctioned no refusal. Delacour stepped closer and added a further inducement.

"You wouldn't mind living among the Eminent Protectorate, would you? Enjoying the luxuries and liberties of such a preferential assignment; eating meat and drinking wine?" Captain and lieutenant looked at each other with unspoken acknowledgment. They missed The Bastion and couldn't wait to get back to the comforts it afforded. Phillippe, who had been eating insect protein meals for years since joining the service of The Protectorate couldn't resist their skillful temptation.

"Yes. I, I believe I would." He looked down at his armful of notes. "I've already made some, well, intriguing discoveries."

Year 2445.
The 95th Year of the 4th Era after the Great Cataclysm
The Road to Marçais

Pain enveloped him like a thick fog, cutting him off from reality and disorienting him. Unlike any sensation he had ever experienced, it gripped him so tightly he could barely breathe. When he did draw breath, each was a jagged blade entering his body. He couldn't think clearly or give his attention to anything other than how to survive the unrelenting waves of agony washing over him like a ferocious tide. The waves pulled at him ruthlessly, as if intent upon drowning him, wrenching him into the depths of their seething core of confusion through repeated assaults of merciless torment. Blackness consumed him on more than one occasion and his innate sense of time and place was shattered.

He had very little perception of where he was, although he knew the vicious humans who attacked him had hurled him into some vehicle of conveyance without a single thought to his needs. Tears of shock and pain flowed freely from his violet-hued eyes, the acrid, metallic taste of blood filled his mouth, and a loud rushing-buzzing noise caused his head to pound. He struggled against it, fought to retain some portion of the being he knew he was, but each breath severed his thoughts into splinters of serrating distress, separating him from everything he knew and cutting him off from himself.

Time, that incalculable enigma that had for most of his life been a measure he rarely considered, dragged its lazy heels across his abused frame, extolling with unspeakable clarity the fragility of the human form and how vulnerable it was to damage. When he had first assumed the ungainly human form, it had taken many of the earth's cumbersome days to grow accustomed to the awkwardness of the body and many more months to be able to comprehend the myriad sensations to which it was susceptible; yet pain had barely registered on the compass of his experience, until now. Now, his only thought was discomfort, his only sensation aching torment, and his only need was escape. Escape from the repeating waves of inexpressible pain that held him in the prison he now inhabited. Escape from the cruelty of sadistic domination seeking to oppress him. Escape from these men.

He could escape; of course, he could. Many avenues of action lay at his disposal awaiting only his choice to command them. He could call upon his brother Archangels to aid him and they would come without hesitation. He could invoke the power of the Hashmallim, one of several angelic legions of Heaven that he had led before coming to Earth. He could bring his sword to his hand and wield it to crush those who tormented him or he could speak the incantation that would release the one who waited behind him. With any of these acts every creature giving offense would perish. All that was required was a word from his mouth and the interminable hours of suffering would end. One word and it could all be changed, but that was not his purpose.

His purpose was to find at least one human who comprehended the true meaning of mercy among the masses that remained. He had searched for 95 years before encountering Lévesque, but had not found the one he sought. So, he continued to search. He had not waited millennia to fulfill this sanctified purpose only to be defeated by a lone sensation. He would not allow the actions of men to dictate his fate. He could choose to destroy them all. The means of their destruction waited only for his word.

The choice was his.

He decided to wait.

He accepted pain.

Waiting required a deliberate choice every day and a measure of patience and hope most found incomprehensible. It also required submitting to all the vile offenses the humans could hurl upon him. For more than a week he lay in the back of an open wagon, untended and unprotected. The glare of the afternoon sun was a blessing, as the sun's radiance aided his healing processes, but when torrents of rain poured down no measure of comfort was provided. He was abandoned to wait out the long, cold hours alone. It also required allowing himself to be imprisoned in a tower cell once they reached their destination. It meant permitting humans to force requirements upon him that no immortal had been asked to submit to in countless eons.

Phillippe had discovered his ability to regenerate by utilizing the sun's energy during their journey to Marçais and it only took a few weeks before he devised a way to balance the intensity of the torture they inflicted with the length of time he was allowed to absorb the sun's energy and recuperate. Forcing him to endure abuses that would have proven fatal to any human, they kept him in a perpetual state of weakness that required the full span of the day to recover from and gave him no opportunity to actually renew his strength. It was a twisted, merciless routine overseen by Lévesque, but executed by Phillippe. He had learned in a very short span of time that the medic effectively hid from his superiors a personality disorder marked by aggressive, sadistic tendencies and a complete lack of empathy. He was the epitome of every failing humanity had embraced and was exactly the opposite of the sort of person he had come to earth to find.

It was an irony that tormented him every single day.

Year 2446.
The 96ᵗʰ Year of the 4th Era after the Great Cataclysm: Tower Obligar, Le Bastion de la Résolution, - Marçais, New France

"His level of endurance continues to increase, Sir," Phillippe reported dryly after coming off the night shift. Lévesque, who was just coming on, stood in the office that had been provided for him nearly a full year ago and glared hatefully out into the chamber beyond. There, his captive lay bound to a stone table several hundred years old that had been specifically designed for torture. "He's gotten used to the treatments."

Phillippe nodded. "I haven't, uh, moved him back to his cell yet. Wasn't sure if you might want to, I don't know, increase the length or intensity of the sessions?"

Lévesque considered while staring out into the chamber before he spun on his heel. "We decided on this yesterday. You're to reduce their intensity and shift to first thing in the morning."

Phillippe shook his head. "I know, Sir, but it, it isn't enough."

"My fine military career reduced to overseeing a torture chamber," Lévesque growled under his breath.

Phillippe frowned, unable to hear him clearly. "Sir?"

Silence answered him for many moments before Lévesque forced himself to swallow his anger and turn back to face Phillippe with a feigned expression of indifference. "What do you recommend?"

Stepping forward, Phillippe referencing the notes he had diligently taken and they spoke casually about their horrifying options, having gotten so used to the cruelty they inflicted that it never once disturbed their conscience. As they discussed ways to increase the intensity of the 'treatments', the young servant who had been assigned to The Tower moved with conspicuous hesitation towards the stonework table, trying hard to go unnoticed. In her shaking hands she carried a bucket of water and several scraps of cloth, which she used to clean the prisoner's blood from the floor. In spite of the number of times she had been forced to repeat the duty during the past several months, the horror of the situation still distressed her greatly and she wept as she stooped to clean up the blood that had pooled on the floor beneath the table.

He was so close, yet she could not bear to look at him. The terrible things the EP officer had done left open wounds she could not force herself to see. His screams echoed in her ears and she wanted nothing more than to be as far from that place as possible, but she was as much a prisoner as he. As she crept closer, daylight sparkled through the ancient windows of the fortress, spilling inward in a progression that streamed across the cold stone floor. Gradual as the slow hands of time, its radiant luminance shimmered upward along the base of the stone table and when its glimmering rays touched him, he sighed out loud.

The sound startled her and she muffled a shriek that spoke more loudly than any complaint she could have voiced. Tzadkiel opened his eyes, becoming more aware of his surroundings even as unconsciousness sought to overpower him. He sensed her distress and could not force himself to ignore her. Whispering indistinctly, he moved his hand against the iron manacle closed tightly around his wrist, seeking to somehow assuage her misery, but his action caused the heavy iron chains that bound him to rattle and the sound echoed in the now quiet chamber. Gasping in terror at the unexpected noise, she scurried away from him like a frightened animal and it took many long moments before she gathered enough courage to return.

"Seems you're right," Lévesque agreed with a tone of surprise upon hearing the metallic echoes that betrayed his captive's movements. Phillippe merely nodded, then turned as an unannounced visitor strode in. Dressed in the leather uniform of the Eminent Protectorate's Private Guard and holding his braided cap beneath his arm, the youthful officer who was barely in his prime scanned the chamber hastily, grimaced, and turned his critical green-eyed glare onto the pair of them.

"Who's in charge here?" His stare went to Phillippe who lowered his gaze and, with an inclination of his head, specified Lévesque who answered unceremoniously.

"I am. Who's asking?" His petulant attitude did little to intimidate the intruder as it might have been intended. Instead, the EPP Guard raised a single eyebrow and strode to within a few feet of the captain, taking up an aggressive stance in spite of his stature, which barely reached Lévesque's shoulder. His belligerence stood in stark contrast to his boyishly handsome features and curling light brown hair that fell over his forehead now that it was not confined beneath his cap.

"Your host, The Eminent Protectorate, that's who. State your name."

Bristling in response to the guard's insolent demand, Lévesque provided what was required of him, but then brazenly posed a question of his own. "Captain Lévesque of the 32nd. What do you want?"

Phillippe's expression shifted from impassive to astonished and he stepped back from the pair cautiously, fully anticipating the conversation to explode into hostility. The EPP Guard, however, merely scoffed before returning to the doorway leading out into the chamber beyond.

"You've had nearly a year with the prisoner. What progress have you made toward controlling it?"

"We control it just fine." Lévesque's uninformative response made the guard pause. Twisting with unmistakable annoyance, he waited for more, but was not given anything further. After a tense moment, he snapped impatiently.

"How?"

"Through the measured application of subduing action." The unenlightening response snapped the young officer's patience. Spinning on his heel, he returned to Lévesque in three quick strides.

"I haven't got all day," he growled before continuing with a well-rehearsed explanation of his orders. "The Marshal's sent me to ascertain whether or not you're making progress and through what means such progress is being achieved. You'll provide the information I require or I'll drag you before the Marshal himself."

Lévesque turned lazily away and gazed out the barred window, unwilling to yield to so young an officer. "I've been here for 362 days, following no other orders than to control my prisoner."

"The Eminent Protectorate's prisoner," came the immediate correction. It was ignored.

"No questions have been raised about my methods and no reports have been required. One might think the Eminent Protectorate isn't concerned about what's being done here."

"The Eminent Protectorate sees and hears all." It

was a stock response, but it made Lévesque pause. Deciding to be practical for the simple reason of being rid of the impudent upstart, he turned with a complete shift in his attitude.

"Like to see for yourself? Phillippe, here, just explained that the prisoner's grown accustomed to the routine. I was just about to suggest an alteration."

The EPP Guard's eyes narrowed with suspicion, but he nodded brusquely. "Proceed."

Lévesque gestured at Phillippe and the three men moved out into the chamber. At their approach, the young servant kneeling at the base of the torture table snatched up her cloths and rushed into a far corner, leaving a large, red stain upon the floor she had not had sufficient time to remove. They watched her with marked silence before Lévesque continued more conversationally. "We had a devil of a time getting him here."

"Why? Was he resistive?"

Shaking his head, Lévesque gestured towards the magnificent sword lying atop a small stone dais they had draped with a black velvet cloth at one side of the chamber. "Moving him wasn't the problem. It was his sword that gave us the most trouble."

The EPP Guard stopped to examine the weapon with greater interest. "A sword?"

Lévesque nodded. "Not just any sword. The weapon of an Archangel." He waited, allowing the young man to gaze at it for several moments before continuing. "It required three draft horses spelled every six hours in continual rotation to haul it here and the strength of sixty men on a winch cable to get it where it is now." Such a declaration was nearly beyond imagining and the guard's forehead wrinkled with skepticism as he turned his doubtful gaze back to the captain.

"A sword?" he repeated incredulously, to which question Lévesque smiled magnanimously.

"Please, by all means, see for yourself. I invite you to take it in hand."

The youthful officer glanced across at Phillippe who was busying himself with the practical matters of preparing their captive for another session, checking the tension of the manacles confining him and placing a leather harness across his head to hold him down. Unable to accept such an outrageous claim, the EPP Guard stepped closer and grasped the hilt of the sword firmly. Try as he might, however, he could not move it. Not a fraction of an inch. It was a mountain resting atop velvet without as much as a bend in the delicate fabric.

"Astonishing. Yet, he can wield this weapon without effort?"

Lévesque nodded. "Well, we suppose as much. We've never actually seen him do it. He took it in hand on the day we detained him and didn't struggle with it."

The guard's curiosity was piqued. "And since then?"

"Since then he's not had the opportunity."

The EPP Guard stared at him as if utterly at a loss. "Why not?"

Lévesque's patience dissolved. "Would you like an Archangel to have full command of his strength and weapons within these walls?"

Unintimidated, the young officer's steely gaze locked once again with the captains and he spoke once more with a practiced tone. "If it gives us the opportunity to learn how better to utilize that strength for our purposes, then yes, I would. That, Captain, is the reason for my visit. The Protectorate feels you're under-utilizing this opportunity."

Lévesque smiled long-sufferingly. "Really? You'd rather we permit the prisoner to recover more fully?" he questioned derisively.

"It seems the best way to study his abilities."

"I see, and you feel qualified to make that decision having never witnessed those abilities?" It was clear the guard wanted to agree, but the wide-eyed expression frozen on Phillippe's features gave him reason enough to pause.

"What I feel qualified to do is assess the situation by witnessing a demonstration of those abilities and strengths."

"A judicious notion." Lévesque motioned for Phillippe to continue as he undertook, at last, a fuller explanation of their work. "Our efforts here haven't been entirely wasted, as you might suppose. During the past year, we've learned that sunlight is directly linked to the prisoner's recuperative capability. His treatments up to this point have typically taken place at night, which provides several hours of darkness to keep him in a weakened condition before he is given time in the sun to regenerate." Lévesque moved casually toward the table upon which their prisoner was bound, speaking as if he were nothing more than another article of furniture in the room. "Over the course of the last year, Phillippe has been able to develop several potent combinations of treatments."

The EPP Guard interrupted incredulously, "Treatments?"

Lévesque shrugged and made an offer with a markedly sarcastic tone. "Would you prefer I used the word torture? It is more accurate."

Looking down at Tzadkiel for the first time since entering the room, the guard's stare took in the definition of his physique, the bleeding lacerations crisscrossing his body, as well as the unhealthful pallor of his skin, the exhaustion in his pale lavender eyes, and the similarly hued crystal that hung around his neck, pulsing indistinctly. Upon seeing it, he raised a curious brow.

"What's that?" Pointing at the amulet, he questioned, without verbally asking, why they hadn't removed it. Lévesque shrugged again.

"It's linked to his regenerative abilities. We've tried removing it; even used a bolt cutter, but it's as impossible to move as his sword." Levesque continued in a nonchalant, business-like manner as he strode unhurriedly around the table. "His treatments are designed to tax his limits and keep him in a weakened state. Phillippe has several routines he runs through over the course of a week's time."

Tearing his gaze from the Archangel, who tracked their movements like a wild animal, the EPP Guard turned his attention back to Lévesque. "And you've decided to keep him in a weakened state because...?"

Lévesque stopped in his tracks, twisting around to stare at the young man with exasperation. He was too young to remember the Great Cataclysm, but he had clearly forgotten his histories.

"*And the seven angels, who had seven trumpets, prepared themselves to sound, and I heard a great voice saying to them 'Go your ways and pour out the vials of the wrath of God upon the earth.'*" Quoting the ancient book of Revelations, Lévesque hoped to remind the young man of what he had clearly forgotten, but his unblinking stare showed plainly enough that he had never bothered to learn his histories and he thought the captain, quite possibly, off his hinges. Irritated beyond diplomacy, he gestured emphatically at the Archangel.

"This is one of those damnable creatures, sent to destroy our world and all of us along with it!" His vicious growl echoed through the chamber. "Do you really want him strong enough to wield his sword just so you can see him do it?"

Looking down again at the prisoner again, the EPP Guard stepped back and motioned for them to proceed without asking anything further.

The exhibition that followed nearly caused him to be ill.

It would haunt his memory for the rest of his days.

As would the Archangel's screams.

3

In the early decades of the 21st century, a disturbing change had begun. Weather patterns grew erratic, tides and wind currents shifted back on themselves, and global temperatures intensified dramatically. Droughts and floods, mudslides and wildfires grew more and more common. The warmer temperatures melted the polar icecaps and brought devastating changes to the global ocean ecosystems, causing widespread extinctions and vast plumes of red algae and jellyfish. What was even more calamitous was the electromagnetic solar storms that wreaked havoc with the planet's electrical grid for nearly an entire week. The disturbances caused widespread blackouts and power interruptions. Digital and electrical technologies across the planet were damaged beyond repair and rendered useless.

Attempts were made by many governments to restore power, but even though nations worked together and scientists and engineers labored for months, every mechanism on the planet capable of producing electricity had been rendered inoperable. The devastation caused by the intensity of the storms was unprecedented, causing riots and worldwide chaos. Security systems failed to restrict the frenzied and frightened masses that descended on installations and their uncontrollable actions destroyed what remained of the infrastructure.

Without the technology humanity had grown so dependent upon, entire governments began to crumble. Martial law and dictatorships replaced democracies around the world. Entire countries disintegrated and were claimed by tyrants. In the year 2050, under the shadow of such irreparable changes, insidious epidemics of varying degrees began to sweep across countries and continents. Small outbreaks of diseases long thought to be entirely controlled grew into vast pandemics. Deadly plagues of maladies no doctor had ever seen decimated entire populations. Blame for these illnesses shifted from populaces where medical care was scare, to the unvaccinated, to wild claims of alien infiltrations, but it was the lack of medical technology, which the world had long relied upon so heavily, that caused the greatest problems. As the scale and frequency of epidemics escalated and thousands, and then tens of thousands, perished it had become inescapably clear.

The Horseman, thought so long to be nothing more than religious myth, was riding.

Year 2060
The 1st Era of the Great Cataclysm
Regional countryside outside Chambon, France

"I saw him! Dear God, it's true!" A petite woman with graying chestnut-red hair and distinctive, caramel-colored eyes dropped her bundle of firewood on the porch and called to her husband. He was a man of silver hair and handsome features, who, at that precise moment, was starting a fire in the living room grate. It was an unassuming farmhouse nestled on the margins of a vast woodland, but it had been home to them for more than forty years. Startled by his wife's shocking pronouncement and speedy return from the forest where she collected firewood every evening while he tended to the remaining livestock they owned, he dropped the flint he had just struck and watched it fall into the unprepared kindling before he started up from his crouched position.

"Saw who? Annabella, what are you shouting about?"

She hurried inside, gesticulating frantically. "Him, you absent-minded imbecile. The Horseman."

The man's hazel eyes grew wide as he stepped forward unsteadily, as if at any moment the legendary rider would come galloping out of the woods and into their living room. "Pestilence? My God! Where? What were you doing? I thought you were collecting wood. When did you see him? Was he coming this way? Are you sure? What color horse was he riding?"

Shaking her head at her husband's barrage of questions as she twisted around to flail in the direction of the forest, she moved back onto the porch and its timeworn boards creaked beneath her bare feet. "I was collecting firewood. What else would I be doing at this hour, you ninny." She berated him sharply, but he never flinched; their arguments long having become battles of verbal affection over the many years they had spent together. "He rides a white horse, you know that."

Her husband nodded and drew close to her, intending to embrace her before the onset of their demise, but she pushed away from him urgently and hastened down the stairs. "Where are you going? Shouldn't we..." he tried to question her, but she motioned for him to follow as she hurried towards the barn that stood at the opposite end of their yard.

"We've plenty of grain stored. We can fill the trough with water and...Gabriel, what are you doing?" Turning, she watched as her husband stood frozen on the stairs of the porch, staring in the direction of the forest with fear in his pale eyes unlike any she had ever seen before.

"He's coming. I hear hoof beats on the woodland road."

"Then hurry, you handsome half-wit!" She raced back to him and, grabbing his hand, pulled him along with her towards the small barnyard they had, in their younger years, filled with goats, cows, horses and chickens, though now it housed only a handful sufficient to their needs. "Fill the trough. Hurry! I'll get a wheelbarrow of grain." Her frenzy of activity caused him to gaze at her with a raised eyebrow.

"Why?"

She stopped at last. Moving back to him, she raised herself to her toes and kissed his mouth tenderly. "I've no idea why I should think this. There's no shred of proof he can be reasoned with or dissuaded from his purpose, but if we give him food and water for his horse, if we show him kindness and act with respect instead of hatred and fear, perhaps...."

He smiled, wrapping his arms around her as he drew her close. "Your spirit amazed me the first day we met and it does to this day, beautiful woman."

A blush warmed her cheeks as they considered each other affectionately, then he stepped away towards the well, even as she headed into the barn.

Year 2446
The 96th Year of the 4th Era after the Great Cataclysm
Le Bastion de la Résolution, - Marçais, New France

Lourdes reported to the Head Housekeeper's office as she did every day, as she had done since she began working in The Bastion of Resolution ten years earlier. It was part of her daily routine where she would gather her supplies for the day before beginning her shift. Absently smoothing the wrinkles of her uniform and fussing with the lacings of her cap in order to appear as tidy as possible and escape any verbal reprimands the Head Housekeeper might choose to throw at her, she stepped through the open door with her thoughts still distracted by her earlier contemplations.

How could she possibly gain entry to the restricted Tower Obligar? Would she really be able to help the one they tortured or would she simply be endangering herself? What would she do if she could gain entry? How could she free a prison of The Protectorate and where could she possibly hide him if she succeeded? Her thoughts were a maelstrom of confusion, but as she stepped inside the windowless room that was Madam Ornaly's office the muffled sounds of weeping seized her attention and she slowed her footsteps. Someone was crying.

"I don't honestly care how much it distresses you. It's your assignment and I'm not about to change it."

Lourdes paused. Should she continue inward to collect her supplies or return in a few moments when, perhaps, those speaking would have completed their conversation?

"But Madam, it's so horrible," the voice of a young woman wailed and Lourdes could not help listening more closely. Did she recognize that voice? "I can't

CYNTHIA A. MORGAN

sleep for the nightmares I'm having and now I'm exhausted and can't do my work."

"You knew what was required when you accepted employment here," Madam returned heartlessly, but their conversation trailed off and Lourdes looked up uneasily to see both women watching her. Madam Ornaly was a tall, slender woman of mature years with graying hair that she wore in a loose bun. She had a fine complexion, despite the fact that she was beginning to wrinkle, and her steely gaze glinted with inner fire. She enjoyed the luxury of a supervisory position, though she had worked for many hard years as a servant to gain such status. Because of her experience, she had a perpetually cross expression and her temper was hard and unsympathetic.

"Something you need, Lourdes?" Madam asked sharply. Her first reaction was to shake her head, duck, and hasten to her work, but when she realized the other speaker who stood wiping her tears with her apron was Brigyda, she stammered uncertainly.

"No Madam. Um…That is,"

"Make it quick, I've already got my hands full here and it's not even seven A.M."

Brigyda watched with a disbelieving stare as Lourdes stepped forward uncertainly.

"It's just…may I help in some way, Madam?" Her cautious question made both stare at her as if she had taken leave of her senses and it was very likely she had. The risk she assumed by intruding into matters that were not her business was substantial, but the words were spoken and she couldn't unsay them.

"Help with what?" Madam snapped irritably. Brigyda shook her head with frantic subtlety, but to no avail. Clearing her throat, which suddenly felt like she had swallowed a flagon of sawdust, Lourdes proposed the preposterous.

46

"Madam, if it would help, perhaps Brigyda and I could switch assignments for the day?"

Madam Ornaly looked back at the young servant behind her with a critical gaze, evaluating her observable tremors, even paler than usual complexion, and red eyes. Her ability to perform her duties was certainly in question and, although she didn't have a reputation for coddling anyone, she turned to glare suspiciously at Lourdes. "Why?"

Taking another tentative step forward, Lourdes knew she was pressing her luck. The best rule to follow was to keep your head down and mind your own business, but she couldn't just turn away, not from her friend. Attempting to appear as innocent as possible, she shrugged. "Only to help, Madam."

Madam Ornaly clearly didn't trust either one of them. "Help? You mean to say you're tired of finding food under the table and would rather wipe blood from the floor?"

Lourdes gaped with sudden confusion. "B...blood, Madam?"

Waving her hand with exasperation, Madam chuckled unsympathetically. "That's what you get for volunteering before thinking," she snapped. "Switching is out of the question, there are rules to follow and I'm not about to start changing things."

Lourdes opened her mouth brazenly as if to argue, but Madam continued with a petulant tone before she could find anything to say. "But since I need the work done and this one," she sneered, pointing at Brigyda balefully, "is as unreliable as the north wind, the two of you will work together until I decide otherwise. If you fall behind, you've only yourselves to blame. Now, get out of my sight before I really get angry."

Appalled and relieved all at the same time, both servants bobbed swift curtsies and fled from her presence, hastily gathering their supplies from the provisions closet before rushing out into the corridor. Proceeding along the narrow passage until they were well out of ear-shot of Madam's office, Brigyda took hold of Lourdes by the arm and pulled her to a stop. Her tears had doubled and she shook fiercely. "Why did you do that? You could've gotten in so much trouble?" Her tremulous tone betrayed her confusion and Lourdes pulled her to the side of the hall to speak surreptitiously, even as footsteps echoed from farther along the passage.

"You needed help and I'm not one to turn away from my friends. Here." She raised her apron to the girls face and wiped the tears from her cheeks, noticing for the first time how hollow those cheeks were and how thin she was beneath her dress. "You could use some table scraps, that's certain. C'mon, or we'll be late and Cook won't stand for that."

"But Lourdes, what about my assignment? How're we gonna get both done at the same time?" She drew several ragged breaths as Lourdes considered her valid question thoughtfully.

"I'm not sure, but we'll figure something out." Starting off down the hall again, she looked sideward at the younger servant as she trotted to keep up with the hurried pace Lourdes had set. "What is your assignment, anyway? What did Madam mean, 'wiping blood from the floor'?"

Brigyda stared at her vacantly and then slowed to stand looking at the floor. Several of her blond curls had escaped her servant's cap and trembled about her face, betraying just how distressed she was and Lourdes watched her with mounting dread.

"Lourdes, I never want to go back there," she wailed piteously.

"Where? What did they assign you?"

Brigyda shook her head, looking around cautiously before answering, as if no one could overhear their conversation. Stepping forward, she leaned closer to her friend to speak in whispers.

"Tower Obligar."

Lourdes' eyes widened in cold dread. "What? But you're so young. Madam never should have given you such an assignment," her whisper was harsh and she couldn't disguise her anger as she began to comprehend the girl's fear. Little wonder she was having nightmares and could barely sleep. The horrible things they did in that tower would scar anyone emotionally. How Madam could ever have thought….

Her musings were interrupted as from further along the hallway, rapid strides echoed off the stonework as someone hastened towards them. Lourdes grabbed the younger servant's arm to pull her along beside her. "We've got to hurry. Give me time to think about this. We'll figure it out, ok?"

Torchlight shimmered as the one coming toward them rounded the distant corner and shouted in a tone that was not to be ignored. "You there, what are you doing? You're needed this instant. Why are you dawdling in the corridor?" His harsh tone held them on the precipice between flight and fright, but when he called out again, Brigyda squealed in panic. "Did you hear me? Come at once and bring your bucket!" In less than ten paces he was upon them and Lourdes looked up at the Tower Guard who towered over her as if she were only a toddler. Dressed in dark leather and bearing a glimmering torch, her gaze fell to watch the sword, daggers and multiple other weapons that hung from his belt and clanked ominously when he stopped. He was exceptionally large, his bulky muscles bulging beneath the leather uniform he wore and his head was bald. Glaring down at them with disdain in his dark

CYNTHIA A. MORGAN

eyes, he reached to pull Brigyda along with him, but
Lourdes stepped in front of her boldly.

"She's ill and cannot do her work today." The
tremors in her voice belied her audacity and he
scowled down at her with impatience even as Brigyda's
crying increased.

"Horse shit. She's assigned to The Tower and to The
Tower she'll go." He yanked the girl away from Lourdes
and began to drag her behind him.

"Madam Ornaly has assigned her to the kitchens today," Lourdes informed hastily, rushing after him, then
doubling back to collect the bucket and bundle of rags
her friend had dropped before running to catch up
with them. Trotting beside him, she continued her
breathless explanation, "please, Sir, I've been assigned
to you instead. I was just taking her to Cook before I
reported to The Tower door."

Without pausing, he growled at her irascibly. "Ornaly never notified The Guard of this change. Far as I
know, this one's with me."

Brigyda's knees buckled in terror and she stumbled,
her legs scraping along the stone floor for several yards
as he dragged her behind him.

"Please, Sir, if you let me explain," Lourdes gasped
in desperation, but he merely shoved her away from
him like a ragdoll. Twisting around, he glared down at
the girl he dragged bodily behind him and finally
stopped.

"Damnable, worthless, swine-fodder! On your feet!"
Raising his hand over his head, his next action was
alarmingly clear, but he never followed through. Stepping out of her office with chilling nonchalance,
Madam Ornaly addressed the guard with a low tone.

"Is there some way I can assist you?"

Turning even as he lowered his hand, the Tower
Guard considered her with a narrowed gaze, recog-

nizing her immediately and dropping the sniveling girl to the floor. "This one's late. I was sent to collect her."

Madam nodded unhurriedly as she approached, her demeanor entirely altered from what it had been only moments before. She reached for the girl tenderly and Lourdes watched with disbelief as she drew her into her arms like a protective mother. "I do apologize for the inconvenience of not notifying your office sooner. She only just came to me for reassignment not fifteen minutes ago. She is quite unable to satisfy the conditions of her duties today and I've given you, instead, that one over there."

He turned to look at Lourdes with an openly scrutinizing gaze, his examination dropping from her rose-tinted cheeks to the supple curves concealed beneath her dress and the twisted grin that fleetingly turned his lips caused her to shiver. Grunting with acceptance, he turned back to the Head Housekeeper and snarled. "Shift changes are to be reported immediately. Is that one fully trained?"

Madam stepped back with Brigyda even as she turned a caustic glare onto Lourdes. "She's a scullery maid and untrained in the tasks you specify for Tower servants, but, if mopping up is all that's required, she's perfectly capable." Indicating artfully that she was fully aware of what went on in the infamous Tower, Madam gestured toward Lourdes generously who stood gaping and looking from one to the other in wide-eyed dismay.

"Bring your bucket, girl," the guard snapped at her harshly. Turning without another glance at Madam or the servant he had so brutally handled, he led Lourdes away down the corridor, his pace so rapid she was forced to run to keep up. As they retreated into the shadows, Madam lowered her gaze to Brigyda and her warming embrace fell away, replaced by the coldest of stares.

"Report to the kitchen at once and if I hear another peep out of you, I'll trade you for one of the regimental whores without another thought!"

Lourdes was gasping for breath by the time they reached The Tower doors. The Tower Guard took little notice of her beyond ensuring that she was still there before he brandished a large ring of keys, which he used to unlock the doors that remained secured at all times. As they swung open with a low groan, Lourdes' gaze scanned the interior hastily. She was both terrified and curious what she might see, but the only sight that met her eyes was a stone stairwell leading upward to the left and a narrow corridor leading inward to the right. Turning to glare down at her impatiently, the guard reached to shove her forward.

"That way." He shoved her toward the corridor and she stumbled forward awkwardly, unsure where to go or what was required of her, but he followed close behind her. She took in the long corridor and the dark shadow of a chamber ahead as she approached a narrow side room and before she could pass it, he grasped her by the shoulder tightly.

"You'll need to draw water from the well to fill that bucket. Well's in there." The room was dark, illuminated by only a small glimmer of light from the corridor. It was a windowless room and was barely bright enough see. She peered inward unnerved by the shadowy alcove nearly as much as she was by the guard who stood so close behind her she could feel the heat of his body. It wasn't hard to guess what he wanted or why he had stopped her by the dark room and she

couldn't contain the trembles that suddenly raked their
icy fingers over her.

"Did you hear me, girl?" he growled and her heart
lurched in her chest as fear reached out of the dimness
as if trying to strangle her. What could she possibly do?
She had no options; she was alone and no one other
than Brigyda and Madam Ornaly knew where she had
been taken. Clutching her bucket tightly, she twisted
around with a caustic reply and her words met his
broad chest.

"You're practically standing on top of me. How
could I not hear you?" It wasn't the smartest idea she'd
ever had. The words had barely left her mouth before
both his hands came down heavily on her shoulders.
Leaning even closer, he spoke with a rasping tone in
her ear.

"I'll be doing a lot more than standing close to you."
Pushing her into the shadows towards the only thing
inside the room she could see, a circular well with a
low bench to one side, he pursued her aggressively and
captured her in his arms as his mouth grazed the back
of her neck. The squeal of panic that escaped her only
made him chuckle.

"Mmm, scream all you like, girl. That's what hap-
pens in The Tower." He forced her against the well,
wedging the bucket she still clutched tightly in her
shaking hands between the ancient stonework and her
body. Bending over her from behind, his hands ex-
plored her youthful curves as she twisted and bucked
against him, trying to elude him, but her struggling
only served to entice him. Grasping her breasts harshly,
he growled and pushed himself against her. The sensation caused her to shriek loudly. Writhing against his
restrictive hold on her, she sought any avenue of escape, but she could not oppose his strength any more
than she could fight the tears running over her cheeks.

Her predicament became horrifyingly clear. Forced to endure his exploration of her body, she shook violently when his hands followed the curve of her waist to the roundness of her bottom.

"That's a good girl. Give me what I want and I won't hurt you…. much." Tugging the loose fabric of her dress upward, he held the hem of it against the small of her back with one hand. Pinning her in place with the weight of his body, he used his free hand to unlace the front of his pants and she fought him more frantically.

"No!" she shrieked loudly, the word echoing throughout The Tower, but he only laughed and leaned heavily against her as he tugged her remaining garment downward.

"Oh yes!"

Struggling against the weight of his body, she felt the heat of him press against her and she couldn't control the shocked sob the unfamiliar contact produced. He laughed at the sound. "Struggle for me." His heavy tone slurred against her ear as he pushed into her and he enjoyed her resistance as much as her cries of pain. Her senses spun in a bedlam of shock and desperation, the violation of her body so furious and unrelenting she nearly passed out.

Rounding the corner outside the dim alcove, the commander of the Tower Guard, a ruggedly handsome man in his prime, looked into the shadows interestedly and scoffed. Shaking his head, he watched for a few moments before he drew a dagger from his belt and knocked the hilt against the framework of the door. "Finish up there, Ghislain, she's got work to do."

The sound of his voice drew her out of the nightmare into which she had sunken and she cried out with renewed vigor, desperate for someone to help her, but the commander was not the least bit concerned over the rape of an insignificant servant girl. Ghislain grunted his acknowledgement, but continued merci-lessly, as unhindered by his commanding officer's re-buke as he was her pain-filled crying and he didn't pause until he had fully satisfied his lust.

Releasing her, he stepped back as she crumpled to the ground and he stood watching her cry for several moments as he leisurely redressed. Outside, the com-mander reappeared and the two men observed her cal-lously before Ghislain stepped aside. Moving into the darkness, the commander approached her slowly, crouching down in front of her as he reached to place his fingers beneath her chin. Raising her head slowly, he watched very closely as she wept, his handsome fea-tures twisted by a sadistic smile.

"Such pretty tears. You'll do quite nicely, I think." His cold blue-eyed stare dropped to examine the bodice of her dress barely covering her and a perverse grin turned his lips as he used his free hand to expose her more fully. "Cry as much as you like. You'll get no sympathy from me. Girls serve only two purposes here, to obey and serve their masters." Watching the tears that slipped down her cheek, he moaned with pleasure and traced their passage with his thumb. She stared at him in horror, the scar that crossed his handsome face from his right temple to left jaw sending another shudder through her. "You understand, cherie, while you are inside the walls of The Tower, *we* are your mas-ters. It is your job to obey and serve us."

The cruelty of his words stabbed her like a knife and she leaned away from him, but the fingers beneath her chin reached outward and grasped her by the throat, holding her tightly as he leaned closer. With de-liberate slowness, he licked her mouth and the tears on her cheeks, thoroughly enjoying the way she whim-pered and tried to turn her face away.

"Yes, you'll do very nicely. Best get to your work before I decide you can serve me better right here." Rising, he stood over her and watched as she grasped the splayed bodice of her dress in an attempt to close it. "Leave it open."

The soft tone of his voice turned instructive with a harsh edge she knew better than to disobey. Swallowing hard against her dismay, she scrabbled up, collected her bucket and moved to the ancient well so she could fill it. Turning away without a shred of concern, the two men stepped out into the corridor and waited until she had successfully filled the container and turned to look at them. Gathering as much of her composure as still remained, she took several unsteady steps towards the entryway before she looked down the hall. "What is my work?" She asked in a hushed and shaken voice.

The commander of the guard ran a hand through his shoulder-length brown hair and shook his head. "What is my work, *Sir?*" he corrected with evident disparagement, then waited for her to repeat the phrase before giving the information she sought. His belittlement tore at her as ruthlessly as what they had just done to her, but she refused to allow him to see her devastation.

"What is my work, *Sir?*" she whispered hoarsely as she struggled to restrict the flow of any further tears. Not entirely successful, her display caused them to smile wickedly. Pointing toward the locked doors of The Tower, the commander finally divulged what her duties would be.

"You will report here each morning by the start of rotations. 6 A.M. to be clear, and await our pleasure. Only when I've decided you've fulfilled your requirement to obey and serve your masters will you be allowed to proceed to the chamber beyond and clean up the mess left by those on the night watch." His calm explanation of his plan to rape her on a daily basis sent a violent shudder through her, but she would not give in to her revulsion and fear by squalling in terror and running for the door, though she wished to do nothing else. "Do you understand me?"

Forcing herself to nod, she made no further sound or motion and he inclined his head at her as he set another requirement.

"Very good. Now thank me and you may get to work." His calm disregard of her feelings made her stomach twist. She struggled to force the words to her mouth, but it took several attempts before she was successful and the entire time he stood watching her, waiting for her to degrade herself further. Though she tried, she could not keep the tears his demand created from washing over her cheeks anew.

"Th..thank...thank you, Sir."

Smiling at her heartlessly, he moved a step nearer. "Curtsy now, like a good girl."

His demand unsettled her so prodigiously that she could manage only an unbalanced stoop before she backed away from him like a frightened animal. Hurrying along the corridor as quickly as the heavy bucket she carried permitted, she could feel their cold stares following her every movement, but when she turned the corner into the main chamber, the sight that met her eyes made her fear and pain entirely irrelevant.

4

Patience was his essence, clemency his soul. He had never known resentfulness, rage, or hatred. All the years of his long life, which numbered in countless ages, he had been the exemplification of compassion, empathy, and forgiveness; yet now as the dark hours of agony and loneliness dragged on, his thoughts churned in a tumultuous commotion of wrath and determination. Those who abused him deserved the wrath that pierced his benevolent essence like furious bolts of lightning from a tempestuous sky, but the one he had come to find deserved all the determination he could muster.

He had to wait, to continue the search he had so audaciously started. To ask the Almighty to be given any measure of time to search for something commonly accepted to be lost was, by its very nature, brazen; yet he could not accept that so valuable a concept as mercy had been abandoned. He could not stand by silently while hope burned within him. The strength of his resolve had prompted him to speak, just as it now convinced him to wait, despite his intensifying desire to pour out the ferocity of his wrath on those who abused him. It was an alarming circle of vehement emotion and it became a maelstrom that threatened to undo him, separate him from everything he knew about himself, and create in the void a beast of abhorrent violence.

It took every measure of strength he possessed and countless hours of intense meditation to silence his mouth from speaking the words that could end his suffering and free him from the monsters holding him captive. Over and over again, he reminded himself of his purpose, a purpose for which he had sacrificed his sanctified state and assumed human form; a purpose for which he now chose to suffer. He had asked to be allowed to search for any human beings left among the dwindling throng of humanity who understood what mercy was and who lived with compassion and empathy. Even just one.

His request had been granted. 100 years has been appointed and the final Horseman, Death, had been required to wait until the Archangel's search was completed. The Horseman's brothers, those Riders who had preceded him, had a purpose just as he did. They wrought justice for all those who had been victimized during the ages since the beginning. They condemned the children of the wicked and punished the descendants of the compassionless by unleashing the consequences of their violence and hatred upon them.

Humanity had sown the seeds of their own destruction through their despicable actions. The sickness and perversions they poured from their souls like plague were returned to them as plague. The violence they perpetrated on the meek and innocent was repaid through violence, and the deprivations suffered through their cruel neglect, greed, and corruption were revisited upon them through harsh years of want, need and starvation. Pestilence, War and Famine had thundered across the abyssal plane, leaving turmoil and ruin in their wake.

All of beautiful creation was not subject to the trials the Horsemen unleashed. Only human beings felt the full measure of their resolve. During the three catastrophes that had already passed since the onset of the Great Cataclysm, the earth's population had diminished on an alarming scale, but plant and animal-life recovered from the subjugation they had suffered under the ungainly dominion of humans. Nature slowly recovered from countless generations of pollution and exploitation as those responsible bore the penalties for their disregard.

Tzadkiel had chosen a different course. Death waited behind him, ready to ride upon his pallid horse, but his own purpose had yet to be fulfilled. He needed to find one that matched himself; one who still understood compassion. Although he had searched for nearly a century, he could not accept there was no one. None, but him? It was incomprehensible. So, he continued to search, to wait, and through waiting he continued to accept the abuse forced upon him by the children of the lost.

Year 2060
The 1st Era of the Great Cataclysm
Regional countryside outside Chambon, France

Great clods of earth flew behind the thundering hooves of the massive white charger that broke through the tangle of green forest and galloped into the clearing of their yard. Annabella and Gabriel stood clasping each other's hands tightly, facing the Rider with palpable resolve as he approached. He was terrifying to behold and breathtakingly beautiful; a representation of male perfection that gave them both a staggering sense of insignificance. He raced closer, but taking notice of them standing near a weather-beaten barn on the far side of the clearing, he sharply reined in the great horse upon which he rode. The courser bellowed in outrage, but obeyed and skidded to a halt upon the lush grass crumpling beneath his enormous, golden hooves.

Considering them with an expression that mingled surprise and curiosity, the Rider urged his mount forward more judiciously as his brilliant cobalt gaze that studied them reflected the brightness of the sky above. Annabella struggled to remain standing beneath the weight of his intense stare, but Gabriel, who was always bolder in the face of adversity than he ever anticipated he could be, raised his free hand to cover his heart and bowed respectfully. Several yards away from them, the Rider tugged the reins and the immense stallion stopped once more, blowing and tossing his head in defiance at the pair.

They looked at each other for only a moment, but it seemed an eternity. In that brief span of time they took in the Rider's powerful physique, the cobalt blue cape flowing from his broad shoulders, the waves of his white, shoulder-length hair, his hands gloved in golden leather, and the uniform of cobalt, stark white, and sparkling gold he so proudly wore. They also saw the blood that stained his striking uniform drawing attention to the seemingly fresh wound he bore upon his shoulder. Gabriel noticed the size of the sheathed sword he had strapped to his horse's side where it was within easy reach while Annabella observed the youthful blush of his high cheek-bones, the fullness of his lips, and the determined gleam in his vivid gaze.

Crossing one leg across his steed's withers, he leaned forward in the saddle and watched them with marked interest before he chose to speak. When he did the sound of his voice echoed as if he stood in the center of a vast hall. Only after several words did the resonance fade and his voice became more humanly typical, although his rich baritone seemed to fill the clearing in which their small farm was constructed.

"You greet your demise honorably, humans."

They glanced uncertainly at each other before Gabriel raised his wife's small hand in his and replied with an averted gaze. "Noble Rider, we are paltry blots upon this fair globe and unworthy even to speak with you, but we offer what we have to give in reverence for the One you serve."

Raising a brow at this unexpected response, the Rider straightened and looked around him, noticing a small wagon of hay and oats located next to a trough filled with water. He studied this closely, as if he had been lured by other humans who, in the hope of averting their fate, had first offered gifts and then sought to attack him when he took his leisure. One such attack had apparently resulted in the gunshot wound he now suffered and he was visibly skeptical of their honesty. Searching the surrounding clearing with evident caution, he spoke with a firm tone. "Who resides here with you?"

Gabriel shook his head. "No one. Our children have moved away and we live alone."

The Rider's gleaming gaze narrowed and he shifted his attention to the woman standing so quietly beside the man. She had not spoken, but her benevolent essence announced itself to him with an unmistakably clear voice. Intrigued, he considered her more carefully.

"This is your husband, woman?" The question was a test. She could not know his intent or reason for asking and might assume something unworthy of him, which would tell him a great deal about the nature of her being and the depth of her heart. She lowered her gaze modestly; then looked at the man beside her. Before she could answer, he saw in her expression the years she had loved him, the joy they had shared in raising their children, and the unconditional trust she had in him. She nodded, but he posed another question before she could find words to articulate her sentiments. "What are your names?"

They looked at each other with a glint of fear, but she answered quietly. "He is Gabriel and I am Annabella. Please, Good Rider, you appear to be injured. May I tend the wound for you?" Her honest compassion caused him to raise an eyebrow yet again, but as if he had heard enough, the Rider nodded and smiled. The beacon of glimmering beauty sparkled in their small yard more radiantly than the setting sun. Releasing the reins from his powerful hands, he leaped down from the saddle and patted his charger with his uninjured arm. The horse nickered softly, turned his head to gaze at the waiting fodder and whinnied with delight when the Rider responded to him.

"Yes, my friend, you may indulge yourself. I have a feeling all will be well here." Turning his attention back to the humans standing before him, he took a few strides closer to them. They trembled observably, but the warmth of his smile didn't fade as he closed the distance between them. Approaching as if they were family he had not seen in far too long, he moved to stand before the man and offered his hand, which he took with visible hesitancy.

"Gabriel." The Rider spoke his name portentously, studying him with a piercing gaze that seemed to see straight into his soul. Turning slowly, he looked at his wife, his expression softening though he didn't reach to touch her. "Annabella." Speaking her name with a tone that reminded her of both her father and her sons, he inclined his head with evident gratitude. "Your greeting is unexpected, but very welcome. It has been... a difficult road." His voice trailed off as he glanced at his shoulder. Returning his penetrating gaze, Annabella found herself issuing an unforeseen invitation.

"You must be tired and hungry. We don't have much, but I can make a meal of bread, wine, fruit and cheese if it appeals?"

Again, he studied her incredulously, looking between them for several tense moments before he shook his head and visibly relaxed. Stepping back from them, he bowed formally and smiled magnificently once again.

"I was told I would meet 'the unexpected', but I didn't anticipate it would be the warmth of a woman's kindness and the reminder of friends." He looked back at Gabriel before continuing. "You bear a noble name. My friend Gabriel smiles at me through you." This caused the man's eyes to widen in surprise and he stammered to formulate a response, but the Rider looked past him towards the small house they called their home. "My shoulder does, indeed, require tending and I have not eaten in nearly two days. I gladly receive your generosity, though I fear I may leave you with little for yourselves." His tone lilted with mirth and they looked at each other in astonishment, never anticipating they might sit down at table with the dreaded Horseman of the Great Cataclysm, let alone enjoy his company.

Year 2446
The 96th Year of the 4th Era after the Great Cataclysm
Le Bastion de la Résolution, - Marçais, New France

Early morning sunlight streamed into the broad chamber through several large windows secured by iron bars. Its radiance illuminated the man who lay bound to an ancient stone table centrally located in the room. The light reflected an odd, glimmering aura emanating from his body and pulsing through an amulet he wore, but the beauty of this inexplicable glow stood in stark contrast to his ghastly bleeding wounds. The sight of them caused Lourdes to gasp loudly and she raised her free hand to cover her mouth as she stopped in her tracks and stared at him in wide-eyed horror. Blood spread across his skin, running down onto the table and collecting in small grooves that were carved into the stonework before seeping down its flanks to form crimson pools at its base.

"You understand your duties better now." The commander's voice from directly behind her caused Lourdes to shriek in dismay and jolt away from him violently. In her fear, she dropped her bucket onto the floor where it splashed much of its contents outward onto his boots. Glaring down at them, he raised a threatening stare to her and allowed his anger to intimidate her for many long moments while he enjoyed the way she cowered away from him with tears rimming in her eyes once more. Immeasurably pleased by the opportunity to torment her further, he smiled sadistically and shook his head.

"Good thing that's clean water. We wouldn't want you wasting time cleaning my boots when there are more important things for you to be doing." He paused ominously while his dark gaze dropped to the still open bodice of her dress, "like serving and obeying your masters." The clarity of his intentions sent violent trembles coursing over her and the sight of them twisted his smile wickedly before he aggressively shouted at her. "Get to work!"

Her startled screech made him laugh before he strode away without a second look, leaving her standing there with fear stifling her unlike any she had ever known before. It pierced her like a blade, stole her breath and left her shaking uncontrollably. It was not only the fear of him and what he could so easily to do her, but fear of what she saw before her.

The man lay unmoving on the table, his arms and legs secured in iron manacles that were held fast by heavy chains fed through holes drilled into the table's stonework. These chains were fastened to the floor to keep the prisoner immobilized and a leather harness lay behind his head, the blood-stained straps secured to the underside of the table. Above his head, other manacles lay waiting and unused. Naked and bleeding profusely, he lay unwatched and untended, breathing in deep shuddering gasps that shook his body. She couldn't tell if he was awake, but hoped for his sake he was not. Sickened with dread and frozen in horror, she stared at him, unable to bear the sight of him and incapable of looking away.

The tears that fell from her caramel eyes were no longer for herself. How could anyone do something so horrible? How could someone even think up such cruelty? Long, deep lacerations crossed his body, leaving little of him unmarred. In the places where there were no bleeding wounds, his skin was vivid red as if he had been scorched by severe heat. The unbearable pain he must have endured and now was suffering made her stomach twist into a tight knot. Even as she tried to force herself to her knees to focus, instead, on cleaning his blood from the floor a wave of sickness heaved inside her. She moaned against the surge, bending forward and covering her mouth as she squeezed her eyes tightly closed and concentrated every ounce of strength she possessed on not becoming ill.

The sound of her moan drew him out of the dark well of agony he had fallen into and he opened his eyes to look up at the ceiling uncertainly. He thought he'd heard speaking, but the heavy darkness pulling him downward was disorienting. Even as the soft sound drew him back, blackness clawed at him, trying to drag him back down into its abyss. His thoughts were unfocused, blurred by intense pain he could not ignore, but surely the soft moan he'd heard hadn't been a manifestation of his mind. Had it? Was this sound some indication that his mind was attempting to disengage from his tortured body? Was it a figment of his imagination, like the screams he'd heard, or thought he'd heard, only moments ago? Had it been only moments ago or had he slipped into unconsciousness and they had actually been nothing but a dream?

His mind was a tangle of pain and confusion that made him doubt himself, but another soft noise beside the table captured his full attention. Was it crying? Had the young servant returned? His thoughts spun for a moment as he considered. Was this even the same day as when he'd seen her? He had no point of reference. His memory was a disjointed haze of agony, torment, and severing isolation that fragmented his thoughts into pools of jagged darkness. They spun slowly, reaching for him, drawing him into the quiet calm at their center where it was peaceful and irresistible.

He closed his eyes.

Silence deep and soothing enveloped him.

Stillness.

"You do not need to suffer this." A deep, resonant voice filled the obscurity surrounding him. It encircled him like spiraling smoke, waking him from the stillness that enshrouded him. As his senses returned, he realized he was himself again. He was once more the spiritual embodiment of mercy in its purest form. He no longer suffered wave after wave of inescapable pain, but felt vibrant and strong. Powerful. Standing in thick blackness, he turned slowly, searching the emptiness for the one who spoke.

"I know." His voice was resonant and echoed in the darkness.

"They only hurt you because you allow it." Again, the deep voice echoed into the gloom. He nodded distractedly. The sensation of not having any pain was euphoric. He could barely concentrate on anything else.

"I know." At his repetition, the darkness surrounding him transformed into an ominous red murk.

"I wait!"

He suddenly understood. It was the one who stood behind him waiting to be released, waiting for him to be satisfied that there were no longer any living souls of mercy left among the lost multitude of humanity, but he wasn't convinced. Not yet. He repeated himself more assertively. "I know."

"Time grows short."

He understood this as well. He had been given 100 years. If a single soul could not be found in so long a stretch of time, it would be accepted that none remained and the final Horseman, Death, would be released. He had waited all this time, but was obviously growing impatient. Squaring his shoulders, Tzadkiel pierced the darkness with his deep violet gaze and spoke formidably. "100 years has been appointed and I shall not be rushed."

Slowly the murky-red haze diminished back into darkness as a low growl acknowledged the final Horseman's acceptance that he would continue to wait. The darkness thickened and, as it intensified, the sense of liberty he had so briefly enjoyed was replaced by a heavy mantle of pain once more. He had chosen this suffering and allowed it to return to his body, unsure how long he could continue to endure, but determined to wait for the one he sought even as tears fell from his now pale, lavender eyes. The crystal he wore round his neck pulsed softly, glowing faintly lavender in the morning light.

Beside him, from the direction of the floor, another soft noise drew him back into consciousness more fully and he turned his head slowly, gritting his teeth against the discomfort even such a slight movement caused him. He could hear the sound of water and a shushing noise he could not identify, but whoever was there was not within his visual range and the iron manacles restraining him kept him from moving any further. The sound of water created a sudden, desperate need within him that was so intense he couldn't silence the moan that escaped his lips.

"Water," he whispered; his voice an unrecognizable, raspy thread. The sounds below him instantly stopped. There was no indication of any movement at all, but he was sure someone was there. The noises he heard weren't simply his imagination, just as the need within him for water was not. Despite the fact that he required neither food nor drink to sustain his life-force, the urgency of his inexplicable desire for water forced him to speak again. "Please."

Not a sound.

Rising from her stooped position, a young woman straightened to look at him with misery evident in her eyes. Their stares locked and she sniffled repeatedly, swallowing hard against her own tears. He stared at her as if she were an apparition, disbelief and desperation mingling in his eyes with an intensity that belied his weakened physical state. She trembled as she stood staring at him; then looked down to the floor before she searched the corners of the chamber for any sign of guards. Oddly, The Tower seemed empty.

"Please," he repeated more softly, regaining her distracted attention for the briefest moment before she ducked out of sight once more. The disappointment he experienced at her rejection was far more painful than any wound he had ever received and he could hear resonant laughter echoing in his mind from the one who waited behind him.

Bending to collect her sodden rags and the bucket, Lourdes straightened and leaned closer to him before she whispered in a soft voice so only he would hear. "I'll return shortly and bring you fresh water."

He opened his pain-filled eyes to stare at her as if unable to comprehend her words. It would not have surprised her if he was delirious. The pain he must have endured was incomprehensible. Glancing over him with dismay, she reached to touch his arm in a gesture of reassurance, but drew back with a start. Was she crazy? Touching him would only cause him more pain. Unsure what else to do, she returned his penetrating stare for a brief moment before hurrying away.

Hastening back to the well room, she dumped the blood-stained water into a drain she discovered near the outside corner of the small alcove before returning to the well crank. Lowering the pail down into the darkness, she glanced round her repeatedly, nervous energy fueling her haste. Ignoring her own situation and the discomfort she felt with each movement, she worked the well crank as quickly as she could and cursed under her breath at the dry creaking noise it made.

It took several pails of water to rinse and then refill her bucket. Pouring the water she drew from the depths of the well one final time into the larger vessel made of wood and twine, she hoisted it from the low bench beside the well and began to make her way back to the main chamber. Rounding the corner of the alcove, she stopped suddenly, nearly colliding with the commander of the guard who stood in the corridor to bar her way. His dark stare moved slowly over her body, inspecting her openly. "Finished so soon?" he asked with a heavy tone. She shook her head, answering with a timid squeak while she focused her eyes on the floor beneath his boots.

"No, Sir."

He stepped closer, his threatening proximity causing her to shudder. "No, Sir? What are you doing, then?" Not waiting for her answer, he raised a hand to touch her trembling shoulder, lightly tracing the subtle curve of her collarbone as she struggled not to lean away from him. His touch made her skin crawl.

"Just...just getting fresh water...S...Sir."

"Mmm. I'm quite lucky you're so conscientious." He looked down at her with a heated stare, his fingers lingering on the soft spot of her neck before he allowed them to slide downward toward her bosom. Whimpering, she could not force herself not to evade him by turning away, but her action only caused him to grasp her shoulder tightly. Pulling her back abruptly, he purposefully moved the fabric of her dress aside to reveal the full paleness of her breasts. "Stand still."

His demand was firm, although slurred with desire, but she was unable to control her reactions. Straining

71

away from him, her disobedience caused an instant frown to darken his expression.

"Put your bucket down. You aren't going to need it for a while."

"Please, Sir." Pleading with him was the last thing she wanted to do, but the words slipped past her lips before she could contain them. He twisted them into a perverse request.

"Ssshhh, I know. Be patient. I have no intention of rushing like a mad beast." Leaning in, he held her securely as he slovenly licked her mouth and the tears from her cheeks. She squirmed in protest.

"Please stop."

Drawing back slowly, he watched as she began to cry in earnest, smiling lasciviously and raising his hand to cup her face as if adoringly. "No, I will not. Cry for me."

5

It didn't take long for technology and the wantonness of waste that had been so prevalent in the late 20th and early 21st centuries to become a thing of the past. Natural resources dwindled rapidly. Without electricity or fossil fuels to power all the machines that created so much of what the world took for granted and used on a daily basis, rationing quickly became ineffective. Entire populations turned to hoarding and scavenging in order to survive.

Although there were a small number of wealthy families who enjoyed the comforts their money could still buy such as security from the looting and riots that became nightly occurrences, clean water and working sewerage, the vast majority of the world's population survived however they could. Life without electricity forced humanity to return to a way of living they had abandoned hundreds of years earlier.

Candles and clean water quickly became more valuable than gold. Monetary wealth was replaced by a system of barter and trade. Coalitions and factions replaced most major governments, breaking down large barriers while building an even greater number of smaller ones. Fragmentation and isolation became the new reality. Where it used to take mere moments for current events and information to circle the globe, it now took days and sometimes weeks for news to spread. Humanitarian groups dissolved and justice became swift and inescapable.

Trust was shattered by greed.

Hope suffered decimation through apathy.

Sympathy and compassion became virtues of the past.

Year 2060.
The 1st Era of the Great Cataclysm
Regional countryside outside Chambon, France

Gabriel placed three wine glasses on the table beside a bottle of red wine he had retrieved from the cellar, then he sat down. The small kitchen table was as time-worn as the home itself, but it was a cozy place they shared together in the midst of the world's increasing chaos and there was nowhere he'd rather be. Looking at the Rider seated beside him, he wondered what would become of them now. Would the enigma of flesh and myth seated with them at their humble table decide to show them mercy? Would they live to enjoy another quiet evening at home together or would he fulfil his purpose as Pestilence?

While Gabriel went to the basement, Annabella hastened to collect the few medicinal provisions they had from upstairs, leaving the Rider alone in their humble living room. He stood with his hands clasped behind his back, looking about the small house with interest and examining the photographs displayed on the fireplace mantle. His inspection was cut short when

MISERICORDE

Gabriel returned, but the two men didn't speak to each other in the brief span of time that passed before Annabella returned from the upper floor with the medical supplies, several cloths and a small washbasin. Rejoining them, she filled the basin with clean water from a large pitcher on the kitchen counter before setting everything down on the table before the Rider. She hesitated beside him, disinclined to ask the obvious as she looked at his blood-stained coat and shook her head subtly. "I fear the only way to remove such a stain is to soak this for several days."

He shook his head before she could continue. "It shall have to remain marred. I have little time to tarry." Seeing her hesitation, he got up and unfastened his cape, draping it over the back of the chair before he began to unbutton his coat. She stepped back from him nervously, only then realizing how tall and strongly built he was. She'd grown accustomed to her husband's slender build and average stature, but standing beside a man who was easily over six-foot-tall and whose physique was twice that of her husbands, she couldn't help staring in spite of her uneasiness. He didn't seem to notice her apprehension, however, and continued to disrobe, removing his blood-soaked shirt while she tried not to stare at the perfection of his form. Focusing her attention, as well as she could manage, she examined the injury before proceeding.

The bullet had pierced him just below his left shoulder and exited through his back creating two angry, bleeding wounds. She wasn't skilled with sutures, but knew the injuries required cleaning and a generous application of salve before she could properly knit and bandage them.

"You have tended injuries before?" he asked curiously, watching her closely. She nodded.

"With two sons, injuries are a daily occurrence.

Though I'm not entirely convinced I know how to stitch this properly"

The Rider nodded and looked at Gabriel who had gotten up from his chair and stood watching them as if he were on guard. Considering this judiciously, the Rider turned his attention back to Annabella. "I wouldn't worry about stitchings. I heal rather quickly and your kindness is appreciated. As you see, most do not welcome me as you two have." He winced suddenly and jerked away from her when the antiseptic ointment she applied stung unexpectedly. Her apology was instantaneous, but Gabriel wondered at this evidence of his humanity.

"Many have tried to kill you?" His question brought the Rider's gaze back to him and he felt the weight of his stare before he answered with a nod.

"They cannot, of course, but having taken human form I am vulnerable to injury." Annabella sighed despairingly and he looked back at her with confusion. "You disapprove?"

She frowned as she began to wrap his shoulder in bandaging, struggling to express what it was that disturbed her so greatly. "I disapprove of the way we've become, so full of hatred and violence; so ready to hurt another with so little cause. Where has our compassion gone?" Tying off the bandage, she redirected their conversation back to his injury before he had time to answer. "This will keep your wound clean for a day or two, but should be changed after that."

He examined her work and nodded, rising to his feet once more as he reached for his shirt. "In a day or two it will be fully healed," he replied matter-of-factly and she stared at him with astonishment.

"Fully?"

He smiled and agreed. "I am in human form, but am

not human." He moved his arm in several directions as if testing the efficiency of her work. "Thank you. It feels much better because of your ministrations."

Sharing a glance of amazement with her husband, Annabella smiled and moved to the kitchen counter, fastidiously cleaning up before assembling their supper. It was little more than a board of cheese with fruits and vegetables from their garden and a few cuts of cured meat, but it was all they had. The village market was half a day's ride and they only dared travel such a distance and leave their farm untended a few times each month. Instead, they relied on the stores they had from their garden and the game Gabriel was able to snare. They lived a simple life and were thankful for what they had.

It was more than many enjoyed.

As they waited for her to complete her task, Gabriel opened the bottle of wine and poured a generous amount into each of their glasses. The Rider watched him intently, as if waiting for him to ask something, but he didn't, so instead, the Horseman turned back to Annabella. "Your sons, are they the ones you have pictured on your mantle?"

A bit surprised that he had even noticed, she agreed they were, but before she could think of anything else to say, Gabriel interposed with a question of his own. "I have no right ask, but am curious. Why have you taken human form if it leaves you vulnerable?"

Piercing cobalt locked with his hazel gaze and the Rider considered for several moments before answering. "My native state of being is not easily understood. It was decided that Horsemen would be better comprehended." His enigmatic response caused both of them to pause and look at each other in surprise. Gabriel would have queried further, but Annabella prevented him by setting the board down on the table amid the glasses, bottle of wine, and a loaf of day-old bread that she immediately apologized for as she stepped back and looked toward the Rider.

"It isn't much, but we gladly share what we have with you."

Gabriel gazed at her with open affection and nodded, getting up from his chair even as the Rider smiled once more and followed his lead, getting up until she settled comfortably in her chair. Only then did he sit down as before without offering anything further on the subject. An uneasy stillness settled over them as several birds outside in the yard began to serenade the evening. Gabriel took it as signifying something portentous and lowered his head. "May we show our thankfulness through kindness and appreciate our blessings through generosity."

Annabella nodded subtly before unfolding her napkin. The Rider nodded as well.

"A simple, but powerful blessing," he said approvingly. "I see more clearly now why my path has crossed yours."

Their curious stares compelled him to further explanation, but he reached for the loaf of bread and tore it into three pieces, offering instead a far more trivial subject of conversation. "Have you lived in this place very long?"

They shared another uneasy glance as Gabriel took the bread offered to him by their guest and agreed they had, but his nervousness left him more than usually non-conversational. Annabella was quick to supplement her husband's quietness.

"We've lived here since we were married and raised our children here, before..." her voice trailed off and the Rider nodded with comprehension as he took several pieces of cheese from the board.

"Much has changed, but you seem to have adapted well."

They nodded mutely, eating in awkward silence for several moments. Undaunted by their apprehension, the Rider raised his glass and inhaled the aroma of the wine he had been offered, tasting it with caution before he closed his eyes and smiled. "I'm very glad to discover not everything has changed." Feeling their stares on him, he sighed, relenting at last. "Fear not gentle Gabriel and kind Annabella, you may rest easy in your bed tonight....and for many nights to come." He could see their relief as well as their confusion, but took another drink from his glass before continuing. "Many have tried to impede my purpose, their fear outweighing any compassion left within them."

Gabriel couldn't contain the question that immediately flew from him. "Your purpose?" His startled expression at having asked such an impertinent question only made the Rider chuckle.

"Yes, the purpose for which I was created. To render justice for all those who have been offended by the sickness of greed, cruelty and disregard." It was not the answer they had expected.

"Justice?" Annabella posed the simple, yet poignant inquiry and the Rider turned his cobalt stare to her, considering for many moments how best to explain before responding further.

"For thousands of years the innocent and meek have suffered under the sickness of cruelty and disregard of those who thought only of themselves. I am the embodiment of that sickness, sent to plague the uncaring multitudes. We Horsemen are justice for the poor, the helpless, and the innocent, wrought upon a world that has forgotten kindness and turned away from compassion. We condemn the wicked."

It was clear she was beginning to understand, but

Annabella couldn't keep the empathy within her silent. "But surely there are many who are still kind and compassionate, aren't there?"

Again, he stared at her for a long moment, the intensity of his gaze stealing her words and Gabriel motioned for her to be silent, but the Rider turned to face him and set his anxiety at ease. "Her questions do not anger me. They show the depth of her love, something the world has scorned." Having said this, he turned back to Annabella, the warmth of his expression falling into shadow. "You may ask what you wish, kind woman, but you must know this: there are far fewer who are still kind of heart and compassionate of spirit than you dare think." His ominous words stabbed at both of them and Gabriel, seeing the dread that crossed his beloved's fair features, got up from his chair and crossed quickly to take hold her shoulder from behind her chair.

"Please, speak no more of such awfulness. We may live in ignorant hope, but it's far better than the darkness of fear."

Leaning back in his chair, the Rider raised a gaze to him that expressed not only his surprise at Gabriel's bold rebuttal, but also his approval of the manner in which he protected his wife with his quiet strength. Inclining his head, he raised his hand to cover his heart. "Forgive me. The intensity of my resolve serves me well. It must be so or I could not fulfill such a resolute purpose, but I will speak no more about it. You have proven to me that mercy still breathes among the multitude. I believe this is why I was brought to your land." Pushing back from the table, he stood up and strode toward them with palpable determination, reaching out with both hands to lay one upon Gabriel and the other, very gently, upon Annabella. He could feel their fear through more than their trembling, but didn't release them. Instead, he spoke in a clear and commanding voice that echoed as it had when he'd first spoken to them.

"I am the embodiment of disease and infection. I am malady, misery and plague. I am the personification of all forms of Pestilence sent to expunge and renew." He paused when he realized that Annabella had begun to weep. Looking down at her with gentleness she had never seen in the eyes of another living being, he moved his hand to her cheek reassuringly before setting it once again upon her shoulder and continuing more softly. His words filled the house and he spoke as if making a proclamation for the world to hear.

"These two are one. They stand apart and shall be untouched. They will remain unharmed. They will be blessed with vitality for many years to come. They will live unscathed upon this sanctified and fertile land that will yield its bounty to them in abundance and will shelter them within its verdant dominion. They will live in the protective embrace of mercy, loving and bringing forth love, anew!" Looking up at Gabriel, he smiled an unexpectedly impish grin, patting him on the shoulder as if to congratulate him and Gabriel could not help but understand his unspoken suggestion.

Stepping back, the Rider placed his hand over his heart and inclined his head to them. "We shall know this land as the Place of Mercy. It is now set apart and I and my brothers shall pass by it. It shall be a sanctuary for all those who comprehend the values of compassion and generosity as you do. You and all those of your line who abide here are safe because of the greatness of your mercy."

Then, without another word, he turned and strode from their house.

Year 2446
The 96th Year of the 4th Era after the Great Cataclysm
Tower Obligar, Le Bastion de la Résolution, - Marçais,
New France

After several hours of being allowed to receive the regenerative effects of the morning sunlight that
streamed into the chamber through its barred windows, Phillippe returned to move Tzadkiel to his cell
for the remainder of the day. It was a routine both had
grown used to and few words were needed to prompt
the recovering Archangel to get up from the table upon
which he had been bound. Unsteadily he staggered
across the chamber to the holding cell awaiting his return and he didn't bother to turn back to face his tor-
mentor once inside.

It was not a large cell. A mere 8x8 cube of stone and
iron, the only comfort it offered was a pile of straw
heaped on the floor that served as either bed or bath-
room. There was not enough straw provided to serve
as both. Originally designed to hold prisoners awaiting
their turn on the rack or whatever other device of torture had been deemed their lot, the cell was intentionally a small, cramped space with a door that was
secured by the mere turn of a key. It was an insult
added to the injuries he suffered each day. Yet, to further torment him Phillippe hung the key to the cell's
door on a nail he had driven into the wall adjacent to
the cell, leaving the means of freedom visible at all
times and just out of reach.

In his perfected state as an Archangel, the ordeals he
now suffered would have been unthinkable. In his native realm his strength renewed itself in moments. His
words were never questioned and the potency of his

thoughts could alter physical realities. Now, however, he was limited by the frailties of the human form and silenced by his own decision to endure what they did to him. The sense grew stronger every day that by waiting, by enduring, he would find the one he sought. It was only an impression, an insubstantial notion backed by no evidence whatsoever, but he would not abandon his mission. He would not give up hope until the final seconds of the ninety-ninth year of his search when he would be forced to concede that humanity was lost. Then, when everything he could possibly do had failed, the final Horseman would be unleashed and these insignificant mortals tormenting him would suffer the wrath of the righteous.

They would suffer his wrath, for although he was the embodiment of mercy, he had just cause for vengeance. The thought gave him some level of comfort, but this was not that moment. Though his anger flared when he looked around the dismal cage into which Phillippe locked him, he had barely enough strength to keep himself upright. Stumbling the mere thirty feet from the table of his anguish to the cell of his despair had drained the small portion of strength he had recovered. Phillippe said nothing, closing the door behind him and hanging the key on its nail before walking away without a second glance, heading for Lévesque's office where they would devise some new brutality for tomorrow. He could hear their voices and had he listened closely enough he would have heard what they discussed, but he couldn't force himself to want to know. Horror was horror, regardless of how it was delivered.

Standing in the center of his small cell where Phillippe left him, he faced the blank wall and sought to center himself with the meager portion of energy he had absorbed from the radiant morning sunlight. His injuries no longer burned into him with intense agony. The sun's energy had already closed them and blood no longer flowed from his body, but his strength was barely more vital than a single flame lit against the darkest night. They never gave him time to recover fully.

They didn't dare.

Again, rage twisted inside him with vehemence so extreme he could scarcely contain it. Standing motionless against the onslaught of physical, emotional and mental fragility he battled, he sought to regain the serenity of his essence; to re-establish the discipline he had always practiced in his native environment, but he was exhausted. Depleted. Shaking. Lowering his weary gaze to the straw-littered floor, he sighed prodigiously. He was so tired. Tired of the pain that never completely left his body and filled him with dread. Tired of the filth they forced upon him; tired of the cruelty and callousness of this world. Worst of all, he realized he was tired of waiting.

He had no proof that he would find the one he sought within the walls of so dark a place as this, yet a subtle whisper from the depths of his being compelled him. Although after ninety-six years, he had no evidence that mercy even remained, not in the form he sought, a persistent hope he could not ignore urged him to wait. The fact that he had spent nearly a year locked into a prison where those who detained him spent their days devising sadistic ways to harm him was far more persuasive than the barely perceptible notion whispering deep inside him that his search was nearly over, but that whisper never altered and never grew silent. He knew the source of the internal whisper and he sighed again. It had to be nearly over; he didn't have the strength to continue.

She said she would return.

She told him she would bring him water.

She hadn't and the torment was intense, but the insistent whisper was impossible to ignore.

The loud, hollow sound of the Tower doors alerted him that he had been left alone. No guard stood on duty. No one watched to ensure his recovery. Those who secured the Tower always left when they locked him into his cell. They were free to leave. Free to go where they wanted; free to refresh themselves. He was not. He was abandoned without even so much as a cup of water. Though he had spent millennia tending the sick, ministering to the neglected, and reassuring the down-trodden, he was deserted without a single thought to his needs and the betrayal was piercing.

Behind him, a soft sound captured his attention. Little more than a quietly drawn breath, the sound made him listen, but he didn't turn around. He had so little energy and he couldn't be sure if the sound was real or if his mind deluded him. Then, another noise sparked his interest further. It was the hushed knock of wood against stone and a faint splash of water. Having not been aware that he'd closed them, he opened his eyes. Could Phillippe have returned with water? They provided so little, only enough to either wash away his blood or a meager portion to drink. It was never enough to do both and that frustration fueled the indignation burning inside him. He wasn't sure he wanted to know who it was; he wasn't sure he wanted to permit the outrage after all the others he already accepted, but he turned anyway and the surprise that met his wearied gaze was one he truly didn't expect.

It was the young woman he'd seen earlier that morning.

She had returned as she said she would.

She had brought him water.

The astonishment and relief he felt at seeing her

was replaced with dismay seconds later when he saw the bruises that marred her lips as well as the paleness of her bosom that was scantily covered by the torn bodice of her dress. Her left cheek was vivid red and she had an unmistakable bite mark on her neck just above her shoulder. The servant's cap she had been wearing earlier was gone and her chestnut-red hair tumbled in askew chaos. Beside her on the floor was a bucket filled with water, but his desperate thirst vanished when he saw how violently she trembled and the bruises that marred her lips and neck.

The sight of her caused him greater agony than anything Phillippe had ever done to him and the combination of shock, compassion and rage that swept across his expressive features seemed more than she could comprehend. Swaying unsteadily, she closed her eyes. The possibility that she might collapse right there in front of him brought an alarmed "oh!" from his lips. Reflexively reaching out for her, he moved to the iron bars that separated them, but his instability nearly matched her own. He could do nothing for her. All he could do was watch as she sank to the floor, stifling a sob as she raised her hands to cover her face.

He had witnessed atrocities many times, too many times. He was no stranger to anguish; other's anguish and more recently his own. He had stood quietly beside deathbeds, had shared the fear and loneliness of the abandoned and the lost, and had sought to comfort those who were mistreated and ill-used, but the helplessness he felt in those few moments was a torment he found nearly impossible to bear. What made her so different he couldn't comprehend.

Drawing a ragged breath, she uncovered her face and looked up at him miserably, her tearful gaze flickering over his naked body. He became painfully aware of himself. They hadn't allowed him the dignity of clothing since they captured him and had all but destroyed with gun fire what he'd been wearing. Forced to endure the cold, the hard stone of his cell, and the abrasive discomfort of straw against his unprotected wounds, he had gotten used to being unclothed. It was just another way they could oppress him, but it wasn't what she expected to see and, given what had obviously just happened to her, he didn't want her to be more uncomfortable than she was already.

Moving to sit on the floor in a less flagrant position, he found he could barely hold himself upright and slumped forward upon the iron bars of his cage, oddly thankful for their support. He had so little strength left that even such a simple task as sitting down exhausted him. She watched him silently, worry plainly evident in the reddened depths of her distinctively hued eyes. Looking beyond her own distress, her gaze strayed over his bloodied body and the misery of her expression doubled. It was plain to see it was not his nakedness that disturbed her, but the abuse he had suffered. She seemed to want to say something to him, but the emotion she so clearly battled prevented her and she averted her attention to the bucket on the floor between them. Leaning forward to push it closer to him, she whimpered at the discomfort it caused her and the sound tore at his heart.

Reaching cautiously through the iron bars, he stared at her with immense concern, but the tears rimming in her eyes deterred him from any thought of touching her, even if his intent was only to try to comfort her in some way. Instead, they stared at each other with silent dismay, words unattainable and, in truth, unnecessary. Instead, he focused his attention on the bucket. Dipping his hands into the cool water it contained, he brought a small portion of the liquid to his mouth.

It was sweeter and more refreshing than anything

he had ever tasted and an irrepressible urge to drink suddenly overpowered him. The only thought in his mind was insatiable thirst, all else faded. He didn't heed his exhaustion, which had only a moment ago been nearly unmanageable. He didn't notice her astonished gaze as he reached again and again and again into the bucket, drinking as hastily as he could manage. He also failed to see her blush when he shifted to a kneeling position and leaned against the bars of his cell so he could use both hands to scoop up the life-restoring water more efficiently. Indeed, if he had the strength to pick the bucket up and pour the contents into his mouth he would have, so great became his need.

Far too soon the water was gone.

Closing his eyes with immeasurable relief, he sighed heavily. Such a simple comfort, water, but one he had been denied for far too long. No, he didn't require it, but as soon as the replenishing liquid filled his stomach the sensation of irrational thirst diminished. He felt a measure of relief no amount of meditation or sunlight had been able to provide. Perhaps he needed it after all. Moving to sit down as he had been before; he raised his hand to wipe his mouth and chin and looked at the young woman once more. He was surprised that she hadn't moved, but when he looked more closely, his surprise faded. She returned his gaze with a half vacant expression, the furrows creasing her brow betraying the amount of pain she suffered and it was more than he could bear seeing. Slowly, cautiously, he reached through the bars another time.

He didn't speak. He didn't need to, and even if he should have said something, he could find no words to express himself adequately. Besides which, though the water eased his voracious thirst, it did little to bolster his strength and after using so much in the process of drinking, he now felt even more exhausted than before, if that was possible. The effort of holding his hand out to her claimed what little energy remained within him, causing him to shake though he strained to keep his hand steady. Like a frightened animal, she looked at it hesitantly; then, in spite of her obvious pain and uncertainty, she raised her hand to his. Their eyes met as he touched her.

"Thank you." His deep voice sent a tremor through her that he could feel and she pulled away, looking behind her as if to ensure no one else was there. Wiping the tears that had slipped down her cheeks, she pushed herself up from the floor. Not without a great deal of effort.

"I must go before they see." Her voice was a harsh whisper, strained with emotion and pain. He stared up at her, unable to rise.

"Are you alright?"

She considered, but could not bring herself to answer his question.

"I'll come back tomorrow." Looking at him with an expression he found unfathomable, she picked up the bucket and walked slowly away. He watched her go, praying she would meet with no further misfortune before finding her way out of The Tower. When the sound of the heavy door confirmed her escape from that dreadful place, he looked back to where she had been and stared for long moments at the crimson stained stones with a tempest of unexpectedly merciless thoughts raging within him.

How she managed to climb the ten flights of stairs leading up to her chamber, Lourdes didn't know. The pain she felt was nearly unbearable. It was so intense she actually considered returning to Madam Ornaly's office to see what aid she might offer, but the thought of walking all that way deterred her. In any case, she knew better. Servants were as insignificant to Madam as they were to everyone else who oversaw within the walls of the Eminent Protectorate's stronghold. Servants were to be used until they could no longer work and then be disposed of; they were easily replaced.

She couldn't risk losing her position, not for something that would be considered her own fault. Female servants were given no greater protection than male servants and all were expected to be smart enough to avoid being raped. EP Guards were known to be ruthless opportunists. Though rape or any other form of violent crime was not openly sanctioned, they were just another of the many actions The Protectorate could take that would not be questioned. Not by anyone.

The only thing she could do was rest and keep well away from the commander of the guard when she returned in the morning. She didn't want to return, but, as with most everything else, she had no choice. Failing to report for an assigned shift was as good an excuse as any to be replaced. More importantly, she had told him she would. She knew the man she brought water to was the one she'd been hearing for so long. He had to be; he was the only prisoner she saw inside The Tower and the ghastly injuries he had when she first saw him were more than enough to make his harrowing screams understandable.

Closing her door securely behind her, Lourdes moved to her bed and lowered herself cautiously to the firm straw mattress, gritting her teeth against the discomfort of sitting and lying down instead. She wanted to curl up in a knot and wail. Everything inside her screamed in protest. She had managed to live a full decade in this place and not only had she gone untouched, but she went practically unseen; yet now she dreaded going beyond her own door. How would she survive being raped day after day? How could she avoid it? Little wonder Brigyda was in the state she was in, and she was barely older than fifteen!

Poor, poor Brigyda!

Growling in outrage, she clenched her fist and pounded it repeatedly against the unyielding mattress, but it didn't help. It only hurt. Turning her face into her small pillow made from an old flour sack she had stuffed with feathers collected from the kitchen, she screamed with all the force she could muster, but the pressure of such a loud cry made the internal pain she felt even worse. All she could do was cry.

And cry.

Cry, until crying seemed pointless and she ended up lying on her bed, staring at her door vacantly. She didn't notice the afternoon slip away. She didn't remember to go to the servant's dining room for supper, even though her belly was empty, and she didn't answer when a light knock broke the silence in the room. The knock was repeated and a hushed voice came from the other side.

"Lourdes? Are you there? It's Brigyda."

Blinking with confusion, she focused on the door and struggled to sit up, but her body was sore beyond moving.

"Lourdes?"

"I'm here, Brigyda." A breathless reply was all she could manage. At the sound, the door was pushed open and her friend stepped inside, her expression immediately shifting to startled concern when she saw her lying on the bed, pale and trembling.

"Lourdes! What happened? Oh god, don't tell me. I know, I know what happened." They cried together for longer than either of them could gauge. Both had suffered at the hands of the EP Guards and neither could do anything about it. This was the way the world was and nothing they could do would change it. As servants they had no specific rights. They could only enjoy whatever freedoms their supervisors decided to extend, but they could make it better for each other. They could help each other survive. It didn't matter how, not at that moment. How was not important. They simply had to because the alternatives were even worse.

Brigyda helped Lourdes tend her injuries, wash, and change her clothes. Ensuring her friend was as comfortable as she could be, she returned to the door and retrieved a basket she had dropped at the entryway when she first came in. Returning to Lourdes, who was reclining on her bed propped up against the wall, she showed her what she had brought. "You didn't come down for supper and I knew, I just knew something was wrong. So, I brought you what I found today." She held the small basket out for her to see. It contained a heel of bread, two small apples that had imperfections, and the edible trimmings from several carrots. It also contained a few rinds of cheese, a true treasure of a find, but Lourdes shook her head.

"I can't take this. You need it more than I do." Her voice was a thread of a whisper. She was in no condition to argue.

"Don't you say no, not when they should be yours anyway. If you hadn't switched with me, they would be and you wouldn't be...." Brigyda's voice trailed off, watching her friend worriedly before redirecting her thoughts. "Besides, I had supper today, you didn't." Adamantly refusing to be refused, Brigyda placed the basket on the table and turned to look at her friend with genuine concern. "Will you be alright, Lourdes?" She suddenly sounded like a little girl, seeking reassurance from her older sister and, in many ways, Lourdes felt she was; they were the only family either of them had left. Lourdes smiled weakly and nodded.

"Thank you for coming to check on me," she whispered, emotion stealing her voice as tears once again tried to overrule her. Brigyda stepped closer and laid her hand on her shoulder gently.

"I will come get you in the morning. Make sure you're alright and help you downstairs, ok? Don't you dare leave this room without me." Receiving a weary nod in answer, Brigyda smiled encouragingly and stooped to gather the torn uniform they had discarded earlier. "I'll mend this for you." She moved to leave, then stopped and turned back to her friend, hesitating uncertainly before she returned to her bedside and hugged her reassuringly.

The night grew dark and Lourdes managed to lie down again, refusing to move so her body had some few hours to heal. She tried to nibble on the food Brigyda had brought her, but she was not hungry. Her thoughts were a tangled knot that she wanted to hurl into the darkness and forget. It would do no good to think about what had happened. There was nothing she could do to change it and lingering on it would only result in her crying the night away. She had never been one to crumble under pressure and she certainly wasn't going to allow someone like the commander to change her into someone she was not. Instead of crying, she attempted to focus on something more useful and distracting.

Him.

She didn't know much about guard shift rotations or the routine those in The Tower followed, but she could pay attention and figure it out. She needed to if she was going to get him get out of there. Concentrating on guard rotations would keep her focused on something other than fear and trying to avoid the commander and Ghislain. She couldn't allow herself to be defeated by their merciless actions; yet even as she determined to be strong her mind betrayed her and the memory of their heartlessness sent her spiraling into a well of despair.

More than an hour passed and the candle Brigyda had left burning on the table guttered and went out. At first, the darkness felt stifling, but it was enough to distract her. Drying her eyes with her sleeve, she drew several deep breaths and tried once more to redirect her thoughts onto something more productive. Anything would help, but thinking about how she could help him made her feel better. She wasn't sure where she could take him if she could manage to somehow free him. The only places she knew were frequented by other servants, so she couldn't hide him in those areas, but if she brought him to her room, they would have to ascend ten flights of stairs. She had barely managed it after what she went through; how he would get up ten spiraling flights of stairs after being tortured for so long? The notion made her scoff. If he went missing, her chamber would be one of the first places they'd search.

As she lay quietly considering the few options available to her, she found herself also thinking more curiously about him. When she brought him water, she hadn't been in a frame of mind to notice details about him and hadn't even thought to ask his name, but now all the things she didn't know preoccupied her. She couldn't recall the color of his hair, except that it had been drenched with blood. She couldn't remember the shade of his eyes, though he had looked directly at her more than once. She did notice, however, how tall he was, although being barely five feet tall herself, anyone was taller than she. Although she was not in the frame of mind to appreciate it, his striking physique boasted of beautifully defined muscle that was neither bulky nor sinewy, but the shock of realizing he was entirely naked had kept her attention fixed on the floor for most of the time they were together.

He was in his prime, early to mid-thirties, which was about the age she had expected. Although The Protectorate was brutal, they didn't typically make a habit of torturing children. They apparently had no problem brutalizing him, however. She wondered what he had done to 'deserve' such treatment or if he had done anything at all. Certainly no one deserved to suffer the way he did. Her thoughts came back around to when she first saw him, how appalling his injuries were, and the shocking amount of blood that had covered him and the floor! She squeezed her eyes closed against the memory and shook her head, trying to dispel the thought, but it refused to fade. How could he survive such torture day after day?

She paused as the obvious finally occurred to her. How could he? The injuries she had seen were too severe and the amount of blood he had lost too great. He couldn't survive such injuries if they were inflicted as often as she heard him screaming. She considered what seemed implausible, then reconsidered what she had not noticed at the time and an inescapable question began to form in her mind.

When she first saw him, his wounds were ghastly, fresh and bleeding. Bleeding quite profusely, yet when she had taken water to him only a few hours later, they were no longer open and angry as she expected them to be. Though they should still have been oozing and inflamed, and though he should have been practically immobilized by the pain they produced, he was not. He had been visibly weak, but he seemed able to move as if he suffered little or no pain at all. The insatiable manner in which he had drunk all the water she pro-

95

vided was proof of that, but what confused her was his wounds.

They were not as they should have been.

They were half healed!

How could that be?

6

Year 2446
The 96^(th) Year of the 4th Era after the Great Cataclysm
Tower Obligar, Le Bastion de la Résolution, - Marçais,
New France

Lévesque stood with his hands clasped behind his back looking out the small, barred window of his equally small office, contemplating the visit he had been paid by the EPP Guard three days earlier. The display they had made of their captive had seemed judicious at the time, even though he had not fully recovered from the night before. Yet now, as Lévesque waited for the Marshal of The Protectorate to come to a decision about how they would treat the prisoner going forward and what their goals should be, he wondered if he had made the right decision. Perhaps it had been too harsh a choice, too heartless, which is why he now found himself in the position he was in with his supervision of the prisoner in question.

It mattered very little that he had, just the day before the EPP Guard's visit, instructed Phillippe to back off on the intensity of the prisoner's daily 'treatments' and to shorten them to just a few hours in the early morning so he could spend the rest of the day absorbing sunlight and healing. He had noticed, although they had thought him indestructible, that the prisoner's health seemed to be in decline and he'd thought it prudent to alter their process. He didn't, after all, desire the prisoner's death, just his continued inability to cause any more havoc in earth's history.

He knew The Protectorate. He thought he understood their protocols and their underlying principles and he tried to live by them, which made having everything he had done for the past year scrutinized, questioned and potentially changed not only irritating, but infuriating. He had been told to wait. It was his only directive at the present time. Wait. Wait for what? Wait to be told his decision to keep their prisoner too weak to be a threat was not only unacceptable, but an irresponsible waste of time? Wait for The Protectorate to decide how best to use a prisoner they had no interest in for nearly an entire year? Wait to be told what to do like a regimental dog?

Grating at the outrage, he clenched his hands tightly and growled under his breath. He hadn't served in the ranks of The Protectorate for nearly twenty-five years only to be told what to do like a first-year cadet. Worse, to be ordered to change his strategy by a superior who had no information other than what a junior-grade subordinate decided to tell him was more vexing than having to wait for that same order. Turning on his heel, he glared out of his office toward the place where the prisoner was being held and fought to suppress the desire mounting within him to take his baton in hand and use it in the manner in which it was intended, liberally. Beating their prisoner to within an inch of his life would serve no useful purpose, but it might satisfy his frustration.

As he considered, the commander of the Tower

Guard turned the corner from the entryway and strode purposefully along the hall leading toward the armory. His air of confidence was not only apparent, it was palpable, and it was the only excuse Lévesque needed. Grasping his dagger from its ornate scabbard slung along with his sword on his baldric, he shouted after the man with a tone he dared not ignore. "Commander Sauvage!"

The younger officer, who had more arrogance than ability, stopped, turned slowly and returned to stand in the doorway. "Captain?"

Lévesque had never spoken to the man before. He knew very little about him, other than what his own men had reported. His arrogance made him difficult to work for and he was clearly more interested in promoting his own interests than those of his men. More disturbingly, he had a penchant for raping young servants, male or female. It didn't seem to matter to him. Whatever else he might be, Lévesque didn't approve of such behavior, especially when it involved servants who were practically children. Knowing this about the commander was enough to warrant disliking him, but he also had reason to be suspicious because he had been recently posted to the position in The Tower with very few reasons given for the transfer. It had happened very quickly and very quietly.

Attempting to put his aggravation to better use, he inclined his head and gestured for him to come inside. "We haven't had the opportunity to speak since your assignment here. I thought it best we do so," he offered nonchalantly and the younger officer raised a brow, but nodded and stepped inward.

"What may I tell you, Sir?"

Lévesque smiled ineffectively, visually inspecting the commander with an openly critical gaze. He was of an average height around 5"10" with a trim, athletic physique. His uniform was immaculate; his weaponry and boots polished, and, at the present moment, he held his braided cap under his arm just as any officer worth his salt should do.

"I was curious, that's all. Your transfer was rather... how shall I say?"

Sauvage, unwilling to offer any aid to the captain he already knew he should be wary of, stood silent.

"Covert. Perhaps you would be willing to provide me some additional information?" Lévesque's formal inquiry made little outward effect on the commander. He only repeated himself cunningly.

"What may I tell you, Sir?"

Looking down at the dagger he offhandedly held Lévesque twirled it between his fingers adeptly. "Anything you feel your commanding officer ought to know, I suppose," he returned with equal art, squaring off with the younger officer more perceptibly.

Sauvage's gaze narrowed, but he forced a congenial smile to his lips. "There really isn't much to tell. I grew tired of watching over the under-utilized regimental depot and requested reassignment."

Nodding as if he understood, Lévesque posed another question without a moment's hesitation. "Because you want to be of better service to The Protectorate." His suggestion made the commander grin and he inclined his head, accepting his rationale without verbally answering. Lévesque continued, "and because you want your specific skills to be utilized more effectively."

This further proposal made Sauvage's smile broaden. "Yes, of course."

Stepping out from behind his desk, Lévesque moved casually to stand beside the commander as he took up a cloth from the desk and began to polish the flawless blade of the dagger he held. "Every weapon should be used to its fullest potential, wouldn't you agree?"

Sauvage smirked, but refrained from answering other than to offer a snap of a nod that caused his shoulder-length dark brown hair to momentarily fall across his brilliant blue eyes. Ignoring this, Lévesque continued around him and spoke in an even tone.

"It would be truly unfortunate to allow such a weapon to become blunted from disuse, or misuse, would it not?"

Sauvage twisted to follow his movements, his gaze narrowing with growing distrust. "It would, unless it was being used in a manner not immediately apparent."

Lévesque paused, recalling suddenly the EPP Guard's warning that The Protectorate sees all. Turning to look directly at the commander of the guard, he considered his next question carefully. "As I said, you may wish to provide whatever information your commanding officer should know."

They stared at each other like two wolves with hackles raised and neither blinked or backed down.

"You wouldn't ask me to disobey the direct order of an officer superior in rank to both of us, would you?" Sauvage posed his own question, then stood silently waiting for Lévesque to try to overrule him, but he shook his head without hesitation, fixing an innocent expression on his face as he replied with astonishment.

"Oh, certainly not. After all, obeying such an order could ensure one's career." He turned and moved back behind his desk, looking once again at the dagger he toyed with so purposefully.

"I'm glad you understand, Sir."

"Of course." Nodding forbearingly, Lévesque paused with dramatic flair. "Although, you may wish to clarify the liberties of such an order. Taking advantage of such latitude may be considered... presumptuous."

Sauvage, unable to bite his tongue, retorted before he could temper his response. "I don't take your meaning, Sir?"

Lévesque leaned over his desk with greater animosity. "Don't you? Perhaps I should question the servants Madam Ornaly sent us recently? They may be able to provide some insight."

Bristling, Sauvage merely grunted, but before he could formulate an answer, Lévesque straightened and continued.

"The floor was not cleaned properly yesterday and I understand you had some hand in detaining the servant assigned to that duty."

Sauvage answered with constrained belligerence. "I may have."

Lévesque raised a brow with disdain. "Blood draws insects and generates disease. We can have neither here, do you understand."

Snapping a single nod, Sauvage said nothing.

"Good. What you do off hours is your own business, commander, and I could really care less about it, but while you are on duty you will follow protocol."

"Sir." Acknowledging his superior, Sauvage didn't break eye contact for a second, waiting to be dismissed before he turned and left the office without looking back. Lévesque watched him go, a satisfied grin twisting the corner of his mouth.

He barely slept. Not because the residual pain from his injuries was any worse than usual. He had grown accustomed to the aching of his body that lingered even after the energy from the morning's sunlight initiated his physical regeneration process. Not because of the alarming rage turning his thoughts into a demonic version of himself. His anger towards those who tortured him and had so brutally mistreated the young servant who brought him water was well justified. Not because he had begun to suffer a gnawing hunger he could neither dispel nor ignore. It was vexing. He had never felt either hunger or thirst before and had had little need for food or drink; yet now they were impossible to ignore.

He tried to rest. He tried to calm the rage within him and to ignore the exhaustion that went far beyond physical weariness. He sought to understand his sudden need for nourishment, but he was unsuccessful on all counts. Standing in his small cell like a caged animal, he stared beyond the bars at the key hanging from the nail Phillippe had driven into the stone wall. In his true form he could simply have commanded that key to his hand and his freedom would have been instantaneous. He could also at any time call his sword, Jshunamir, to his hand and his captors would soon find themselves in a desperate state, but his decision to wait silenced the word before he spoke it. It was his choice. He could obtain his freedom at any time, but he had an innate sense that his search was nearly over and the one he'd been searching for was within his reach. He'd learned to trust those senses that were not flesh and blood. He knew they stemmed from what he had been before; he trusted them.

Having taken human form, he accepted the limitations and frailties of a physical body. Well, nearly. The nature of his true state of being could not be completely altered. He was perfected energy in its purest form, regardless of whether or not he wore the mantle of a physical body. As such, he had the innate ability to adapt energy to sustain his life-force, but after all the years he had spent on earth he was learning that even the transmutation of kinetic solar energy into physical strength had its limits. In just the last few days, his physical body had made it very clear that it had requirements he could no longer disregard. Although he had been able to live many years without the necessity of food or drink, relying on the energy of the sun to sustain him; the stress and abuse his body now suffered on a daily basis was taxing the limits of his regenerative ability. Each day, the torture his captors inflicted was more difficult to endure and, each day, he healed more slowly and less completely.

He required more than the kinetic force of sunlight alone. He needed food, drink, and sleep just as any human and he needed them desperately. The weariness he felt was like an ocean of water weighing down his body and obscuring the clarity of his thoughts. He was not entirely certain how much longer he could continue on the course he had set for himself. As the hours of night waned and the faint light of morning began to brighten the dark chamber, he stared fixedly at the key, a sensation of dread taking hold of him unlike anything he had experienced before. He knew what the early morning hours brought with them; the demon Phillippe and his instruments of agony, and every atom of his being seemed to tremble.

How long could his human body survive the repeated horrors of their merciless torture?

How long would he accept what he didn't deserve?

How long until he saw her again?

Waking with the dawn as she did every morning, Lourdes opened her eyes slowly and peered round her small room at all the familiar shapes and items that made up her world. They were insignificant, but used to give her some measure of comfort, reassuring her that her life was not as bad as it might be and she had blessings to count. Today, however, they felt more like the bars of a cage. Even before she sat up, she sighed miserably.

Suddenly, everything about her life felt terribly wrong. She felt trapped.

Closing her eyes, she shook her head. Trapped or not, she had to get up, had to face the day and hope to make the best of whatever it brought. It wasn't much of a rule to live by, but it was something she had learned before her family had been stolen from her. They had taught her to live with gratitude and kindness in her heart and when she was left alone in an unforgiving world, she had learned the only way to survive was to fight her battles with whatever measure of positive hope she could muster.

"Show thankfulness through kindness and welcome blessings with generosity." She repeated the phrase she had been taught as a child while she attempted to ig-nore the soreness of her body and sit up. Kindness and generosity; they weren't usually all that difficult for her to manage, but this morning they felt very far from her. Gritting her teeth, she forced herself up from the bed and took a few steps towards her washstand, scoffing at the notion. Kindness and generosity? They were what had gotten her into the mess she was now in. If she hadn't tried to help Brigyda she would never have ended up in The Tower. She would never have ended up suffering the sadistic perversions of the commander of the guard or worrying what he might do to her next. She wouldn't need to be afraid to leave her room or fear that she might not survive the day.

Sighing sharply, she shook her head to try to scatter her dismal mood. She was not facing so difficult a day, not compared to the man being held in The Tower who suffered far greater pains than she. If she didn't go to

The Tower, she wouldn't be able to help him and, after wishing for so long that she could, she would not turn away now. The thought rallied her spirits and she repeated herself more determinedly.

"Show thankfulness through kindness and welcome blessings with generosity!" A soft knock on her door made her shriek as she jumped backward and nearly toppled the water pitcher from the washstand.

"It's only Brigyda." Her friend announced through the door before she pushed it open and peered around it. "Lourdes, are you ok?"

Gasping to catch her breath, she agreed she was, although she leaned on the back of one of her table chairs as if she might topple over at any moment. Hugging Lourdes as if they had been separated for years, Brigyda laid the uniform she had mended on the table and asked in a soft voice. "Did you sleep at all?"

"Not much." She decided not to share what had largely preoccupied her thoughts during the night or her plans to help a stranger. It was a decision that could potentially create an even worse situation for her than the one she presently faced and she didn't plan to drag Brigyda into it, so the less she knew, the better. If anything unfortunate happened, her friend would be safe.

"I did a bit of scavenging last night." Brigyda announced with a hint of pride in her melodic voice.

Lourdes looked at her with dismay. "You did what? You could have been caught!"

Brigyda shook her head. "Not likely, I wait until after midnight, when everyone important has gone to bed."

"What do you mean?"

The younger servant grinned slyly and unveiled a small pile of bread heels she had folded into the mended uniform to hide them. "I snuck into the kitchen. There's usually a guard, but I waited until he went off to use the privy." It wasn't much and the risk Brigyda assumed was great, but it was a far more rational hazard to risk than the one she was planning.

Ready as she could make herself, Lourdes took two of the bread heels and tucked them into her uniform pockets, which were well hidden by the apron she also wore. They went down to the servants' dining area together, taking the stairs slowly despite the growling in Lourdes' belly prompting her to hurry. Breakfast was never much; bland oatmeal, lukewarm tea, and, if they were lucky, an egg or two, but it was far better than nothing. Today was not much different in what was provided. Oatmeal, tea and an overcooked croissant from an entire batch of croissant's burnt by the new kitchen maid that were deemed unsuitable to serve the families of The Protectorate. As she carried her bowl and cup to the table and sat down beside her friend who was already eating as if she hadn't seen food in several days, Lourdes marveled at her good fortune. She had bread from last night's dinner table and now, a fairly fresh croissant. She would watch the table vigilantly and, if fortune was on her side, she might manage to snatch an extra croissant or two she could take with her into The Tower.

For the man.

The man?

Frowning with dissatisfaction, she decided, if she achieved nothing else this day, she would learn his name. She would have to be extremely careful trying to talk with him, let alone attempting to give him anything to eat, but it was a risk she was willing to take. Why she was willing, she truly could not explain to herself, but she needed something good to focus on and that was reason enough for her. Perhaps it was because it helped her not think about what she might be facing when she reported to The Tower or how she might elude what seemed to be her fate.

She could focus on something else, but she couldn't ignore the twisting knot of nervousness writhing in her stomach. Forcing down her small breakfast, she carried her empty dishes to the sink, washed them, then turned and scanned the table for any leftovers. Nothing. Sighing, she shrugged. She couldn't blame anyone for not giving up bread, even if it was over-baked. They got so little, even what was deemed unpalatable was invaluable. Surreptitiously tucking her croissant into her pocket, she nodded at Brigyda and indicated she was ready to go. She wasn't truly ready, but she had to be. As with so much else here at The Bastion, she had little choice. Bidding her friend a silent good morning, she walked out of the room and bolstered her courage for what was to come.

———————

Phillippe stood before their captives' cell, looking in at him with a critical gaze, scribing notes into the journal he carried with him everywhere. He never asked any questions. It was best not to engage in conversation with prisoners, but he could formulate hypothesis and draw conclusions based upon his observations. Lévesque never wanted details anyway, all he wanted was enough data so he could make decisions and this morning wasn't any different. Their routine seldom varied, until recently. He reported at six in the morning, made some few observations and recorded his notes; then provided this information to Lévesque. After the visit from the EPP Guard when Lévesque was ordered not to proceed until hearing from the Marshal, he had been told to perform the 'treatments' in the morning and to cut the time they took by half. He had also been told to back off on their intensity.

It was left to him to decide precisely what 'backing off' meant and how greatly or insignificantly to decrease measures, but he was still required to give his morning report and garner Lévesque's approval. Thus, he stood visually inspecting their captive with cold objectivity. He never really believed in the mythology of an all-powerful entity that ruled the universe. Even taking into account their captive's unique regenerative abilities, he was not entirely convinced he was an Archangel. He could simply have a genetic mutation humanity was not aware of that allowed him to heal quickly.

Turning without a word, he made his way to Lévesque's office, noticing as he went a young female servant hesitantly coming in through the main entryway. Looking round him to see if any of the guards were present to direct her and finding none, he nodded to her and asked if she knew her duties for the day. Seeming horrified by his inquiry, she turned white as a ghost and nodded before standing and looking at him as if waiting for his next actions. Perplexed by her reaction, he stared at her for a brief moment, then continued into Lévesque's office.

"Good morning, Phillippe," came the customary greeting, to which he nodded respectfully in his usual way.

"Sir." Stepping backward he looked once more down the hall at the young servant. She stood where she was, trembling profusely and holding onto her bucket as if for dear life while she waited. Cocking his head slightly at her odd behavior, he stepped back into the office with a confounded expression.

"Something the matter?" Lévesque asked as he stirred his morning cup of tea. He gestured outward.

"It's this servant, Sir. No, no one's around, so I asked if, if she knew, um, her duties," he haltingly explained, far less apt at communicating than delivering 'treatments'. "She indicated she did, but now, well, she's standing there looking, how shall I say…" he fumbled for the right word.

"Looking?" Lévesque prompted impatiently, to which he shrugged.

"Like a frightened rabbit."

Frowning at this, Lévesque rounded his desk and moved unhurriedly to the door to look for himself, watching as the young woman stood waiting with an unmistakably terrified appearance. He considered this for a moment and then shook his head. "What are you doing there?" He directed his question to her without approaching. Shuddering, she looked down at her feet.

"W…Waiting…t, t…to serve, Sir." Her stuttering reply confused him.

"Well, get to it, then. Do you know your duties here?"

Swallowing with difficulty, she nodded and stepped forward as she blinked away the tears he could see welling in her eyes. Puzzled, he frowned and held out his hand to keep her from drawing any nearer. "What have you been told your duties are?"

Staring at the floor, she forced the loathsome words from her lips as strangling emotion reduced her voice to a soft murmur. "T… to obey and…s…serve my… masters, Sir."

Phillippe returned to the door as well and looked with baffled surprise first at the young woman and then at Lévesque who returned his stare with an incredulous raised brow. After considering further, a glimmer of realization made him sigh sharply and scowl with dissatisfaction. Stepping forward, he asked in a notably less forceful tone. "Who told you this?"

She glanced up at him fleetingly, her entire frame shivering violently. "The...c-c-. commander of the guard, S-Sir."

Closing his eyes to conceal his anger, Lévesque struggled to muffle a growl of agitation. He was not quite successful and the sound caused her to flinch backward from him. Raising his hands in a mollifying gesture, he shook his head. "Hear me now. Your duties are to tend the prisoner's needs and clean the floor. That is all." Looking more closely at her, he noticed the bruises that marred her rose-blushed lips and the black and blue marks on her cheek and the curve of her neck. He stepped closer, looking more closely at the mark on her neck and, when he confirmed his suspicion that it was a bite, his anger could scarcely be contained. Turning away abruptly, he looked at Phillippe who stood watching them with an unreadable expression.

"Phillippe will explain how you should tend the prisoner and show you the well so you can fill your bucket." As he passed the medic, he spoke under his breath, "we'll discuss your report when you're done."

Phillippe acknowledged this with a reluctant nod before fixing his gaze on the young servant. Trembling like a leaf in a November wind, she visibly struggled to suppress her emotion, but emotion was something he had never been able to connect with very well. This lack of empathy served him in his current assignment, but he felt ill-equipped to handle this particular situation. Mimicking what he had seen Lévesque do to solicit her trust, he raised his hands and spoke in a gentle tone. "Are you all right?" He considered mentioning that he was a trained medic, should she have need, but quickly abandoned the notion when she only nodded, sniffled spasmodically, and used her apron to wipe the tears that had slipped down her cheeks. "You can fill your bucket at the well, just there." Pointing toward the small room that housed the well, he thought better of taking her inside alone. Instead, he gestured toward the main chamber. "Leave your...the bucket here. I'll show you the rest of your duties."

He watched as they approached, both alarmed and curious. He didn't know why Phillippe was leading towards his cell the young woman who had brought him water the day before, but he could not moderate the sensation of panic that took hold of him. Had he noticed her kindness and now sought to chastise them both? What form of cruelty or perversion would he employ? What twisted punishment would he devise for them? He might never ordinarily think such a thing, but with Phillippe the depraved and unthinkable was often the norm.

Watching and listening keenly, he realized he was explaining duties to her and pointing out where she would find the things she would need to perform those duties. Sighing with relief, he continued to watch them, curiosity replacing the brief chaos of panic that had gripped him. It was better than admonishment, but knowing she was being given such responsibilities didn't make him feel any better. It meant she would be present while they implemented their vicious cruelty and, although he barely knew anything about her, he didn't want her to see or hear the things Phillippe did. It seemed to him she had already suffered enough dreadfulness.

"While the prisoner is out of his cell, you'll clean it. Rakes are in that storage closet there. There's a small chute to one side of the cell, see there, against the outside wall. That's where you rake the straw that's fouled. Collect more from that repository." He pointed around the chamber in several different directions. Noticing then that she was staring at the prisoner rather than listening to him, he stopped in his tracks and raised his voice. "Are you listening to me?"

Jumping at the harsh change of his tone, she lowered her head. "I'm sorry, Sir. Please forgive me." The honesty of her apology seemed to appease him and he nodded before continuing to walk about the chamber with her in tow. Tzadkiel watched her with a sudden, keen interest, tracking her movements and listening carefully to her quiet interactions with Phillippe. In spite of what she had already suffered and the fact that she had every reason to mistrust all of them, she followed him attentively, responding to his questions genuinely and politely.

He stared at her, transfixed.

He wasn't sure why he hadn't noticed it the night before. Perhaps his exhaustion had made him less perceptive than usual. Perhaps her emotional distress had overwhelmed everything else. Regardless of the reason however, he perceived it now and it was unmistakable. Her gentleness of spirit whispered to his essence in a way no others had in all the years he had been searching. It was what he'd been listening for, but had not heard for nearly a century.

He heard it now.

Distinctly.

"We'll begin shortly. 'Til then, fill your bucket and stay out of the way." Dismissing her without so much as a second glance, Phillippe returned to Lévesque's office, leaving her standing in the middle of the chamber. She drew a deep breath and exhaled prodigiously, closing her eyes as if collecting her senses before she looked around nervously. They were alone. Turning a shy gaze to him, her worried expression took on a warm blush and she averted her attention to the floor.

"Are you alright?" The softness of her voice and concern with which she spoke soothed him in a way he had never experienced. Nodding wordlessly, he didn't need to say he would not be for very long; she already knew it. Glancing around again to ensure they were not being observed, she looked at him with visible curiosity and seemed confused by what she saw, but before she could say anything more Phillippe reappeared and she dashed towards the well room.

It was time.

Drawing a deep breath, Tzadkiel bolstered his courage to face his captor with no sign of fear in his eyes, but today was entirely different. His body still hurt from the extreme abuse Phillippe had inflicted three days before when they had made a show of their torture techniques and their ability to cause injury without killing their prisoner. The continued abuse they inflicted each day since had not given him enough time to recover fully. His weariness was consuming and his weakness alarming. He could not disguise his dread. Though he knew he could at any time call out to his brothers for their aid or call his sword to his hand and Phillippe would face an outcome few humans had ever suffered, he stood silenced by the oppressive weakness weighing him down. His eyes closed involuntarily and for an instant time seemed to stop.

Blackness consumed him fleetingly, but the metallic sound of the lock opening jolted him back into reality. Shaking his head in astonishment, he tried to clear his thoughts. Had he nearly fainted? Attempting to focus his vision, he expected Phillippe to wait for him to kneel. It was the protocol they had made mandatory, whether to protect Phillippe from any sudden attack or to force the Archangel to submit, but Phillippe did not wait today. Rushing at him with startling ferocity that caused Tzadkiel to step backwards, Phillipe grasped a handful of his hair and yanked his head back sharply. Before the Archangel could even cry out, he forced a knotted piece of fabric into his mouth. Tzadkiel raised his hands to try to wrench free from the overpowering hold he had on him, but Phillippe was prepared for his resistance.

Striking him forcefully in the stomach, Phillipe knocked the wind from his lungs and took advantage of his doubled over position to secure the make-shift gag with a leather belt he pulled from his pocket. Tugging it closed tightly, he stepped back and smiled maliciously at him. "You know where I want you."

He expected him to walk to the table and lay down of his own free will, but he couldn't force himself, not today. Not when the object of his long search was so close. Not when what he submitted to was no longer necessary. Phillippe's attack, however, left him few alternatives. He could no longer call on his brothers or his sword and he wasn't strong enough to oppose Phillippe. He would only call the guards who would cause injuries of their own before securing him to the table where he would still endure the torments Phillippe waited to impose.

Phillippe cleared his throat. The man's patience was chilling. Watching with the cold detachment of a demon, Phillippe turned slowly as he passed him and approached the table. Tzadkiel wondered if he could see the trembling he could not control? Did it please him to know he was afraid? Turning to face his captor, he stood unmoving, staring at Phillippe with the last measure of courage he could demonstrate, but he stared at a stone. Raising his hand to gesture at the table, Phillippe spoke in the same cold voice as he always did, unshaken and undeterred.

"Lie down or I'll call the guards." Without waiting to see if he was obeyed, Phillippe moved to the head of the table where he waited to secure the harness that would bind his head to the stone. Closing his eyes, Tzadkiel fought to suppress the fear that twisted inside him. He raised himself to sit on the cold stone table, fighting back a rush of sickness when his stomach lurched in true terror.

"I'll not tell you again." Phillippe seemed impatient. Perhaps it was because the sun had already risen and its light was beginning to stream in through the barred windows of The Tower. Perhaps he feared he didn't have as much time as he might want. It didn't matter; he would take as much time as he wanted regardless of sunlight.

While Tzadkiel tried to force himself to lie down, the commander of the guard returned from the armory, crossing the floor with a brisk pace as he strode purposefully towards the well room, but when he saw the prisoner sitting unrestrained on the table it caused him to stop abruptly. "Everything in order here?" His hand moved to his hip where several weapons were secured. Phillippe turned his head, fixing a direct stare on his captive.

"Do you need the commander to help you?" His question was enraging, but he didn't have the strength to resist either of them. Drawing a shuddering breath, Tzadkiel lay back and didn't struggle when Phillippe secured the leather harness around his head and cinched it tightly. No longer able to see what went on, he listened as Phillippe moved around the table. Allowing his wrists and ankles to be shackled in the iron manacles that were chained to the floor, he wondered where the young woman had gone and hoped she would not see what was about to happen.

Phillippe nodded as if satisfied and moved away, crossing the chamber to a cabinet set on the other side of the room. Tzadkiel didn't need to be able to see what he was doing, he already knew, but Sauvage, who had relaxed his stance and clasped his hands behind his back as if intent upon observing, watched with increased curiosity as he unlocked the cabinet and swung the door open. He revealed a nightmarish spectacle. Within the cabinet hung a variety of devices whose only purpose was torture. Whips, both barbed and smooth, single leather strap and multiple, hung waiting. Leather hoods of varying shapes and sizes that were fitted with razor blades. Several daggers, scalpels and a variety of clamps with both smooth and barbed surfaces were displayed. A supple lamb-skin cloth that could be dipped into scalding hot water or oil before being applied to the skin and numerous other devices of a more sadistically devious nature awaited selection. Phillippe stood for a moment contemplating his options before drawing out a serrated dagger, a sharply honed scalpel, and a multi-strand whip. He then returned to the table and lay the items down near his prisoner's feet.

Not bothering to look at him as he spoke, Phillippe prepared to begin. He always explained in great detail what he intended to do each day, seeming to enjoy tormenting him with the horrifying knowledge of what was to come before actually proceeding. He was a calculating, merciless monster and Tzadkiel tried not to listen, but he could not wish himself into deafness any more than he could regain his strength through the force of will alone.

"Although it's the day we typically employ the hot oil lambskin and barbed lash, I'll be conducting an experiment, instead." He looked at his captive with a scrutinizing gaze, running his fingers along several of the lacerations he had inflicted the day before. "Your wounds from yesterday's session don't seem entirely healed, which I find quite interesting.

I'd like to know why, so I'll be reopening them to-day. Of course, I'll do this very slowly. I don't want to deprive you of the exquisite pain it will cause." The unsettling calmness of his voice echoed with insidious laughter no one else seemed able to hear and Tzadkiel's eyes widened in horror. Recognizing the sound, he could not hold his silence.

Hissing viperously at him through the gag stuffed into his mouth, he strained futilely against his bonds and his reaction satisfied his tormenter immensely. The malevolent smile that turned the corners of his mouth turned into an evil sneer as Phillippe paused to study him with a cold gaze. He ran his fingers along one of the lacerations he'd created the day before. It stretched across his upper thigh and had not fully healed and the impassive glare of his gaze turning almost loving. His dark eyes shimmered with a crimson gleam as he continued his callous description and picked up the dagger he'd placed by Tzadkiel's feet.

"I want to see if shallow wounds heal more quickly than deep ones or if they heal at the same rate, but I also want to know if wounds that are cleanly made heal more rapidly than exacerbated ones." He paused, his silence ominous and when he spoke again, his voice was a hiss that chilled Tzadkiel to his core. "Thisss should be delissssssiously painful for you, Archangel." Turning his attention to the incision site, he ran his fingers lightly along the half-healed wound crossing the width of his powerful thigh and licked his lips.

"Let'ssss begin."

7

Year 2067
The 1st Era of the Great Cataclysm
Regional countryside outside Chambon, France
The Family Farmstead- Le Lieu de la Miséricorde

He left them in confusion, but they were extraordinarily thankful. Instead of promoting their demise, The Rider had blessed them. Exceedingly. Perhaps it was predestined for them to meet him when he was in need or perhaps it was mere happenstance, but he said he'd been told he would meet the unexpected and they were, apparently, it. Who could have told him this, Gabriel and Annabella could only suppose, but as he was one of the Horsemen of the Great Cataclysm it was not terribly difficult to draw certain conclusions. They had always believed in a power greater than humanity and, although no proof existed, or at least no proof existed until The Rider became an irrefutable fact, they had always lived with gratitude for their blessings.

It was a simple philosophy. Showing thankfulness through kindness and appreciating blessings through generosity kept their lives in focus. When they met The

Rider, it was not extraordinary that they should treat him with the same kind generosity they showed everyone and everything else. Perhaps it was this simple philosophy that had swayed him from his purpose. Perhaps it was something they could never fathom. They might never know, but regardless of the reasons why, the blessing he bestowed was far greater than they would ever have expected.

Not only had he commanded they would not be touched by the virulent strains of disease that swept across entire countries in his wake, for he was Pestilence of every form, he had spoken their vitality for many years to come. Already having seen sixty plus years when he came to them, they expected to see their health begin to decline as age had its way. They were astonished, however, to find themselves renewed and rejuvenated, as if restored to their youth. Like their physical state of being, their love blossomed anew and in the spring of her 67th year, Annabella gave birth to a daughter whom they named Lourdes.

Gabriel often recalled the smirk The Rider had given him before departing. Perhaps it was all fated to be so, or perhaps The Rider caused these events to occur through the blessing he bestowed. Either way, they lived in a protected oasis from the remainder of the country. They named the unassuming farmstead upon which they had lived most of their lives *Le Lieu de la Miséricorde*, the Place of Mercy, just as the Rider had named it. In response to the Rider's blessing, it poured forth its bounty upon them in abundance that seemed inexhaustible and, true to their philosophy, Gabriel and Annabella shared this profusion. Not only did they share it with their friends and neighbors, but any they learned to be in need and they taught their daughter the great rewards of living simply and generously.

Year 2446
The 96th Year of the 4th Era after the Great Cataclysm
Tower Obligar, Le Bastion de la Résolution, - Marçais,
New France

She spent more time than she should have filling her
bucket, but she couldn't help it. She had to be sure she
wouldn't burst into tears when she went back out into
a chamber where torture was about to take place. Despite the fact that she really just wanted to hide, she
knew if she lingered too long, she would only be providing an excuse for someone to come looking for her.
God help her if that someone was the commander of
the guard! Leaving the bucket on the low shelf beside
the well, she directed her steps toward the main
chamber and the cell she had been instructed to clean.
It would keep her away from the commander, at least,
and she would manage, somehow, to block out everything else. Turning the corner, she stopped in her
tracks.

The commander of the guard stood in the main
chamber, not only watching what was about to happen,
but blocking her route to the cell beyond. Hesitating as
she scanned the room for another way she could go,
she saw him turn to look at her, but he only smiled de-
viously, running his hand through the lengths of his
brown hair before returning his attention to the table
he faced. The last thing she wanted was to go anywhere
near him, but with no alternative route accessible, she
had no choice. Having few choices was a situation she
was growing used to, so she gritted her teeth, straightened from the cowering position she had already assumed, and walked with feigned confidence into the
chamber.

Turning his head to watch her with an openly hungry stare, the commander made no threatening move when she passed by him, but he made it clear he had every intention to. She could have pressed herself up against the wall to keep as far away from him as physically possible, but she refused to give him the satisfaction of seeing her fear. Instead, she raised her chin defiantly and strode by him within easy reach. Her path took her close to the cabinet set against the far wall, which now stood open, and her determined stride faltered when she saw the implements of torture it displayed so callously. She tried not to stare or to wonder at the use of the unfamiliar items she saw, forcing her steps forward to the storage closet where she would collect the rake she was supposed to use to clean the cell.

She had only just taken it in hand when a loud hissing of breath and shuddering groan forced her to stop. Grasping the handle of the rake tightly, she squeezed her eyes closed and spun on her heel to face the wall. She could hardly bear to hear his screams from her tower window, but to be forced to listen to every sound he made within the same room where he was being tortured caused her stomach to wrench violently. It was nearly impossible to force her steps toward his cell as if his cries meant nothing to her or to remember how to use a rake once she got there. Shaking prodigiously, she worked with distracted agitation, paying little attention to what she was doing while at the same time desperately trying to focus on anything other than his wails.

His screams.

His bitter crying.

They tore at her heart. They twisted her insides and her tears flowed as freely as his blood. His torture lasted far longer than she ever imagined someone could bear such pain. Phillippe transformed into a monster more terrifying than anything her mind could have conjured. He took perverse delight in the pain he inflicted and frequently stopped to watch his victim's suffering with disturbing interest. Several times he spoke to him quietly, bending close so his voice would not carry and, although she could not hear what he said, the growling reactions and sudden clangor of chains his words prompted when the man strained against his bonds to reach him betrayed their vile nature. Even the commander of the guard eventually disappeared, but she didn't have the freedom to leave.

When she finished refreshing the straw of his cell, she replaced it with twice as much fresh straw, unsure how much to use, but certain the small amount she had removed was not sufficient. It kept her occupied, but not long enough and all too soon she had nothing left to do. Retreating to the well room, she crouched down in a corner, pressing her hands to her ears and humming loudly in an attempt to drown out the sound of the lash and the man's harrowing cries. She cowered so long that her limbs grew numb, but she was too horrorstruck to move. Only when a man came to stand in the doorway and looked in at her with silent contemplation did she stand up and drop her hands from her ears.

It was Phillippe. His hands were covered with blood and his uniform spattered. Shaking violently at the sight of him, she backed up against the corner, unable to force herself to go near him in an attempt to flee the room. Instead, she stood with mute dismay and watched as he casually entered the small room and made use of the water she had drawn to wash his hands. A full bucket of water was not enough to clean them thoroughly and he turned to her and spoke in a dispassionate tone. "I require more water. Dispose of this and draw more."

Shuddering, she could barely force herself to obey, but after seeing what he was capable of she dared not refuse. Stumbling forward, she took hold of the bucket and hauled it to the corner where she poured its scarlet contents into the drain. When she returned, he stepped back to allow her access to the well and didn't speak, but watched her with an unreadable stare as she worked the crank and drew several pails of water to re-fill the bucket. Only then did he step forward again and continued washing the blood from his hands and arms, requiring three full buckets to properly cleanse them.

"You've plenty to keep you busy today." He told her with more pride in his voice than should have been natural. "Clean the floor well. No stains should remain. Do you understand?"

Sickened by him, she nodded wordlessly.

"Good. When you're finished, you'll spend the re-mainder of the day tending the prisoner's needs." He hadn't shown her any medical supplies and, wondering how she was meant to care for him properly, she cocked her head slightly to one side.

"Tending his needs, Sir?"

He stopped in the doorway and looked back at her; his voice suddenly sharp. "I'm not a nursemaid. If he has needs, they're your concern and you'll tend them. Is that understood?"

Backing away from him, she nodded frantically. "Yes, Sir."

He snapped a nod at her, then turned and trod off in the direction of the office where she had first seen him that morning. It was both a good and terrible thing. She wouldn't have to try to sneak into the man's cell or hide the water she wanted to provide, and she would be able to help him by soothing his injuries, if such a thing was even possible, but the thought of seeing him again in such a distressing state left her trembling even more fiercely than before.

Unwilling to invite reprimand for loitering when there was work to do; she filled the bucket another time and hauled it with her into the main chamber. She intentionally didn't look up, not initially, but her tactic of avoidance only brought her attention to the blood on the floor surrounding the table, which caused her to gasp audibly and raise her hand to her mouth. Such a quantity pooled on the stones at the table's base that she wondered how he could even still be alive. His bonds had been loosened; nothing restrained him, but nothing needed to. His body was scarlet from his own blood! Her stomach turned and she closed her eyes tightly, swallowing repeatedly to keep from being sick. No wonder Phillippe had instructed her to tend his needs. He was in a wretched state! Stepping closer with monumental hesitation, she watched his chest for any indication that he still breathed, which brought her attention to something very strange.

The light of the morning sun, which was streaming in through the barred windows, forms ribbons of radiance that enshrouded him in its glimmering luminosity. It seemed brighter than it ought to and she stared at it with wonder. The light enveloping him softly pulsated and sparkled though nothing obstructed its shimmering streams to cause such an occurrence. What was even more peculiar was the similarly pulsing lavender crystal he wore around his neck, though its light was weak and nearly indistinguishable against the bright sunlight.

To her astonishment, he turned his head slightly to look at her. She cried out, covering her mouth another time and shaking her head helplessly as his pale lavender gaze locked with hers. How could she possibly help him? How could anyone inflict such ruthless harm on another? What could she do to ease such injuries? Stepping closer still, she stood beside the table and set her bucket on the floor, returning his penetrating gaze while she struggled to find words.

His face was wet from tears, smeared by spatters of blood that had soaked into the lengths of his hair. His mouth was gagged and the cloth scarlet from blood. She shook her head and choked back a rush of sickness, her anguished gaze flickering over his body, but before she could figure out what she could possibly say his eyes closed and she cried out once more, fearing the worst.

From behind her, Phillippe's sharp tone redirected her attention. "Clean the floor! You can tend to him when you are finished."

Jumping at his unexpected chastisement, she sobbed audibly and lowered herself to her knees, afraid that he had just slipped from life into death. Even as she reached for the crumpled rags she had been given to sop up his blood from the floor, she closed her eyes and struggled against the whirlwind of emotion swirling inside her. How could anyone do something so utterly horrible? How could they possibly live with themselves? Why treat him so? What could he possibly have done to justify such gruesome cruelty? Her thoughts spun helplessly, fueling the tears that fell while she mopped up the pools of his blood from the floor. It took more than an hour to remove so much blood and many trips to the well room where she drained the crimson water from the bucket, pumped clean water to rinse it and her few ineffective rags, before refilling the container another time and returning to the table to continue her work.

Each time she rose from the floor, she sought to re-assure herself that he still breathed and, each time, she was astonished to discover that he still did. Each time she returned from the well room, she watched the glimmering sunlight shift and spiral around him like eddies of smoke from an extinguished candle and wondered at the extraordinary phenomenon with bewildered curiosity. Each time, before she knelt down again, she hurriedly glanced over his body, attempting to comprehend why it seemed with each trip she made his wounds appeared less irritated and as if they were already beginning to heal.

He remained motionless the entire time she worked, unconscious or unable to find the strength to open his eyes. She worked with fervent haste, well aware that she would not be permitted to give him any measure of assistance until his blood was cleaned from the floor. It was a ruthless stipulation from a ruthless man, but she didn't dare argue with him. He reappeared several times from the office he and the other officer occupied, watching her progress and pointing out places she missed with cold scrutiny until the sun's progress towards its noon-day pinnacle stole its radiance away from the chamber. Only then, when its streaming light could no longer reach the man lying in his own blood on the table, did Phillippe approach once more.

"Time to go back to your cell," he said heartlessly, waiting for the man to get up without offering any aid whatsoever. When he didn't stir, Phillippe leaned closer and spoke menacingly into his ear. "Don't make me call the guards. You won't appreciate it."

Opening his eyes, he looked up at Phillippe blankly, who straightened and twisted around as if searching for guards. Lourdes watched aghast, unable to believe Phillippe's cruelty could have gotten even worse, but when the man didn't move, he leaned closer and whispered something she could not hear. The man squeezed his eyes closed tightly as if fighting back his emotions. He breathed in a deep, rapid succession, groaning with prodigious effort as he attempted to push himself up from the table, but he had no strength. Managing only to turn onto his side, he panted fitfully, shaking violently in pain. Phillippe shook his head. "Very well, suit yourself."

His lack of compassion was chilling and, without thinking her actions through, Lourdes rushed forward from the place she had retreated to and gazed up at him. Folding her small hands in supplication, now stained red from blood, she spoke in a pleading tone. "Please, I'll help him. Please, Sir!"

One brow lifted in an incredulous expression and he raised his hand as if on the verge of pushing her aside, but she repeated herself emphatically.

"Please let me help him. Let me try."

The notion of such a small female attempting to support the weight of a man half again her size seemed to amuse him because he smirked and stepped back unhelpfully. "By all means, do."

His scoff of derision only strengthened her determination. Moving closer to the table, she stooped to look into the man's tear-filled eyes and placed her hand gently on his shoulder, avoiding with diligent care the wound that stretched from his shoulder across his chest to the other side. Softly, she whispered to him. "I will help you."

He looked up at her, shivering.

"I'm going to take care of you, but, please, you have to get up. Don't let him call the guards." Her voice cracked under the weight of her emotion and the misery in his pale gaze seemed to intensify. She tried again. "Can you get up?"

His body was covered with deep lacerations and she wouldn't have been surprised if he could not, but he closed his eyes slowly, drew a deep shuddering breath and pushed up from the table. Crying out against the pain the action caused him, he groaned with prodigious effort as he forced himself to his feet. He waited as she situated herself to support him by pressing against his side and allowing him to wrap his arm around her shoulder. Taking hold of his wrist, she braced herself.

There was no way to avoid his injuries. Everywhere she touched him, she inflicted greater pain and that pain, combined with the effort of standing, caused his breathing to deteriorate into a repetition of panting moans that nearly broke her heart. Barely able to hold his head up, he laid his cheek on the crown of her head and leaned against her heavily, standing unsteadily for a prolonged moment before he took a monumentally shaky step forward.

Her ability to truly aid him was ungainly at best and she couldn't help hurting him. The mere thirty feet from the table to his cell felt like a mile and with each step he gasped and moaned spasmodically. Although his wounds had already begun to close, most renewed their bleeding under the stress of movement and his labored breaths grew even more strained and erratic. He stumbled repeatedly and she only barely managed to keep them both upright. Phillippe watched with his arms folded across his chest, callously enjoying their struggle.

Recognizing the signs that he was going into shock from the loss of so much blood and uncertain how long she would be able to hold him up, Lourdes hastened their pace, half supporting him, half dragging him into the cell. When she reached the heaped pile of straw she had arranged for him, she bent down slowly, attempting to lower him to the floor as gently as she was able, but he released her abruptly and collapsed, lying motionless where he fell.

Stepping forward to stand just outside the cell door, Phillippe clapped leisurely. "Well done. I admit, I didn't think you'd make it." His pitiless disparagement made her glare at him with agitation, but he ignored her ire and pointed at the floor and the bright scarlet streak that stretched from the table to the cell. "You've made a mess. I expect you to clean this up and the table as well before you do anything else."

Lourdes' anger flared at his heartlessness, but she knew better than to turn her fire on him. She'd made that mistake yesterday and had paid far too costly a price for her defiance. Stifling her anger before she got to her feet, she moved closer to the door and looked up at Phillippe with a beseeching expression. "Please, Sir, he's going into shock. If you just allow me to,"

Phillippe shook his head instantly and interrupted with a callous tone. "He's in no danger." He was entirely unconcerned. "Clean the floor."

She stared up at him in disbelief. "But, Sir, he could..." she couldn't bring herself to say the word, but he chuckled.

"Die? Not likely. Clean the floor." Without waiting to argue with her further, he turned away, leaving her staring after him uncomprehendingly.

He returned to consciousness in a haze of confusion and listened to the soft sound of water somewhere close to him. He tried to remember where he was, but the inescapable pain of his body numbed his thoughts. Groaning without opening his eyes, he struggled against the darkness that sought to pull him into its depths even as a sensation of coolness touched first his forehead, then his cheeks. Unable to comprehend such a feeling, he strained against the heavy emptiness weighing him down, struggling to resist the obscurity of blackness clawing for him as he turned his head away from the unrecognized sensation. A soft voice spoke to him, but he was unable to comprehend the words. They echoed in his mind, tumbling over themselves and separating into sounds that made no sense. They disoriented him completely. Raising his hand slowly, he tried to fend off the unknown contact, but his hand was taken in a gentle clasp. Bewildered, he spoke softly.

"Privoweth, shunar rivway?" His voice was barely a whisper, but there was no response to his question. "Privoweth?"

Again, the voice spoke, but he could not understand the words. It was a woman's voice, soft and sweet, but the language she spoke was incomprehensible. He shook his head sluggishly and the darkness tugging at him fell away. Opening his eyes with extreme effort, he blinked in a slow repetition, trying to focus on the person beside him. He recognized the shape as female, but his vision was blurred. He stared at her, unable to remember who she was or to see her clearly. Her entire body rippled like waves on the ocean.

Waves.

He remembered waves. They rocked in a suspiration of sound and motion that further disoriented him. The ocean was gray and foreboding, barren and silent. Everything around him became still and quiet. Involuntarily, his eyes closed and he succumbed to the waves rushing in on him. It seemed so long ago when he stood gazing out over the vast gray waters of the ocean. Time eluded him as his thoughts slipped into a spiraling well, downward, outward and away, melding into a shimmering light. The setting sun, crimson and glorious, cast its light in a final blaze as the wind tousled his hair with its gentle fingers. The ocean stretched out before him, immense and bereft. He bowed his head. Such great loss! So many lives lost, so unnecessarily. Greed, pollution, and apathy all had taken their toll until nothing survived. He grieved at the tragedy.

"Don't cry." An unfamiliar voice drifted on the wind, gently soothing him. The cool spray of the ocean breeze refreshed his cheek. He raised his hand, desperately trying to separate the tangled threads of reality and the beyond, but he could not remember where he was or where he should be. Again, his hand was taken in a tender clasp and a gentle voice spoke to him.

"It's alright. You're alright." The woman's voice drifted on the ocean breeze, mingling with the sound of the waves. Where was he? Who touched him? His thoughts spun in a dizzying haze. He tried to open his eyes, but the sun slipped below the horizon and every measure of strength he possessed dissipated with the last traces of its light. Falling with it, he collapsed onto the sand. Emptiness spiraled into blackness. Time slid away like sands falling through an hourglass.

"They try to impede you now that you are close. Don't give over!" A resonant voice as deep as the darkness engulfing him spoke from the ebon abyss. *"Wake up! Remember!"* It paused as if waiting for him. *"She is near."* The voice spoke forcefully; then faded into nothingness. Stillness infiltrated his very essence as if seeking to melt through him and the silence of the darkness became intense. He felt himself falling.

Abruptly, he gasped.

He remembered!

Gathering what little energy remained within him he drew a deep breath and opened his eyes. *She* was beside him, the young woman who had brought him water and who helped him return to his cell. She sat on the cold stone floor watching him attentively and wiping his cheeks and brow with a cool cloth. Had it been her voice he heard on the wind?

He groaned and drew another deep breath, the task of breathing more demanding than if he had been asked to drag a mountain. Slowly, he brought his hand up a third time, reaching for her to validate her presence, unsure if what he saw and even what he felt was reality or the figment of a dream as his mind separated from himself. She smiled dimly with concern and took his trembling hand in her own. She didn't speak, but watched him quietly as he struggled to remain conscious. His eyes closed repeatedly as he fought the darkness swirling all around him, pulling at him, wanting him. He opened his mouth, realizing the gag was gone and that he was desperately thirsty. After many protracted moments, cognizance returned more fully, but with it came inescapable pain. Although he tried, he could not suppress his sobbing moans any more than he could control his fitful breathing.

He had suffered before, but he'd always been given time to heal under the rays of the sun. Not today. Today, Phillippe had been far more vicious than usual. Like a demon from the pit, he had perversely enjoyed the pain he inflicted. He had taken his time, wounding him far more severely than he had ever done before and by the time he finished the sun was already shifting away from the table. Before he could absorb a sufficient measure of its energy, it was lost and Phillippe returned as soon as it was gone, forcing him up from the table and undoing the light's restorative work. Now, the result of his calculated cruelty was truly unbearable. His entire body burned with indescribable pain. Each breath was a torment. Each second was agonizing.

Opening his eyes, he focused more intently on her, trying to distract himself. The pale skin on the arch of her neck and cheek bore the dark shadows of bruises, yet her unusually colored eyes were gentle and filled with concern for him, rather than with misery for herself. Her lips were bruised as well, but they trembled not because she was under the same distress she had been when he'd seen her yesterday, but because she had witnessed what Phillippe had done to him today. Looking down at her small hand so gently holding his, he realized they were stained from blood, his blood, which she had been forced to clean from the floor. She trembled with evident apprehension, but not for herself. Her attention was observably focused solely upon him and he stared at her, unable to find words.

She seemed equally unable to express herself, but released him carefully and dipped her cloth once more into the bucket beside her. Wringing it only well enough to rid it of excess water, she folded it into a soft shape and brought it to his shoulder, attempting to tenderly clean the wounds that had finally stopped bleeding. Despite the fact that she touched him lightly, it felt as if the cloth was infested with bees and he gasped loudly, jumping from the unexpected sting that spread across his shoulder.

Instantly, she withdrew. "I'm sorry, I'm sorry, I'm sorry." Her voice quavered and tears filled her gentle gaze.

He looked at her with confusion. "Nothing you have done," pausing, he drew a deep breath, "warrants apology." His breathless voice was barely a whisper.

She wiped her cheeks, visibly shaking. "I'm so sorry it stings. I thought it might help." Her voice trailed off as she looked at him, the sight of his wounds instigating more tears. He looked down at himself as well and understood her dismay; he was a horrifying sight. He looked and felt as if wild animals, or demons, had nearly torn him to shreds. Gasping as an unexpected stab of pain stole his breath away, he remembered the resonant voice in his dream.

"They try to impede you now that you are close."

Realizing the speaker had meant demons and not the humans who held him captive, he understood better. Perhaps demons had nearly torn him to shreds. Looking at himself more closely, he saw that she had already cleaned much of the blood away while he was unconscious. God bless her for that mercy! He never would have managed to bear the discomfort of such ministrations otherwise. She had also removed her apron and had laid it across his hips, modestly covering him. Both were considerations he had not been afforded in nearly a year and they meant more to him than words could adequately express. Returning his gaze to hers, he blinked slowly, exhaustion tugging at him. "Thank you."

She looked at her cloth, clearly uncertain. "I didn't know what else to do." She gasped loudly when his eyes closed. He couldn't force them to stay open, but he smiled weakly in the hope it might reassure her and spoke in a halting and breathless voice.

"Your kindness... is a blessing...greater than..." His voice trailed off, the effort of speaking overwhelming him. Her kindness was greater than any he had ever found in all the years he had searched. Greater than vast multitudes of humans he had seen during the ninety-five years he'd spent on earth searching. More selfless than....

"Your shift is over. Collect your things and go."

Starting violently at the sound of Phillippe's voice, he flinched like a frightened animal, covering his face and trying to curl into a protective huddle despite the pain such movements caused him. To his astonishment, she answered him with surprising resolve and Tzadkiel splayed his fingers open to watch her in amazement.

"Please, Sir, he's so weak. You said his needs are my responsibility. Please, let me stay and tend them." She didn't spit her words at him belligerently, though she had cause. She didn't give offence by cursing or calling him vile names, though she would have been justified. Instead, she remained on the floor in the position of a supplicant and, without raising her voice, begged to be locked into The Tower for the night so she might remain and tend to him. Phillippe didn't immediately respond and his silence drew Tzadkiel's attention. He looked not at Phillippe, but at a demon glaring balefully back at him with brazen lust glimmering in his red eyes. He was not entirely startled, but instinctively spoke in his native tongue.

"Keervath uneeya braven." His softly spoken words drew an inhuman growl from Phillippe's throat and the young woman turned to look at him with bewilderment. Behind Phillippe, standing at the table without bothering to look up, Lévesque questioned his delay.

"Something the matter?"

Phillippe's gaze narrowed as he turned to look over his shoulder at his superior. "Sorry, Sir. Trying to, uh, remove the servant from his cell."

Impatient as always, Lévesque frowned and approached. "She should've left an hour ago."

"Yes, Sir, I, I know."

Stopping abruptly, Lévesque stared into the cell, an expression of dismay fleetingly crossing his features. Thoroughly vexed, he turned to face Phillippe. His stare pierced into him even before he spoke and, when he did, his tone was a dagger. "You were ordered to back off."

Phillippe shook his head. "But you don't understand."

Lévesque turned to face him squarely, repeating

himself more assertively. "You were ordered to back off."

Phillippe didn't answer. Watching this exchange from the floor, Lourdes gathered her courage and spoke in a timid voice. "Please, Sir?"

Lévesque glared down at her as if only just realizing she was there and the vexation in his stare silenced her instantly. Shifting his gaze, he examined his prisoner more closely. He clearly didn't like what he saw. Turning back to Phillippe, he spoke with a measured a tone. "You're dismissed. Do not return here until I summon you. Do I make myself clear?"

Phillippe glared at him, his eyes seeming to glow red for an instant, then he stepped back, as if unsure of what had just occurred. Looking down at their prisoner, his brow furrowed with confusion, but he didn't ask any questions or argue. Acknowledging the order he'd been given, he took one final look at the Archangel who was lying in blood soaked straw, his body covered with horrifying, enflamed lacerations, his pale, nearly white gaze locked on him. Turning sharply, he strode away with obvious haste. After he'd gone, Lévesque approached the open cell door.

"You were about to ask something, girl?" His expression of agitation softened, seeming to give her just enough courage to ask once more.

"Please, Sir, may I stay with him?"

Considering her request for several intensely silent moments, he stepped inward to examine more closely the brutal injuries Phillippe had caused, a troubled expression creasing his brow before he straightened and stepped back. "You'll be locked into The Tower the entire night," he explained, clarifying what he felt sure she had not considered, "and I'll not be here to keep Sauvage occupied."

Nodding wordlessly, she indicated she understood.

Lévesque looked down at his prisoner another time. "He needs more than a damp rag, girl."

Turning her head to look at her bucket, she shrugged and attempted to explain. "I had nothing else, Sir."

Barely waiting for her reply, he pointed across the chamber. "There's a medical supply room at the end of that hall. It's unlocked. Take what you need. I'll inform the guards."

Astonished, she got to her feet, but he continued before she could say anything or ask any further questions. "He hasn't had food or water in weeks. I'll have some sent up." Having said this, he turned to face her, considering her for a moment. Taking hold of her arm, he pulled her closer and looked down at her with a countenance of iron. "Try to remove him from this place and I'll order Sauvage to hunt you down and I'll give you to him as a reward. Do I make myself entirely clear?"

Gulping in terror, she nodded mutely and hastened around him when he shoved her away and gestured for her to go. Only then did he crouch down to direct his next words at his captive who stared back at him with a tempest of hatred, terror and astonishment in his nearly white eyes.

"It would seem your God has sent His angel of mercy an angel of mercy."

8

T he medical supply closet was just where Lévesque
had indicated. To the left of the main entrance of
The Tower, it stood open as he'd said it would be, but it
was guarded by two Tower Guards who glared down at
her as she approached as if she were some sort of dis-
eased vermin. Unsure what to do, she lingered in the
corridor, twisting round to look behind her towards
the main chamber to see if he was following her. Was
he going to come tell them she could take whatever she
needed? Should she wait there, under the scrutiny of
the guards or return to wait on him? She dared not. She
didn't want her actions to seem impertinent. He said he
would tell the guards, she simply had to wait.

"What are you doing?"

As she feared, one of the guards stepped forward to
question her and a tremor of fear raked its fingers
down her back as she turned reluctantly to face him.
He was an older man, his hair grizzled with age and his
face wrinkled, but his bright blue eyes were clear and
intensely fixed on her. She stammered incoherently for
a moment.

"Speak up. What do you want?"

"Please, Sir," she began ineffectively, but before she

139

could continue, the other guard stalked forward to interrogate her as well.

"You shouldn't be here. Who do you report to?" He towered over her, fully twice her size, and glared down at her with his weapon in his hand. "Answer me!"

Quavering in fear, she stepped back wishing she knew a name to give him, but she didn't. "The...the captain," she attempted, but the older guard cut her off mid-sentence.

"Lévesque? He spoke to you?" His incredulous tone made his fellow guard snicker.

"That'd be a first." They laughed at the absurdity of her proposition and the younger guard moved closer, looking at her greedily. "You're a pretty little thing, aren't you?"

Cringing, she took another step backward, retorting as bravely as she could make herself sound. "Captain Lévesque sent me to collect medical supplies for the prisoner."

They chuckled at her absurd claim and the younger of the two moved closer to her. "Fiery, too. Oh, come on now, I'll give you all the medical supplies you want. I don't want much in return." They laughed as she backed away from him and in her haste to escape the guard, she turned the corner without looking and collided with Lévesque who was coming to speak with them. Seeing him, the younger guard stopped pursuing her abruptly and snapped to attention, but Lourdes, who didn't know who she had run into and fearing it was Sauvage, shrieked in dismay.

"Moreau, are you causing trouble again?" his stern question caused the guard to step back with a shake of his head, but Lévesque ignored his inept reply, looking instead at Lourdes who had covered her face in terror and was shaking violently. "Calm down."

Gasping audibly for breath, Lourdes looked up at

him uncertainly, her heart hammering in her chest so fiercely she thought she might faint, but he pointed toward the supply closet unsympathetically. "Collect the supplies you need and return to your work." He stared at her as she tried to calm her panic, his impatient gaze piercing into her like a blade. "Hurry."

Forcing herself to move, she turned unsteadily and walked past the guards without looking at them, skimming the wall on the opposite side of the narrow corridor as she went by them. She could hear Lévesque reprimanding them in language that left no room for misunderstanding, but their conversation faded when she stepped inside the supply closet. She stopped in her tracks, astonished.

The so-called closet was a room twice the size of her own. Lined with metal shelves that stood floor to ceiling with a cube of similar shelving occupying the center of the room, it housed more medical provisions than she had ever seen in the whole of her lifetime. A narrow, square path led through the shelving, which she followed haltingly as she examined the instruments she didn't recognize and marveled over the multiple shelves of assorted bandaging and a profusion of medicinal ointments, balms, disinfectants, and herbal tinctures that were stacked neatly on the shelves. Blankets, water basins, pillows, sheets, and rolled up bedding filled other shelves and in the far corner a small white cabinet with glass panels stood locked and chained. Stepping closer, she peered through the glass at the small bottles it contained, wondering what they might be, but before she could discover anything further, Lévesque stepped into the room.

"Quite a spectacle, isn't it?"

She straightened abruptly and turned to face him with a look of dread, but he was gazing around the room and didn't seem to notice her fear, continuing in a surprisingly conversational tone. "Fill a basin with what you need and go. Your patient needs you."

Shocked by his urging, particularly since he was the one in charge of making sure her 'patient' was tortured every day, she stood gaping for a moment. It only took a glare from him, however, to prompt her into motion. Doing as he instructed, she found a metal basin on one of the shelves and carefully selected bandages and ointments from the profusion before her. Stopping beside the shelves laden with bedding, she looked at him questioningly, but he shook his head.

"Don't push your luck."

Bobbing a swift curtsy, she answered with a soft, grateful tone. "Thank you, Sir." Hurrying past him, she returned to the main chamber and crossed the floor to the cell, which stood open and unguarded. Slowing her pace as she drew closer, she looked in at him worriedly, but was unable to discern if he was awake or asleep. The late day sunlight had faded markedly now that the sun had moved to the opposite side of The Bastion and The Tower stood in its shadow. Although the guards had ignited several torches, they only sufficiently illuminated the entryway and the armory on the far side of the chamber. The cell in which he lay had fallen into shadow.

Unsure of his condition, she moved inward quietly, kneeling beside him and setting the basin on the floor. He didn't stir. Studying him closely, she watched for signs of breathing and sighed with relief when his chest rose and fell subtly. He was asleep. Deciding it best not to disturb him, she sat down on the floor beside him and, for the first time since she had woken many hours ago, she relaxed. He might sleep most of the night and if he did, she would do nothing to hinder his rest. Better for him to sleep than to be awake and suffer unbearable pain.

The chamber grew quiet with only the intermittent echo of voices from the far ends of the chamber where the guards remained on duty. Drawing her knees up to her chin, she wrapped her arms around her legs and laid her cheek on her knees, closing her eyes with a deep sigh. All was quiet, briefly. It wasn't often she was able to do nothing. Even if she was locked in The Tower, having no demands on her was so rare it actually felt odd. Several times, she lifted her head and looked around the chamber, making certain no guards were coming to harass her, but none came and she was more than thankful. Her body still hurt from the abuse she'd taken the day before and she shifted repeatedly trying to find a comfortable position. Then, her stomach growled loudly.

It was a common occurrence and she'd learned to ignore it, but she'd forgotten. She had bread. Straightening, she dug into one of her deep pockets and withdrew the crumpled, over-baked croissant she'd saved from breakfast. It was hardly appetizing, but she was hungry. Pulling one of the corners with her fingers, she put the small portion in her mouth and chewed ravenously. Even burnt and squashed, it was still good and within moments it was gone, but the small piece of bread only served to increase her hunger. Fortunately, she still had the crusts Brigyda had brought her that morning.

Poor Brigyda. She would probably be frantic with worry when she didn't return from The Tower. She felt horrible for causing her such distress, but had no way to let her know that everything was alright. Besides, she couldn't possibly explain why she had volunteered to be imprisoned for the night so she might take care of someone she barely knew, risking another confrontation with Sauvage or some other guard so she could sit beside a stranger while he slept.

She shook her head. Why did she care so much? Looking at him again, she contemplated for longer than she could gauge. Why would she put herself at such risk? If she were asked, could she explain her reasons? Did she have reasons or was she simply doing what she had always done, living as she had been taught so long ago, acting kindly and giving generously? Was it really so odd to help someone? She scoffed softly; she knew it was, but why should it be? Perhaps if everyone acted more kindly the world wouldn't be in the state it was in. She scoffed again and heard her grandmother's voice.

'Hoping for the hopelessly impossible is hopeless.'

Her stomach growled even more loudly than before.

Sighing sharply, she dug into her pocket another time and withdrew one of the stale heels of bread Brigyda had given her. It was so hard had she knocked it upon the floor the guards down the hall might have heard it. She looked at it with dissatisfaction. It would have been good with some broth to soften it, or some tea, but she had neither and was too hungry to complain. Breaking off a small piece, she put it in her mouth and held it there several moments before it softened enough to chew. It didn't taste like much anymore, but it was better than nothing at all. Repeating the procedure, she only looked back at him again after several bites.

He was watching her.

Gasping at the unexpected discovery, she immediately frowned at her thoughtlessness. His avid stare was fixed on the bread she held and she cursed inwardly for being so insensitive. Looking down at it, she tore off a piece and handed it to him. "It's horribly stale."

Unconcerned, he took it and ate it in seconds, as well as the additional pieces she tore off and provided.

He ate as if he hadn't seen food in weeks and she drew the other piece from her opposite pocket without hesitation. Handing it to him, her stomach objected loudly even as he took the bread with a ravenous gleam in his eyes, but at the sound he looked at her with a pained expression, holding the bread she had just given him as if he didn't know what he should do.

"It's alright, go ahead," she encouraged gently and he looked down at the small portion he held uncertainly before breaking it in half and offering to hand one of the pieces back to her. She refused.

"Please eat it. I've already eaten today. I'll be fine." Her reassurances were undermined by another grumble from her stomach. Silently considering with an expression that betrayed his hunger and his inability to find it within himself to argue, he raised the heel of day-old bread to his mouth. Tearing off chunks like a voracious animal, he devoured it in moments while she watched with dismay, only then remembering what Lévesque had told her. *'He hasn't had food or water in weeks.'* No wonder he drank the water she brought him the night before so voraciously. Was it possible? Had they not only tortured him, but starved him as well? The cruelty of such a notion was unfathomable. Unable to contain the question, it spilled from her lips. "How long has it been since you've eaten?" It seemed an unsympathetic question and she clamped her hand over her mouth as soon as she asked it, but he only gazed at her, thoughtfully chewing as he sought to recall. Finally, he shook his head.

"I've lost track." His soft answer pierced her heart. No wonder he was so hungry. If only she had more to give him. If only she'd brought the vegetables Brigyda had found as well as the bread. Then she remembered. Lévesque said he'd have food and water sent up from the kitchen. How much would be provided and when it might come, she wasn't sure, but as she watched him finish the bread, she decided not to tell him there might be more. She wasn't entirely certain Lévesque would honor his word and the last thing she wanted to do was promise something she couldn't provide.

Sighing when the bread was gone, he closed his eyes wearily, as if eating had stolen what little strength his sleep had restored. She watched him uncertainly for a moment, hesitant to mention that she now had the means to possibly help him feel more comfortable. She wasn't a nurse maid. She didn't really know how to care for an injured person, especially someone with injuries to the extent he suffered, but she didn't want to just sit there and stare at him. She wanted to help.

"Your wounds look so angry." She stated the obvious and frowned. He only moaned in response without opening his eyes clearly loathe to move unless he had no other choice. "I have ointment and bandages," she stammered uncertainly. "They may help soothe," she never finished. Opening his eyes to consider her with an incomprehensible expression, his stare scattered her thoughts. Unable to bear the intensity of his nearly white gaze, she looked instead at his injuries, wondering if anything would truly help. Some of them would certainly benefit from the medicinal ointment and bandages she'd taken from the closet. Others, however, were so deep they still wept and must have been exceedingly painful.

She felt so useless.

"I want to help." The depth of her emotion made her soft voice quiver. He didn't answer as his eyes closed slowly, then opened once more as he struggled to stay awake.

"What is your name?" His soft question surprised her. Shaking her head, she returned his gaze.

"Lourdes." Her quiet response brought a dim smile to his lips.

"Lourdes, you have helped me…. far more," he drew a slow breath, "than anyone else…has ever done…for me." He spoke slowly, breathlessly, and she understood it was nearly more than he could manage. Watching him with increasing misery, she feared he might not survive the night and the realization of such a dire possibility brought an audible sob to her lips.

"I can do more. Please, just tell me what you need."

His eyes closed again and he answered with barely a whisper. "I need what… you cannot provide."

Unsure what he meant, she shook her head and leaned closer to him. "Please, tell me. I want to help you." He remained motionless and his stillness terrified her. Reaching to take his hand in hers, she whispered in quiet desperation. "Please don't let him die."

Insidious laughter echoed from the darkness clawing at him like a ferocious monster. He felt the sensation of spinning, yet knew he was lying on the cold stone floor of his cell. Strangely, his body no longer burned with pain so intense it threatened to tear his reason from him. Instead, he felt nothing at all. Weightless and spinning, he tumbled into the abyss that yawned greedily before him.

"He is lost." It was the same deep, resonant voice he always heard, but now it spoke from somewhere above him.

"He is not!" Another voice rebuked the first, its tone more determined, but equally far away. He recognized this voice as well and struggled to answer, but he could make no sound.

"He allowed them to vanquish him." The first continued, sounding both angry and accusatory.

"He cannot be vanquished." Again, the second rebuked the first. Then a third voice leeched into the darkness, its words a rasping, guttural hiss

"He is human. He is weak and worthless."

Angry cries filled the darkness in response to the serpentine voice, but it continued more loudly. *"Your plan was faulty and has failed!"* This claim was echoed by peals of rancorous laughter that faded into utter silence.

The silence was long and deep.

The blackness around him was heavy and thick.

"Don't let him die." A small, unobtrusive voice permeated the impenetrable blackness. It, too, was a voice he recognized, but it was overpowered by ruthless shouts of obscenities and derisive howls so vulgar he felt ill to hear them.

Vile demons!

He would not allow them to take him.

He was neither human, weak, nor worthless!

Concentrating with intensity he had not summoned in many eons, he reached up through the darkness. It opposed his effort, pulling at him insistently, but he didn't surrender to it. Straining against its oppressive pull with all the force his essence could summon, he looked upward and saw a shimmer of light. He grasped for it, clawing his way upward through the thick, slurking darkness that clung to him. His determination was greater than its malevolent pull. Exerting himself to his limits and then beyond them, he growled vehemently with effort, reaching for the light, clambering upwards against the energy of a thousand demons dragging him down. He writhed up from the clutching blackness as every ounce of strength he possessed poured out of him like blood.

He awoke screaming.

Beside him, Lourdes gasped loudly and drew back in fear as the darkness of the cell around them hissed menacingly. Casting about in terror, she cringed into a protective huddle as the voices from the shadows faded into obscurity. Utterly disoriented, he panted heavily with exhaustion, trying to clear his head of the tangled images spiraling in his mind that left him shaking uncontrollably. Had he nearly slipped into the tumultuous chasm of death?

The realization was sobering. He had to put an end to this. His physical body was simply not able to sustain such injuries on an unending basis and without the benefits of the sun's energy to sustain him it was far more frail than he ever might have imagined. Beside him, he could see Lourdes watching him with palpable dismay, but before she could question him, he shook his head. How could he explain what had just occurred? He could scarce rationalize it himself and he couldn't possibly tell her that demons from the pit of Hades were seeking to extinguish his immortal life. Such an explanation would not only take far longer than his present strength would allow, it would strain credibility. Gaining control of his breathing, he turned his head to look at her.

"Nightmare," he whispered simply and she nodded, seeming satisfied in spite of the fact that she repeatedly peered into the darkness with evident uneasiness. Deeper explanations would simply need to wait.

"Are you alright?" she asked quietly, to which he nodded, unsure if he truly was or not. Twisting, she picked up a tray that sat beside her on the floor and set it in front of him. To his astonishment, it contained a bowl heaped with food, several pieces of bread, three small apples, a large pitcher he hoped contained water, cutlery, and a metal tumbler. His bewilderment must have showed itself plainly through his expressive features because she smiled dimly and offered a quiet explanation. "This is for you. It was delivered while you slept."

His expression turned even more perplexed. How long had he been lost in the darkness? How had she managed to obtain food for him? "How long?" His confusion was overwhelming.

"Several hours. Do you think you can sit up?" Her soft question was sensible, but hardly possible. The pain pulsing through his body as piercing waves was nearly more than he could endure without crying out just lying there. The last thing he wanted to do was move, even if it meant he could eat. Closing his eyes, he sighed despairingly and shook his head subtly.

"It's alright." She shuffled forward, clearly intended to help him, but as she did footsteps echoed from the direction of the armory and her horrified gaze shot up to see who was coming.

He watched her for only a moment before speaking. "The key," he prompted resolutely. Looking at him uncomprehendingly, she shook her head.

"The key is still in the lock." He drew a rapid breath. "Lock the door."

Scrabbling up, she rushed to the cell door and reached for the key still positioned in the lock where Phillippe had left it. The footsteps rapidly drew closer. Looking down the hall, she saw Sauvage coming towards them and she could not contain the cry that escaped her. He called out to her with a sadistically taunting voice.

"Time to serve your master, pretty slave."

Frantic, she wrenched the key free from the lock, dashing inward as she pulled the door closed behind her and the bang echoed through the dark chamber.

"Lock it," he repeated urgently. He couldn't bear the

thought of lying there helpless to provide her any measure of protection while so monstrous a man took his twisted pleasure from her. Lourdes reached through the bars awkwardly, struggling to find the keyhole in the darkness as Sauvage turned the corner into the main chamber. His piercing stare focused on her.

"Now, what's this nonsense?" He approached with a determined stride and didn't stop until he stood so close to the bars that only inches separated them. "What do you think you're doing?" His conspicuous patience and calculating manner sent a chill through her. Retreating from him with a whimper she could not control, the key tumbled from the lock and clattered on the floor at his feet. Sauvage looked down at it with a wry grin turning his lips and Tzadkiel watched with a turbulent combination of disappointment and mounting anger as he pulled the door open slowly.

"I see. You think because you've done your duties for the day that you're finished, but have you obeyed or served your master today?"

Trying to stifle her crying, Lourdes shook her head as she backed away from him as far as she could go, pressing herself against the far wall. He walked towards her with deliberate slowness, plainly enjoying her fear. "Have you? Answer me." His measured, patient cruelty caused Tzadkiel's insides to churn in disgust as he listened, but what pained him even more greatly was Lourdes' crying and the violent shaking that wracked her body.

"N-no, S...Sir." Her response was barely a timid squeak and his smiled distorted into an evil leer.

"No, you haven't and you're required to, aren't you?" He spoke to her as if she were a child. "Come here."

Lourdes shook her head in a constant motion, unable to force herself away from the wall. In her terror, her knees buckled and she sank to floor. Watching helplessly, Tzadkiel felt a tempest of rage building within him he feared he would not be able to control.

"You're required to obey. Come to me." Holding out his hand, Sauvage stood waiting for her to obey him, but when she remained pressed against the wall, he moved closer to her instead, reaching down to pull off her cap as she turned her head to one side and then the other in an attempt to elude his touch. Tossing it aside, he unhurriedly removed the clasps that held the waves of her chestnut–red hair in a tousled knot, freeing the lengths to tumble across her shuddering shoulders. Looking down at her as he stroked her hair torment-ingly, he watched with obvious pleasure as she cow-ered. "Such defiance of your master warrants punishment. I'll need to discipline you before we be-gin." As he spoke to her, Sauvage traced the tears that rolled over her cheeks, holding her shaking head still so he could stare at her lustfully. "Such pretty tears. You know how much I like to watch you cry."

Tzadkiel truly thought he might be sick. He had to do something. He could not allow such an atrocity to occur right in front of him. The man was such an ab-horrent monster he might even enjoy such a deplorable notion. He saw Sauvage haul her to her feet, lean in, and lick her face. The wail that escaped her as she struggled to resist him was even more than he could bear.

"Leave her." The words hissed from Tzadkiel's mouth more a growl than spoken language. The fe-rocity of his low tone was startling, but Sauvage turned to look down at him incredulously.

"Or what, Archangel? Haven't you suffered enough already? Do you really want me to call the guards to subdue you?"

He didn't respond, but could see the confusion on Lourdes' face before Sauvage pulled her closer.

"I'll do what I want with her and you're welcome to watch."

Never in all the years of his immortal life had he ever felt such irrepressible rage. It was not in his nature to feel hatred or violence, but he was not himself. He was immortal energy bound within a human body and was subject to its unpredictable passions and emotions. Growling fiercely, he pushed himself up from the floor, ignoring the intense pain that shattered through him as many of his wounds reopened. Sauvage had already turned away and was pulling Lourdes against his body, smothering her with a lustful kiss as he tugged the bodice of her dress open viciously.

"Leave her!" Straining to suppress the violent shuddering that wracked his weakened body, Tzadkiel stood facing them and repeated himself with a more imposing tone. He was ignored, but he had not defeated legions of Hell's demons to lie on the floor helplessly and watch so vile a human indulge his wicked lusts. Stretching out his hand, he spoke the word that had been poised on his lips for months. "Jshunamir."

At the sound of his voice the sword, which had rested atop the pedestal created for it for nearly a year, stirred. Holding out his hand, Tzadkiel waited, never doubting the result of the word he'd spoken and the sword glimmered with an inner, silvery light. It rose from the pedestal, spun as if seeking him and then moved with a speed that could scarcely be tracked, slowing the instant before it touched his hand. Looking down at the weapon, Tzadkiel closed his hand around the hilt and clanked the tip loudly against the floor.

The unexpected noise drew Sauvage's attention at last. Twisting to find the source of the clatter, his eyes grew wide when he saw the Archangel standing with his sword in hand, facing him with a bold, unwavering stance even as blood streamed across his torn and naked body. Wiping his mouth with the back of his hand, he held Lourdes by a fistful of hair, pulling her into an uncomfortable backward arch as he shook his head.

"Think you can take me in your condition?" His impudence was only exceeded by his lack of insight. Tzadkiel glared at him, speaking with intractable aggression.

"This sword answers every command I give it. If you do not release her, I shall ask it to bury itself in your spine. Slowly."

Sauvage glared at him for a moment; then he realized the Archangel was not actually holding the sword. It stood upright at his side just below his opened hand, its point several inches from the floor. Tzadkiel didn't hesitate.

"Jshunamir, guard." The sword rose, tilted its point so it was angled directly at Sauvage and, in an instant, poised itself inches from his throat. Arching backward with astonishment, he released Lourdes and stepped away from her hastily, watching the Archangel with sudden wariness.

"If you dare harass her again, touch or harm her in any manner, or allow another to harm her, I shall not hesitate to speak those words." Tzadkiel's voice was a menacing snarl.

Nodding sharply with understanding, Sauvage stepped back again, the sword following his every movement.

"Lock us in and throw the key inside. Jshunamir, return."

His brow furrowed with confusion, but Sauvage didn't wait to question this unexpected command. Even as the sword returned to the Archangel's side, he rushed out of the cell, slammed the door closed, locked it, and tossed the key at the Archangel's feet.

"Go!" The incensed word reverberated within the empty chamber, echoing from all sides of it at once and Sauvage was gone before the echo faded.

Lourdes stared at him, her expression a cascade of fear, anguish, and confusion. She watched with astonishment as he looked down at his sword and spoke the word 'pedestal' in a hushed voice. As if in protest, the sword glimmered brightly and spun at his side, but when he raised his hand and pointed toward the small dais that had been created for the weapon, it returned to its place on the opposite side of the chamber, reoccupying the same space it had previously and with such precision there was no indication it had ever moved. Focusing on her wearily for a brief moment, he sank to his knees with a shuddering moan of pain.

"Oh!" Rushing to his side, Lourdes knelt down beside him, aghast at the severe bleeding his actions had caused. What could she do? Unable to determine how to help him and not cause additional pain, she watched helplessly as he leaned forward, covered his face with his hands, and wept bitterly. The sound seemed to cause the very air to tremble. Outside, a deep rumble of thunder rolled across the sky as torrents of rain drummed against the chamber's barred windows. The darkness of the chamber grew ominous. Watching him with a sense of desolation, she could not imagine his agony or how she could possibly ease it and the helplessness she felt was unbearable.

She had to do something. Anything. He wasn't going to ask her for anything, that much was clear, but she wouldn't sit there uselessly. Unsure whether it was the right thing to do or not she collected the basin she had set to the side and untied one of the many rolls of

bandaging it contained. Uncoiling it, she spread medicinal ointment along a portion of its length and laid it
gently over a laceration that stretched the length of his
arm. Hissing at the unexpected sensation, he jerked in
surprise, but didn't pull away. Remaining in his half-
curled position, he allowed her to wrap the length of
the bandage around his arm and tie it.

"I confess, I don't know exactly what I'm doing. I'm
a scullery maid, not a nurse, but it may help," she whispered hopefully, tilting her head to look at him more
directly. "Can you lie down?" Her soft question drew a
wretched sob from him and he looked at her through
the splayed fingers of his hand as if the thought of
moving was worse than the possibility of bleeding to
death. His entire body shook uncontrollably and she
knew she couldn't force him. All she could do was wait
patiently for him to gather his strength, and perhaps
his courage, to lie back so she could continue to dress
his wounds. It took many protracted moments, but
when he drew a shuddering breath and moved hesitantly, she squeezed her eyes closed and covered her
face with her hands, unable to bear the sight of the terrible effort it demanded from him. Shifting as carefully
as he could manage, he gasped and moaned repeatedly,
in obvious, excruciating pain.

Lourdes could not hold back her tears.

How he had managed to stand or to sound so fierce
when he was suffering such intolerable pain, she didn't
know. How he could have appeared so intimidating just
moments ago when now he seemed so vulnerable, she
was not sure. How the sword had come to him, threatened Sauvage so menacingly, and then returned to
where it had been of its own power, she had no idea.
Why Sauvage called him 'Archangel', she could not
comprehend. Looking at him through the tears in her
eyes, she didn't see an angelic being of light with wings

and a halo; she saw only a shaking, bleeding man who cried in desperate need.

The rest was unimportant, at least, for the moment. The only thing that mattered was helping to ease his pain, if that was even possible. She couldn't be sure her attempts to help wouldn't cause him more discomfort, but cleaning and dressing his injuries seemed vitally important. She might not be a nursemaid, but she understood how crucial it was to keep open wounds clean. When he finally managed to lie back, he panted in distress, his entire body shaking fiercely and she watched him for a moment, utterly at a loss. Could she really help him in any way that would make a difference?

Perhaps it was more to alleviate her own uneasiness than his, but she took a moment to collect her apron, which had fallen to the floor when he had faced Sauvage, and laid it across his hips. He was in such great pain, he hardly seemed to notice or care whether he was naked or not, but it seemed the decent thing to do. Taking up another roll of bandaging and using the same process she had to bandage his arm, she repeated it a full dozen times, dressing the deepest lacerations first and reserving wrappings so she could clean and redress them once they finally stopped bleeding. Her ministrations were as gentle as she could make them, but the hurt they produced seemed nearly as bad as the torture that had caused them. Rocking his head side to side fitfully, he struggled not to raise his hands to impede her actions and turned his head away more than a few times to growl in agitation.

The process took far longer than she hoped and when she finally dressed the last of his deep lacerations, she decided not to torment him with any additional bandaging. She was too inept and his pain was too great. Instead, she gently wiped his brow and cheeks with the damp cloth. "I'm so, so sorry."

He shook his head at her soft apology, but didn't otherwise respond. Visibly exhausted and unable to keep his eyes open, he lay trembling and panting fitfully. The strength he possessed to endure such unimaginable pain amazed her beyond words. It also tore at her heart. Although she wished she could do more for him, she couldn't. She could only watch quietly while he tried to calm his breathing and control the tears he could not suppress. It took many protracted moments, but his shaking finally subsided and when he breathed more easily, she turned to the food tray and poured water into the tumbler that had been provided. Cautiously she brought it to his lips. "Are you thirsty?"

Without opening his eyes, he nodded. The motion was barely perceptible, but it was enough. She brought the edge of the cup to his lips lightly and waited for him to raise his head in response. It was more difficult than she hoped, but he accepted the drink she offered and finished it completely before allowing himself to fall back with a groan.

"Please forgive me for hurting you." Her soft voice wavered with emotion and, after a moment, he opened his pale eyes to stare at her silently. Raising his hand, he reached slowly to touch her. His eyes closed involuntarily several times as he fought to remain conscious and he spoke in barely a whisper. His words were halting and breathless.

"You... have done nothing... to hurt me.... you are... deliverance."

9

L ourdes awoke with the dawn as she did every day
and lay with her eyes closed as she sought to separate herself from sleep more fully. The morning light
that typically streamed in through her window seemed
oddly faint and she wondered if it was still raining.
Rolling onto her back with a moan, she also wondered
why her small bed seemed so uncomfortable and why it
still seemed as dark as night. Perhaps it was not
morning after all and she'd have more time to sleep. It
was a blissful thought. Blinking wearily to clear her
mind from the vestiges of slumber, she looked up at the
ceiling.

It was not her ceiling.

Abruptly, she sat up.

She was still in his cell!

Realizing she must have fallen asleep while
watching over him, she looked around herself and
found she was lying on the floor beside him. He was
still sleeping. At least, she hoped he was sleeping!
Leaning closer to him, she winced as a stab of dull ache
spread through her abdomen, a painful reminder of
what Sauvage had done. Shaking off the memory before it latched onto her, she watched his chest with des-

perate expectation and sighed heavily when she saw him breathing slow and deep. He was relaxed at long last. Nothing could have pleased her more. Nothing, that is, except if they both were far, far away from The Tower.

Straightening, she winced again. She had ignored her own injury to help him and, although she would make the same decision again without hesitation, bearing his weight to help him to his cell had taken an unexpected toll. She ached internally to such a degree it was difficult to ignore. She had to ignore it, though; his injuries were far worse than hers.

Examining the bandages she had so ineptly applied, she was surprised to find they had not loosened or fallen away during the night. Most were scarlet with blood, however, and needed to be changed. It wasn't an unexpected discovery, but she didn't want to hurt him again by having to repeat the drawn-out process of cleaning and dressing his wounds. Perhaps, she wouldn't need to. Allowing her gaze to wander over him, she wished she might find that his wounds had healed as remarkably as they had during the day before when he lay in the morning sunlight, but her examination left her disappointed.

It also left her blushing when she noticed her apron had slipped to the floor. Closing her eyes modestly, she shook her head. Much worse could have happened. She decided to let him sleep. Pushing herself up from the floor as quietly as she could, she stepped away carefully and peered out into the darkness. It was entirely quiet. Were they actually alone? Had the guards gone? Was it even morning? The window of the main chamber glowed with faint lavender light and the sound of rain had stopped, although the panes of heavy glass were streaked with water. Looking back at him, she saw the key to the door lying on the floor where Sauvage had thrown it and she moved carefully to pick it up. She would see to her needs, if she could find The Tower privy, and then collect more medical supplies from the closet.

Opening the cell door quietly, she tucked the key into one of her dress pockets and moved out into the chamber like a timid cat creeping from its hiding place only after all the house's inhabitants had gone to bed. She made her way quietly through the chamber, seeking the privy, and found a tiny closet of a room against the outside wall. It was cleaner than she expected and she took a moment for herself. Given her discomfort, she also made certain she hadn't started bleeding again, which would have been cause for greater concern. To her relief, she found she had not. Continuing towards the supply closet, she tried to put what had happened out of her mind.

The supply room was open and unguarded. Though it was dark, she managed to find what she was looking for and created a small pile of additional bandages and ointment, which she bundled into a clean towel before retracing her steps back toward the cell. The silence of the chamber felt oddly oppressive, as if the walls remembered each scream that echoed from its surfaces and every tear that had fallen during the countless ages it stood witness to man's cruelty. Stopping near the table with the medical supplies hugged close in her arms, she looked at it and sobbed without warning as the sound of his screams crashed over her like a tidal wave. She truly didn't understand how anyone could be as calculating and merciless as Phillippe. The pleasure he seemed to take in hurting him sent a shiver through her. Lévesque seemed little better, although he'd surprised her when he allowed her to collect medical supplies and remain in The Tower to tend his injuries.

Somehow, some way, she had to get him out of this horrible place.

Squaring her shoulders with determination in the face of impossibility, she collected herself and returned to the cell. He slept quietly, so she placed the supplies in the basin and decided to take the bucket to the well room to rinse and refill it. She risked much by leaving a cell she could easily lock, particularly now that morning approached and the Tower Guards would be returning, but she didn't want to huddle in fear. She refused to be intimidated by suppositions. Besides, she wanted to be useful to him.

Him.

She sighed harshly. She still hadn't learned his name, but an opportune moment to ask hadn't really presented itself. Her mind replayed the events of the previous day as she moved hurriedly to the well room where she emptied, rinsed and refilled her bucket. The room stood in darkness and shivers of apprehension raced over her as she worked in the shadowy alcove, memories tormenting her, but she didn't have time to wallow in self-pity. At least, she didn't want to have time. It served no useful purpose to allow misery to overrule her and the last thing she wanted to do was think about Sauvage in any way.

Completing her task as rapidly as possible, she returned to the cell with a full bucket of fresh water, closed the door and locked it. Tucking the key into her pocket with a sense of security she'd rarely experienced anywhere outside her small tower room, she turned to gaze thoughtfully at him. She knew when Lévesque and Phillippe showed up, she would be forced to return the key to them, but at the moment they were safe. Comparatively. Sitting down next to him, she watched him sleep for many long moments as morning quietly stole into the chamber. She closed her eyes and even considered lying down again, but didn't. She was tired, but she was also hungry.

Looking at the tray containing the food that had been brought up for him the night before, she had to fight not to take some for herself. Regardless of the fact that she'd only eaten a small breakfast nearly twenty-four hours earlier, she wouldn't eat the food he so desperately needed. He couldn't even remember the last time he'd eaten; she could. Instead, she sank the tumbler into the bucket of water she'd just drawn and tried to quell the gnawing in her stomach with water. It wasn't much, but it eased the feeling of emptiness in her belly, at least for the moment. Drawing her legs up, she wrapped her arms around them and lay her cheek on her knees, closed her eyes again and tried to enjoy the liberty of doing absolutely nothing for several prolonged moments. More than once, she moaned softly in discomfort and fidgeted, trying to find a better position while her thoughts churned in a jumble of memories she didn't want to remember and possibilities she didn't want to consider.

"Lourdes." His soft whisper roused her from her ineffective respite and she opened her eyes to smile at him dimly.

"Are you alright?" She asked him that question frequently. She knew she did, but it was relevant. He sighed, his expression reflecting the discomfort he still suffered, yet after a moment he refocused on her.

"I'm so hungry."

Turning to collect the tray of food, she pushed it close to him, realizing her error only after he looked down at it despairingly. Shuffling closer to him without speaking, she picked up the bowl and looked at it hungrily. It was filled with a generous serving of oatmeal, berries, and nuts, and was sweetened with a lavish drizzling of honey. Although it was cold, it looked delicious; far more appetizing than any oatmeal she'd ever been served. Cradling the bowl in one hand, she filled the spoon with a small portion and brought it carefully to his mouth.

He looked at her with an unreadable gaze. His eyes were nearly completely white and they sent a shiver through her, but she tried not to let him see it. Nodding at him encouragingly, she offered the spoonful another time and he opened his mouth to accept it. Despite being cold, it must have been delightful because his eyes closed as he tasted it and he murmured a pleased "Mmm." Filling the spoon another time and then another, she fed him with diligent patience, watching him enjoy the savory meal while, at the same time, desperately trying to ignore her own hunger. She might even have been successful if her stomach hadn't betrayed her noisily.

At the sound, his gaze immediately locked on her and his entire countenance shifted from pleasure to dismay. "Have you eaten, Lourdes?" He need not ask; he already knew the answer, but she tried to deny the honesty of her body anyway.

"I'm alright." Her reassurance had the opposite effect than what she intended and seemed to upset him. He shook his head.

"You need to eat," he insisted with greater determination than she expected, but so did she.

"You can't remember the last time you've eaten. I can. It was just yesterday." Attempting to be generous, she raised another spoonful, but he shook his head.

"Yesterday?"

She nodded as if it was the most normal thing in the world, but concern worried his brow and he shook his head another time.

"I'll eat no more until you have some."

She held another spoonful up, but he pursed his lips

stubbornly and turned his head aside, watching her with a sideward stare and refusing to take anything more until she ate several spoonfuls. She couldn't find it within herself to argue.

After complying with his gentle demand, she poured some water into the tumbler and held it steady so he could drink, then raised another spoonful to his mouth with a hopeful expression. To her relief, he relented and ate, though he stopped after every few bites to ensure she ate as well. Together, they finished the oatmeal, two pieces of bread, and the entire pitcher of water, but when she picked up one of the apples, he closed his eyes.

She was satisfied as well. The apples could be their supper. Looking at him with sudden apprehension, she feared what the hours of suppertime might bring. Would he once again be in desperate pain, unable to move, let alone eat? Heaven help him if Phillippe repeated the abuse he had inflicted yesterday. He couldn't possibly survive it and try as she might she couldn't think how she might prevent it. Watching him anxiously, she realized she had not yet learned his name. Although she wasn't sure if he had already fallen back to sleep or if he was just resting, she knew the last thing she wanted to do was disturb him. He needed as much rest as he could get.

Shifting into a curled position once more, she winced uncomfortably. The ache inside wasn't going away, but she tried not to worry about herself. She was just sore. She had every reason to be. The thought lingered and then began tormenting her, forcing memories of what Ghislain and Sauvage had done to her into her mind's eye and she grimaced, fighting back a whimper. She would not give in! Not to them. Not by collapsing into a sea of despair. She had far better things to occupy her mind with and far more important things to do. Opening her eyes that were already red from held back tears, she gazed at him quietly as the dim room began to brighten with the light of a new day. Perhaps it would be a better day. Perhaps she would, at the very least, learn his name.

"May I ask you something?" The question spilled from her lips before she could contain it. She bit her lower lip in frustration, but the softly spoken inquiry brought a small smile to his lips, revealing he was still awake despite the fact that he didn't open his eyes to look at her.

"Of course." His response was hushed.

"What is your name?"

He remained silent and she thought he may have drifted off to sleep. Behind them, the iron bars of the cell rattled as the lock was unlatched. A voice spoke from outside the bars of the cell, answering her question in a drawn-out hiss that sounded like a pit of vipers.

"Hissss naaaaame issss Tsssadkiel." Twisting about sharply at the unexpected reply, she found Phillippe watching them with a glowing crimson stare. In his hand he held a key to the cell door that he held out and swung tauntingly.

She couldn't stop herself from screaming.

Having unlocked the door with the second key, which he must have kept with him at all times, Phillippe rushed in at them with a hideous, inhuman snarl. Before he had time to rouse himself properly and comprehend what was happening, Phillippe stood over Tzadkiel, grasped a handful of his hair ferociously, pulled his head back brutally and shoved a torn piece of cloth into his mouth. Ignoring Lourdes's repeated attempts to fend him off, his sole focus was silencing the Archangel before he could call his sword. He secured the gag with a leather belt he cinched tightly around his head, then he leaned in and hissed at him like an enraged demon.

Tzadkiel cringed backwards, shaking his head violently in an attempt to free himself, but Phillippe, or rather, the demon within him, laughed venomously at him. Yanking him up from the floor with ruthless haste, he ignored his muffled cries as he tugged on the leather strap to drag him backward out of the cell and lead him straight towards the table. In spite of the pain his only partially healed wounds produced, Tzadkiel resisted with every ounce of strength he possessed, but it only took one well aimed punch to his severely lacerated stomach to overpower his resistance.

Turning on Lourdes who tried to follow them out into the chamber and hinder Phillippe in any way she could, he struck her forcefully across the face with a backhanded swing that sent her tumbling back into the cell. Slamming the door closed on her, he glared at her hatefully through the bars. "Detesssssstable whore." His voice was a rasping, guttural hiss and Tzadkiel stared at him in horror from his doubled over position. He recognized the voice; it was the same voice he'd heard in his nightmare. Desperately, he tried to pull the gag from his mouth even as he watched Phillippe retraced his steps rapidly. He ducked out of the way once, but was struck forcefully across his face, the blow knocking his hands away from the gag before Phillippe rushed in at him with a harsh curse.

Shoving him backwards towards the table viciously, Phillippe grabbed the leather strap behind his head and dragged him closer to it. Taking advantage of his off-balance stumbling by jerking the strap downward harshly, he forced Tzadkiel to arch backward over the

width of the stone slab and leaned over him to hiss belligerently into his face again. Seizing his wrist, he
pulled his arm savagely, ignoring the Archangel's muffled cry as he stretched him to his limit in order to
shackle his wrist in the manacle in the over-head position. Rounding the table more slowly now that he was
restrained, Phillippe eluded the kick aimed at him and
grasped his ankle. Using a second leather strap he had
already waiting on the table, he secured his leg to the
chains bolted to the floor.

Clearly, he had planned this attack.

Moving leisurely now that he was immobilized,
Phillippe stepped closer and ran his hands up his legs
and across his stomach lasciviously. Tzadkiel growled
at the sensation, but he was ignored. Taking up the serrated dagger he'd used the day before, Phillippe casually cut away the bandages Lourdes had applied, tossing
them aside carelessly while he spoke in a slurred and
threatening tone. "You maaaay be immortal, Archangel,
but you ssssuffer as deliciousssssly as any humaaaan.
We cannot let thissss opportunity paaassss." His voice
was the same rasping hiss as before and his eyes glowed
red in the diffuse morning light. Tzadkiel muttered
something against the gag, but his words were unintel-
ligible. Smiling wickedly, Phillippe licked his lips as he
raised the jagged blade.

"Bleed for ussssss, Archangel."

Lévesque entered The Tower through the armory auxiliary entrance just as he did every morning, inspecting
the unguarded armory and making note of any defi-
ciencies before appraising the condition of the rations
larder and main storeroom. It had become his routine
and, in spite of the fact that a servant had spent the

night locked in The Tower along with their prisoner, he didn't see any reason to not follow his routine. Regardless of whatever the Marshal of The Protectorate thought of his supervisory capabilities, those under his authority followed his orders and the protocols he had laid out upon taking command. Everything was as he expected it to be.

Satisfied that things were in good order, he stirred the cup of tea he carried and moved on towards the main chamber, becoming aware of a peculiar slurping noise as he drew closer. He didn't recognize the sound as something that ordinarily would have occurred and, to add to the mystery, as he continued along the dim corridor he could hear the unmistakable sound of a woman crying. It mingled with the repulsive sound, as did an odd, never-ending echo that sounded like distant laughter. Looking up from his cup of tea through the light of morning illuminating the main chamber and the table, he stopped dead in his tracks. His eyes grew wide and his cup shattered on the floor.

Phillippe had returned!

Not only had he returned, but he had strapped the prisoner across the table precariously and had inflicted even greater damage than he had the day before, if that was possible. Standing between the prisoner's legs, Phillippe was hunched over and covered in blood, his hands and clothes stained crimson. Mercilessly, he manipulated a deep laceration that stretched across the prisoner's thigh, forcing it to bleed profusely. Darkened shadows danced around him reveling in the Archangel's muffled screams. The servant who had remained with him to tend his injuries knelt on the floor between the cell and the table, her hands covering her face as she cried bitterly. The scene was barbaric, but when Phillippe leaned down and with a vile slurping sound drank the blood that ran down the prisoner's thigh, Lévesque shouted in revulsion.

"What in the name of God!" At the sound of his voice, the ebon shadows scattered into the darkened corners of the room and Phillippe paused, raising his head slowly. Turning to look at his commanding officer with no hint of recognition in his scarlet eyes, he allowed the blood smeared upon his face to run down his chin while he laughed with a gurgling jeer.

"God hassss nothing to do with thisssss." The serpentine voice made Lévesque step back in horror, his eyes widening with honest fear, but he only hesitated a moment before drawing his sword and stalking closer, pointing the blade at Phillippe's throat.

"Whatever you are, be gone!"

Derisive laughter echoed through the chamber, but Phillippe...or whatever had taken his place... turned with indifference and stooped once again to drink. Lévesque watched for a brief moment, appalled. Then, he recalled his primary education.

"In the name of the Almighty, I said go!"

At this command, Phillippe turned on him furiously, his dripping hands raised like claws seeking flesh as he hissed and cursed in language so foul even Lévesque cringed to hear it. They struggled for control of his sword, scrabbling backward from the table. As they fought, Lourdes got up and rushed to Tzadkiel's side. Moving directly to his head, she wrenched the tight clasp of the leather strap free and slid it off, pulling the cloth from his mouth so he could speak.

He gasped for breath, then shouted. "Jshunamir!"

Rising from its pedestal with a bright flare of light, his sword moved faster than could be seen to hover over him. The name of the sword caused frenzied screeches and howls to reverberate around the room from the shadows constricting into corners. At the chaotic din, Lourdes stepped backward from the table and covered her ears, cringing in terror while Phillippe and Lévesque continued to grapple for the sword.

"Liberate." Tzadkiel spoke again and the sword responded with another intense blaze of light. It took careful aim, then struck one of the iron chains securing him to the table. The metal shattered like ice and fell in pieces to the floor even as the sword moved to the next chain and repeated its action, liberating him in seconds. When he was free, he pushed himself up from the table with a prodigious groan and extended his hand to take the sword. Crossing one arm across his stomach, he moved with as much haste as his injuries would allow and only stopped when the point of his sword pressed deeply into the back of Phillippe's neck. His deep voice filled the chamber. "Depart, foul demon, before I call upon Michael to have at you!"

The monster within Phillippe squalled loudly in protest, its voice fading into hissing nothingness even as Phillippe crumpled to the floor in a heap. Lévesque stared at him wide-eyed and dazed before looking up at the Archangel standing before him, unable to find words to express either his shock or his gratitude. It didn't matter. As soon as the demon relinquished its control over Phillippe, Tzadkiel fell to his knees, blood issuing from his wounds at a terrifying rate.

Prompted into action by his collapse, Lévesque stepped closer and shrugged off his coat, kneeling down on one knee as he bundled the coat into a ball and pressed it down on the deep laceration crossing his leg. Leaning his weight on it, he ignored Tzadkiel's cry of pain as he cast about the room for Lourdes. She was still standing on the opposite side of the table, watching in wide-eyed horror with the leather strap hanging in her hand, forgotten. Her expression was shocked and she was visibly overwhelmed, but there was no time for feminine delicacies.

"Bring me that strap," Lévesque barked, cursing under his breath when she shook her head in dismay and backed away from him. "Damn it to hell, girl. Would you rather watch him bleed?" He was not accustomed to explaining himself, particularly to servants, but she had cause enough to distrust them. Haltingly, she stepped forward, her pace quickening the closer she got and when she reached them, Lévesque snatched the strap from her hand impatiently. Wrapping it around his coat, he pulled the loose end tight, grimacing when the Archangel cried out against the pain he caused. The wound was horrifying, but if he could decrease the bleeding, even slightly, he might have time to recover. "Make yourself useful, instead of standing there gaping. Bring some bandages."

She stepped back, looking first in the direction of the supply closet, then at the cell, uncertain if the dancing shadows that had filled the corners of the room had also departed, but she didn't see any movement. Dashing into the dim cubicle of a cell to retrieve the basin she had refilled, she returned in a rush and stood trembling as she watched them. Lévesque assessed the situation, then glanced up at her and barked another command.

"We need to get him into the sunlight. Go to the supply closet and bring one of the bed rolls. Find a suture kit as well." She clearly didn't understand him, but he had no patience to explain himself. "Go!"

Rushing away with an audible gasp, she was gone in seconds. She was fast, he had to give her that and the guards must have been late reporting for duty because she came back in what seemed like a moment with a folded sheet tucked under her arm and a half-unrolled pad of bedding.

"Lay it here." He pointed at the floor beside them and she did as he directed, hovering with palpable anxiety as she waited for his next instructions, but he spoke to Tzadkiel instead. He was still kneeling with his arms crossed over his stomach, curled forward and groaning as blood poured from the many deep lacerations Phillippe had caused.

"Can you lie on this?" Their gazes locked briefly, but Lévesque could not bear the excruciating intensity of his piercing white stare. Hadn't his eyes used to be violet? Confused as well as curious, he looked at the crystal the Archangel wore and realized that it, too, had faded from deep amethyst to milky white, but he didn't have time to consider its significance. Tzadkiel managed to shift his weight, despite the evident pain the motion caused, and fell onto the bedding with another deep groan. Lévesque held pressure on his leg and looked around for the girl. If they could get him into the light, he might not bleed out.

The thought made him scoff inwardly as he realized the absurdity of the situation. He couldn't die. That was the very conundrum that had put them all into the situation they now faced. Shaking his head to focus his spiraling thoughts, he looked towards the window and pointed across the chamber at the streaming rays of sunlight just beginning to illuminate the floor. "Assemble your supplies there. Did you find a suture kit?" Not waiting for her to answer or to fully comprehend his order, he cinched the leather strap around the Archangel's leg like a tourniquet and got up. Taking hold of the corners of the bedding near Tzadkiel's feet, he began hauling him across the floor towards the morning sunlight. Lourdes hurried to the place he'd pointed out and set the basin of supplies and the sheet she'd taken from the supply closet on the floor before turning to watch them anxiously.

She screamed.

Scrabbling up from his prone position, Phillippe garbled incomprehensibly while he lurched toward the makeshift gurney, snatching and clawing at Tzadkiel like a wild animal. Startled by this unexpected attack, Lévesque stopped and twisted around, reaching for his sword only to realize he'd left it lying on the floor where the Archangel had fallen. Tzadkiel curled to protect himself, fending off Phillippe's repeated attempts to bite him as he shouted over the inane drivel spewing from his mouth.

"Jshunamir, protect!"

Spinning on the floor where he'd dropped it, the magnificent sword blazed and found its direction, shooting toward the Archangel's attacker like a bullet from a gun. Rising as it drew closer, it spiraled rapidly and buried itself deep in Phillippe's back. He arched backward sharply, the creature within him snarling furiously even as Phillippe's body went slack. Straining to hold the lifeless body off himself, Tzadkiel looked up to Lévesque for help, but he stood dumbstruck, unable to fathom the sequence of events that had just unfolded and too distracted by the incomprehensibility of them to be of any use. With a vehement growl, Tzadkiel shoved Phillippe's limp body away and curled onto his side in agony.

Lévesque stared down at him with dismay. What in the name of Heaven was happening? How had he lost control of the situation? Had he ever, truly, had control? Would more demons issue forth from the depths of Hell through other guards to attack the Archangel? There were no answers to his questions, only more questions, most of which he didn't want to ask or to have answered, but he knew something had to be done. Shaking his head, he refocused on the most immediate concern, keeping the Archangel in the sunlight.

Turning around without a word, he took hold of the bedding and continued dragging him towards the light glimmering through the barred window. Upon situating the bedroll so the light fell across his body unimpeded, he stepped back and watched as Lourdes unfolded the sheet into a rectangle and covered him across his hips. Tzadkiel's head fell back and he closed his eyes as the rays of sunlight enveloped him and the crystal around his neck began to pulse.

"We must keep him in the light."

She looked up at him, confused and shaken. "Why?"

His glare said more than his answer. "Ask him."

Deliciously warm light enveloped him in its glimmering rays, the soothing sensation blissfully euphoric. Lying back against the soft bedding beneath him, Tzadkiel could not contain the profound sigh that rushed from his lips or the tears that fell from his eyes. For the first time in days, he felt the agony of his injuries begin to ebb. The endless hours of pain he had suffered left him utterly exhausted, so much so he could barely think, yet he was cognizant enough to hear Lourdes. He thought she was crying and the sound sent a different sort of pain through him. Unable to find strength enough to open his eyes and look for her, he spoke her name softly.

"Lourdes."

She didn't respond. Where was she? After several prolonged moments, he heard a soft shuffle beside him. "It will...be alright." He hardly recognized his own deep voice. Fatigue had left him weak and breathless. His voice was barely a whisper and he could only manage to get out a few words at a time. Again, she didn't respond. She was terrified; he felt it deep in his essence just as he had felt the gentleness of her spirit and the animosity in Lévesque. He knew he had to do something. The last thing he wanted was to lose her, not after everything he'd gone through. Repeating her name quietly, he forced himself to open his eyes to look for her.

"Lourdes?"

She was right beside him, kneeling quietly with the bucket next to her and a wet cloth in her hand that was dripping onto her dress because she stared at him, visibly overwrought and trembling. Who wouldn't be after seeing and hearing all she had? Studying her more closely, he realized she had stopped crying and was watching the light that spiraled and shimmered around him. Her expression was a mixture of wonder, confusion, and evident fear, but how could he explain it? Such a discussion could take hours and he barely had the strength to keep his eyes open. Regardless of his weakness, he wanted to ease her distress in some way.

"Please...don't be...afraid, Lourdes." His breathless plea made her blink repeatedly, as if coming out of a trance, and she turned her head to look at him, but she didn't speak. Standing several yards behind her, Lévesque watched them with a somber expression, deep in thought. Tzadkiel's eyes closed involuntarily and she gasped aloud.

"Oh! Please don't..." The panic in her voice pained him as much as his wounds, but he didn't have the strength to keep his eyes open any more than he had energy to try to reassure her.

"He can't die, girl." Lévesque spoke from behind them, his tone as irritated as always. Unable to find the strength to offer an explanation of his own, Tzadkiel listened with curiosity for what he would say, but he didn't elaborate and Lourdes didn't respond to his odd statement. Long moments passed and he felt himself slipping into heavy stillness. When she finally did speak, it was with such confusion it wrenched at his heart.

"He can't?"

"No." This terse reply was followed by a statement he could only assume was directed at him. "I know how to suture wounds."

Comprehending his offer, Tzadkiel groaned and shook his head, the movement so subtle it might have gone unnoticed, but Lévesque didn't press the issue. Sutures would not help. He needed only the light and time. Lourdes remained quiet for several additional moments before she spoke again, her voice little more than a broken whisper.

"Why can't he?"

Lévesque didn't answer her. Returning to the only thing he seemed to know, giving instructions and orders, he spoke to her in a tone that dared not be refused. "You'll need to ask him. Don't ask why again. Tend to him. Watch carefully. When the sun moves, come get me at once. We must keep him in the light at all costs."

Had he been able to, Tzadkiel would have stared at him with shocked incredulity. Did he hear concern in the voice of the man who had ordered his torture for nearly a year? Was it possible? Lourdes questioned once more, but was answered with a sharp retort.

"I don't understand."

"Understand later. Do as I say now." Turning away, Lévesque strode to the place where Phillippe still lay held to the floor by the sword standing rigid from his spine. "Can you release him? I'd like to get his body out of here before..."

He didn't need to see Lévesque to know who he was speaking to and he didn't need him to finish his sentence to understand. Speaking in a voice so soft even

Lourdes who knelt right beside him might not have heard him, he commanded the sword with two words.

"Return. Guard."

The sword immediately dislodged itself from Phillippe's lifeless body and returned to the pedestal. As it did, an unexpected rush of anger and hatred blazed deep inside him. He knew Phillippe had been possessed by a demon and how long that possession had been in place he was not sure. He realized everything Phillippe had done could have been orchestrated by the master of that demon and that he may have been completely powerless to control his actions. He also recognized that as the Archangel of Mercy, the personification of empathy and compassion, perfected energy embodying a perfect ideal, he ought to forgive the man, but, try as he might, he could not find even the smallest measure of mercy within him for Phillippe. The inability to forgive was something he'd never been able to fully comprehend about humanity, until that moment.

Now, he understood.

Phillippe had done too much.

He had been too cruel.

The cool touch of a damp cloth returned his thoughts to the moment. In spite of her confusion and fear, Lourdes had not retreated, but was taking care of him. Gently washing away the blood that covered much of his body, she applied a soothing balm and laid strips of bandaging across his wounds. The light touch of her hands no longer hurt and the feeling of relief he experienced as a result of her ministrations was blissful. Breathing steadily for what felt like the first time in days, he relaxed, his head slowly tilting back as his senses spun. The warm touch of the sun on his skin was a tender caress. His consuming exhaustion was slowly fading as energy returned to his body, and the piercing, inescapable pain that had nearly torn away his sanity was finally diminishing.

The sensations were ecstasy.

Unable to quell the sound of his relief, he moaned deeply.

Stopping abruptly, Lourdes withdrew and it took a moment for him to comprehend her disconcertion. Opening his eyes to gaze at her questioningly, he repeated the phrase they had come to frequently ask each other. "Are you alright?"

She hadn't moved away from him; she'd just stopped what she was doing and was staring at his body with bewilderment. He understood why. He was healing right before her eyes. He didn't need to look at his body to see it; he could feel it. The sensation of release that spread through him that replaced the penetrating ache he had not been able to escape in nearly a year was like the warmth of a fine wine and felt equally as intoxicating. He had fallen under its sweet spell, but his expression of pleasure at this release was not well timed or thoroughly thought out considering her recent misfortunes. He wanted to apologize, but she questioned him before he could gather the energy to speak.

"I don't understand." Confusion burdened her words.

"I know. Please...don't be afraid."

She shook her head, looking once again across his body at the wounds that had, less than an hour before, been bleeding so profusely she feared he might die. He looked down at himself as well, realizing just how astonishing the sparkling, pulsing radiance appeared that enwrapped him with its life-restoring glow.

"You're... healing." The extent of her astonishment mirrored her incomprehension and both were betrayed by the disbelief of her tone.

CYNTHIA A. MORGAN

"I know. Please don't be afraid," he repeated himself even more gently. "There's so much... I know... I need to explain." His weariness was fading, but hadn't dissipated altogether and the simple act of speaking with her drained his strength. "I need to...regain my strength."

Her eyes locked with his and the emotions he saw in their depths were as wondrous as they were perplexing.

"By lying in the sun?"

He nodded subtly and she considered this for a moment.

"It'll heal you?"

He nodded again, his gaze never leaving her. "Please... don't be afraid." His third repetition of this appeal refocused her attention away from the incomprehensible spectacle taking place before her. Cocking her head slightly to one side, she returned his searching gaze with an expression of concern that nearly matched his own.

"And you're alright now?"

"I will be." Fearing she might decide that he no longer needed her and take her leave, he reached for her hand. "Please, don't go."

She smiled in spite of her palpable confusion and justifiable uncertainty. Shaking her head, she smiled. "I won't leave. I'm going to take care of you."

It was such a simple gesture, but it exemplified all she truly was and he could not keep himself from smiling.

She was the one he sought.

Year 2097
The 1st Era of the Great Cataclysm
Regional countryside outside Chambon, France
The Family Farmstead Le Lieu de la Miséricorde

G abriel and Annabella's daughter, Lourdes, grew into a kind and generous woman, just as her mother was, and she became equally strong-willed. Healthy and spirited, as soon as she was old enough to travel on her own she began journeying from *Le Lieu de la Miséricorde*. The Place of Mercy, which was the farmstead of her family and her home, but also the source of her strength. Each month she would travel in a different direction, sharing the bounty that had been bestowed upon them; generously giving through kindness. Traveling by horse and cart, she would carry with her any provisions they had in surplus and she would always find families in need as plagues and calamity spread far and wide.

Outside the borders of The Place of Mercy.

Within its sheltering woodlands, however, health and vitality abounded. While countries armed themselves against their neighbors and neighbors locked their doors against their friends, she went quietly along country roads from village to village, seeking those in need and smiling at the distrust and recrimination of those who could not comprehend or appreciate her open-handedness. Naturally, her actions were a great worry to her parents. In such times of distrust and disease, venturing beyond the woodland that protected them became a greater and greater risk, but they understood her desire to share the blessing they had so unwittingly secured. As they grew too old to place limitations on her determination, they entrusted her safety to the same grace that had so richly blessed them and counted themselves fortunate to have such a daughter.

Gabriel and Annabella shared many, many long years together, proudly watching their unanticipated daughter blossom as she created a philanthropic life for herself. Time and age, which seemed to have slowed within the quiet realm of their farmstead, finally caught up with them and one warm summer evening as the cicadas sang and larks serenaded the setting sun, they found rest together, held in each other's arms, thirty years to the day after they met The Rider.

Lourdes had never known such loss or grief, but the mission she had assigned herself to share the rich bounty entrusted to her family kept her focus strong. She sought balance between the responsibilities of the farmstead, which provided the bounty she loved to share, and the necessity of travelling to continue sharing that abundance with those who needed it most. As the years slowly turned, wars spread in the wake of disease and poverty escalated in the shadows of war. Neighbors became adversaries, families fragmented, and those who found themselves in need took what they didn't have, often by force.

Compelled by these unfortunate changes and the fact that she could no longer trust those she had befriended on her journeys, Lourdes was forced to make the difficult decision to end her sojourns and remain on the quiet, sheltered land of *Le Lieu de la Miséricorde*. She lived alone for several seasons, gratefully tending the gift they had been given, but loneliness and grief grew like weeds in a neglected garden and she began to contemplate abandoning her sheltered home.

The Place of Mercy seemed to hear her sorrow. Although its bordering woodlands protected the land the farm had been built upon by turning strangers around and leading them out instead of allowing them in, one cold autumn day she was visited by a young man named Jordan. Somehow, he had found his way through the winding footpaths that lead through the forest from the east-west byway. He came upon the farmstead late in the day, just as an early snow had begun to fall and Lourdes didn't have the heart to close the door in his face. Instead, she offered him a hot meal and cautious conversation, learning that he had a similar philosophy as her own. He offered to help her bring in the harvest and look after the many needs of the farm, which were gradually overwhelming her, in return for meals and a safe place to sleep in the barn.

The needs of the farmstead were demanding. Bringing in the harvest was followed by winter tilling and planting. A winter garden required tending, as did several holes in the barn roof and storehouses. Weeks of building maintenance, trimming and hedging were followed by tree harvesting to fill the wood larder. The Place of Mercy was generous, but it required more care than one young woman could manage on her own. Committing himself to sharing her burden, Jordan worked hard and gradually gained her trust. Though life on the farm was often difficult, he supported her and brought joy back into her life and Lourdes soon found her heart filled by the kindness and gentle devotion Jordan selflessly shared with her.

Year 2446
The 96th Year of the 4th Era after the Great Cataclysm
Day One- Tower Obligar, Le Bastion de la Résolution, - Marçais, New France

After ordering the removal of Phillippe's body, which was challenging on its own, Lévesque returned to his office to face an even greater one. The Protectorate required a full report whenever an injury or death occurred, but he had no idea how to explain such a death. The EPP Guard who had inspected their operation only days before seemed skeptical, at best, about his claim that their prisoner was an Archangel. How would he explain a battle between demons from Hell and that same prisoner, culminating in a death elicited through the use of a seemingly enchanted sword? He could hardly comprehend what happened himself. Would he be able to answer all the questions the Marshal of The Protectorate would justifiably ask; questions he would ask if their roles were reversed? How could he rationalize the irrational? Could he secure his position in the face of such an outlandish incident? More importantly, could he ensure such an incident would not be repeated?

The final question, more than any other, plagued his thoughts. He could command the guards and soldiers under his authority, but he had no authority over the spawn of Hell. That had been proven beyond a shadow of doubt. More importantly, he couldn't guarantee they would not return to try to destroy the easy target he had so inadvertently provided. Moving from behind his desk where he had been standing, staring out the barred windows as his thoughts roiled, he strode to the doorway and looked out at his prisoner with a pensive gaze. When they first brought him to The Bastion, he thought their plan an uncomplicated one. Maintain the prisoner's status by keeping him in a non-threatening state. It was the same for all prisoners, but his case was unique, given his regenerative abilities. He had decided the best way to maintain a non-threatening status was to apply 'treatments' at regular intervals.

Treatments.

It was a callous description of something truly horrible. He couldn't deny it, but given his responsibilities he was often required to be callous. It was the only way he could approve the things Phillippe had done every day and still manage to sleep at night. It was also the only way he could justify the actions he had taken that would, in all likelihood, earn him eternal damnation. In retrospect, he realized he should, perhaps, not have been quite so callous, but how could he have anticipated such an outcome as a result of that objectivity? How could he possibly have foreseen that his chief medic would become possessed by a demon and attack their prisoner in so gruesome a way?

He thought long and hard about that, even as he watched Lourdes studying that same prisoner and the sunlight that had shifted to such a degree that it no longer streamed over his body. Perhaps, given who and what his prisoner was, he should have anticipated such a possibility. Perhaps he had been woefully short-sighted, not to mention dim-witted.

Not waiting for her to come get him, Lévesque returned to the place where the Archangel lay and, without speaking, stooped down to take hold of the corners of his bedding in order to haul him several feet to the side and return him into the streaming light of the sun. Looking down at him wordlessly, he contemplated a notion that had been nagging at his thoughts all morning and his introspective gaze met the faded lavender of his prisoner's.

Intriguing.

He looked to the pendant he wore, which he had not been able to remove even through the use of a bolt cutter, and noted the similar coloration of the stone. The color of his eyes and the crystal he wore around his neck, in some manner, seemed to reflect the Archangel's physical condition. He scoffed. It would have been an invaluable indicator had he been observant enough to notice it a long time ago. As sunlight regenerated his body and renewed his strength, the hue of his eyes and the amulet darkened. Lévesque wondered if they could return to the deep violet they had been on the day of their first meeting, or if the harm they had inflicted would impair such a full recovery.

Studying the progression of his miraculous healing, he turned his attention to the sunlight streaming in through the barred windows. He knew it would aid his recovery process, but because several of the lacerations were terribly deep, particularly the one on his thigh, they would surely require more time to heal than the sunlight would be available. He noticed as well that they had removed his coat, which he had cinched round the injury in an attempt to stop the bleeding, and he stooped to collect it.

"How are you?" His question clearly astonished Tzadkiel, who looked up at him with noticeable suspicion.

"Why?"

Lévesque frowned. He could understand his hesitancy, but he really didn't have time for it. Wanting to respond with a characteristically sharp retort, such as 'Because I want to know', he tempered his irritation with a more candid response. "I don't expect you to believe me, but I'm honestly concerned. Are you hungry? I can have her collect food and drink from the kitchens." He received a prolonged, silent stare as his answer followed by a subtle, single nod. The Archangel's reluctance to trust him was entirely comprehensible. After the way they'd treated him, Lévesque wouldn't have been surprised if he refused to speak to him altogether. A nod was enough. Turning, he instructed Lourdes with the same air of command he used when speaking to his subordinates. At least in her case he wasn't out of line. "I'll give you a written order for food and drink. Come to my office shortly."

She stared at him mutely, seeming dumbstruck by his actions, but he couldn't really blame her either. He had been entirely heartless, up to this point. He had earned their mistrust. Completely. Gazing down at the Archangel for a protracted moment longer, he shook his head and turned away without saying anything further.

Lourdes stared at him in amazement and Tzadkiel gazed back at her with equal surprise. It was a dim hope, but perhaps the nightmare was ending. Perhaps they would not continue to torture him. Oh, how she hoped it would be so!

"You'll be alright, won't you?" Her anxious query brought a weak smile to his lips.

"Yes." His confidence made her brow furrow.

"You're sure?"

He smiled dimly as his gaze swept in the direction of the pedestal upon which Jshunamir perched. She hadn't noticed before; her attention had been entirely distracted by him, but the sword hovered above the small dais as if standing at attention, its silver runes glittering with an internal light. It guarded him.

Getting up from the floor with a wince she could not disguise, she closed her eyes against the discomfort she felt. She was doing her utmost to ignore what she had no control over, but she was unprepared when he questioned her about it.

"Will you?" Again, their gazes locked, but the penetrating intensity of his pale lavender stare was more than she could return. Closing her eyes again, she tried to shrug off his concern, unable to bring herself to discuss the subject for fear of what the pain might mean. Instead, she glanced over him, amazed at how quickly he was healing. Though his wounds had not fully mended, each one had already begun to close. Each that is, except for the one on his thigh. That laceration was so deep and had been manipulated so cruelly it was still open and weeping. It gave her an opportunity to change the subject.

"Will it heal as well?"

He stared at her with an intense expression she couldn't quite distinguish, but then he looked down at himself. He seemed perplexed by the wound's inability to mend, but before he could answer her, Lévesque called out for her impatiently. Turning away without saying anything more, she escaped by hastening to his office where she stood apprehensively in the doorway.

"Sir?"

He gestured for her to enter, holding a folded paper in his hand. "Take this to Madam Ornaly. She'll authorize the release of food and drink and tell you where to collect it."

Bobbing a respectful curtsy more out of custom than actual respect, she glanced down at herself uncertainly before posing a soft question. "Yes, Sir. Please, Sir, may I take a moment to return to my chambers... to...to change?"

His head snapped up as if what she asked was outrageously insolent, but, seeing her blood-stained uniform, he nodded. "Don't dawdle. I expect you back here within the hour. Don't make me send someone to come looking for you."

She shook her head resolutely. God help her if he sent Sauvage! "No, Sir, I won't. Thank you, Sir." Tucking the folded paper he gave her into her pocket, she turned for the door, hurrying to the main entrance and breathing a prodigious sigh of relief when she stepped out into the hallway and The Tower doors closed behind her.

She stood motionless for a moment, closing her eyes as she gathered her composure. Quite possibly, the last few days had been the worst of her life, but whether they were or not, she didn't have time to wallow in sad sentiment. She could feel the guard's stares on her and refused to give them any opportunities to make the last few days worse. Hurrying in the direction of Madam Ornaly's office, she couldn't help replaying the events of the last day and night in her mind, trying to make sense of it all, but she was not successful. There was too much she simply could not understand. Torture so atrocious she could scarcely think about it. More blood than she'd seen in a lifetime. Demons possessing people; glimmering healing light; a sword that moved on its own, and him.

Tzadkiel.

A strange and wondrous name she'd never heard before.

A strange and wondrous man. A man who surprised her nearly every time she looked at him or spoke with him. A man who seemed to be far more than she could see. A man who had occupied her thoughts for nearly a year, regardless of the fact that she had only met him two days ago. It was odd how close she felt to him despite only having just met him, but there was something about him that set her at ease. Something that felt familiar and comfortable, though they barely knew each other. Closing her eyes briefly, she stopped walking and reached out for the wall as images of gaping, bleeding wounds and echoes of heartbreaking screams tormented her mind.

Coming from the opposite direction, Madam Ornaly looked up from the garment she carried and slowed her stride when she saw Lourdes. She called out to her; the tone of her voice characteristically harsh. "Where have you been?"

Lourdes raised her gaze to meet the older woman's. She fully expected to be chastised for not reporting in the morning and for whatever else the Madam felt she'd done wrong. Such reprimands were a daily occurrence. She'd gotten used to them and it did seem that caustic words were poised on Madam's lips, but as she drew closer and could see Lourdes more clearly, her fierce expression shifted to surprise.

"Sacre' bleu! What happened to you?"

Pulling the folded paper Lévesque had given her from the pocket of her uniform, she swallowed her rising emotion. "Captain Lévesque has sent me to you with this, Madam." Holding it out to her, she could not steady the tremor that shook her blood-stained hand. Taking the paper suspiciously, Madam read it and then looked back at Lourdes with observable concern.

"Has he hurt you?" Her tone flared with indignation and Lourdes momentarily considered telling her everything that had happened. She could tell her about Sauvage and the way he'd treated her. That would be easy compared to trying to explain Phillippe and the man they called an Archangel who they tortured, but could not kill. Madam would never believe her and she didn't have time to try to make her understand. Shaking her head, she looked down at herself wearily.

"It isn't my blood, Madam."

Comprehending, Madam Ornaly grunted in acknowledgment and raised the paper she held. "This'll take about an hour. You can pick it up in kitchen A's auxiliary room. Until then...perhaps you should take some time for yourself." Her tone shifted from caustic to uncharacteristically thoughtful.

Looking up at her blankly, Lourdes merely nodded, too tired to be amazed at her odd expression of concern or the offer of personal time. She turned to leave, but gasped in surprised when Madam reached out for her. Taking her by the elbow before she could continue down the hall, she pulled her closer and spoke in a low tone that implied much more than she actually said. "I know how the guards are. If any of them hurt you," she didn't finish, but stood staring at Lourdes who stared back with the sudden revelation that Madam hadn't worked for The Protectorate for as long as she had without learning how they treated servants. She hadn't risen to managerial levels without living through everything she now oversaw. Understanding her better than she had in the full ten years she'd been there, she reconsidered telling her about Sauvage. Before she could form the right words, however, another servant rushed up to them. Breathless from running, she bobbed a hasty curtsy and frantically dove into a dizzying account, her heavy accent slurring her rushed explanation.

"If you please, Madam, one of the scullery maids has toppled the laundry tumbler! There's water and soap everywhere. She was trying to clean it up when Cook found the mess she made and was so mad she started beating her right there in the kitchen with her baking dowel. The other scullery maids ran off to hide, but one of the stable hands saw what happened and ripped the dowel from Cook's hand. Servants are hollering all over the place and Supervisor Carston sent me to find you. She asks, if you please, Madam, come to the kitchen straightaway to see if you can help."

Thoroughly annoyed, Madam released Lourdes' elbow without another glance at her and Lourdes took the opportunity to slip away. Moving toward the stairs that led up to her small tower room, she couldn't moderate the anxious thoughts that spun in her mind. What might she find when she returned to The Tower? Would Lévesque authorize more torture in spite of Tzadkiel's excessive injuries? Would someone even more horrible than Phillippe take over? Surely Lévesque's concern proved he wouldn't order more torture, didn't it? Or was he concerned simply because it meant he couldn't continue? Was he so cold-hearted? Why had he ordered food and drink if he intended to go on torturing him?

How would she ever manage to free him from such a terrible place?

She stopped climbing, her swirling, frantic thoughts focusing on what had eluded her until that moment. Why didn't he free himself? He certainly had the ability. He had a sword that obeyed his every command. Why hadn't he used it to free himself? Why would he allow himself to be tortured in such a way? Why would he submit to something so horrible when he had the means to protect himself? Her thoughts careened as nightmarish images and harrowing screams replayed in her memory, but the momentum of her chaotic thoughts could not be overthrown. Questions swirled in her mind like a maelstrom. Was he truly an Archangel? If he was, how had they managed to take him prisoner? What had he done? Why didn't he use the power an Archangel was supposed to possess to free himself?

Sighing sharply with exasperation, she raised a hand to her head. She had to focus on the moment or she might drive herself crazy. Looking at the blood stains that had turned her hands red, she shuddered. His blood. An Archangels blood. She shuddered again. All she could do was go to her room, wash up and change. She had to get to the kitchens and hope she could find Brigyda so she could talk with her before returning to The Tower. Despite trying to clear her thoughts as she entered her small tower room and closed the door behind her, the questions continued to tumble through her mind. Leaning back on the door wearily, she considered more carefully. If he had a sword that answered his every command, why would he let them torture him? If the means to stop them was right there, waiting for him to speak a mere word, why wouldn't he have spoken it? Why would he let them do the awful things they'd done to him? Why would he have let Phillippe nearly kill him?

'He can't die.' Lévesque's remark echoed in her mind, but she couldn't make any sense of it. Moving away from the door, she went to her washstand and poured some water into the basin, took off her blood-stained uniform and refreshed herself with a bit of soap and powder before putting on a clean dress and apron. It was the same as the one she'd just removed. It was faded, wrinkled and a dull, unflattering gray, but it was clean. Her cap and hairclips were missing. They were still lying on the floor of the cell where Sauvage had tossed them, but she'd have time to collect them later. Bending over, she shook out the lengths of her chestnut-red hair and twisted it into a loose braid, tying it with a length of ribbon she'd found months before on the floor of the Eminent Protectorate's dining hall. She never used it if she was going to be working lest she need to explain how she'd come to possess such an odd treasure, but at the moment, as seemed her lot in life, she didn't have any alternatives.

She either used it or let her hair tumble across her shoulders, which was even more unacceptable in the eyes of Madam. Now, however, she had better insight into why Madam thought it was so unacceptable. Perhaps for the simple reason that tresses spilling over shoulders was more appealing than tightly knotted hair. Perhaps by dressing them in unattractive, bag shaped uniforms and requiring them to wear their hair up under caps straight out of the 17th century, Madam hoped to keep them unsightly. Unsightly, but safe. It was a thought she'd never considered, but she didn't have time to wonder about it.

Turning to look around her small room, she wished she had the time to sit down on the bed and close her eyes. Just for a moment. Just to relax before going back to the awful tower where she had no idea what would happen next, but she dared not. If she accidentally fell asleep and Lévesque had to send guards to find her, she would suffer far worse than Sauvage had managed to do. Unnerved by the mere thought of what they might do to her finding her alone in her room, she moved to the door and pulled it open hastily. Making her way down the stairs she had just climbed, she headed towards the kitchens hoping to find and talk with Brigyda.

Entering the kitchen wing of the basement, she wondered where her friend might be. Where would she have been at this time of the day if she was still working her customary shift? The thought stabbed at her. Where indeed! Had she been following her normal routine she certainly wouldn't be in the situation she now faced. She would be safe, relatively speaking, and not wincing every few steps from the insistent ache Sauvage's ruthlessness had created.

Shaking her head again, she tried to refocus. She couldn't blame anyone for what had happened to her, least of all Brigyda. After all, she had chosen the path she now trod because she wanted to help Tzadkiel. After nearly a year of wishing she could do something to help him, she was helping him. Even if that help came in a form she had not envisioned. Even if that help came at a cost she had not considered.

If he was an angel, why did he need anyone's help?

Stopping to close her eyes and sigh sharply at herself in frustration, she focused, yet again, on finding Brigyda. Where would she be? If she were still on duty as a scullery maid, she would have been in the laundry, preparing the morning basins, but she wasn't sure she wanted to go there now, not after hearing what happened there this morning.

Only then did she realize what she had missed in her weary stupor. Poor Brigyda would have been the servant Cook had taken to beating!

"Lourdes!" A familiar voice cried out in surprise from the opposite end of the corridor and she looked up to find her young friend rushing towards her with her arms outstretched. Hugging her tightly, Brigyda even kissed her on her cheeks before drawing back awkwardly. "I was so worried about you. Where on earth have you been? Are you ok?"

Lourdes nodded, unable to get a word in edgeways

to reassure her before the young servant babbled on excitedly.

"Why you didn't come back to your room last night? I thought so many terrible things might have happened. I barely slept all night. It's no wonder I tripped over the laundry tumbler this morning and turned it over. OH! Was Cook ever mad!"

"Brigyda."

"I swear, I thought she'd beat me three weeks from Sunday. It's a good thing that stable boy was there and saw what was happening."

"Brigyda."

"But who cares about me. What happened to you? Are you ok? That horrible man didn't,"

"Brigyda!" Shouting her name more insistently, Lourdes finally surprised her enough to make her pause.

"What?"

"I can't stay long. I've been sent for food for the prisoner."

Brigyda covered her mouth and shook her head in dismay, her bright, blond curls swinging from her loosened cap. "Oh, that poor, poor man! The things they've done to him. You can't imagine the things I've seen and heard. Oh Lourdes, it's so terrible. That Phillippe is a monster. He's creepy and sick and twisted." Her emotions turned over themselves as she remembered and Brigyda nearly started crying.

Lourdes nodded in complete agreement. "I know. I saw."

Brigyda shook her head emphatically. "You saw? You saw the lambskin? The hoods? The barbed lash? I've never seen so much blood or heard such screams as when they used that horrible thing on him."

Lourdes nodded, then shook her head, but didn't try to explain. "They have me tending his injuries and sent me for food and water. I have to go back straightaway."

Brigyda stared at her with an expression that betrayed her disappointment as well as her fear, but before she could find what she wanted to say, Lourdes continued.

"I wanted you to know I'm alright. I didn't want you to worry about me."

"Why didn't you come back to your room last night?"

She shook her head. "I couldn't leave him. He needed help so desperately and they would have left him alone...."

"You stayed in The Tower all night?" Brigyda interrupted in wide-eyed astonishment, her tone of disbelief ringing down the hallway. Lourdes gestured for her to be quiet.

"Yes, and I may need to stay again tonight. I don't want you to worry, that's all. I'm alright."

"But what about that man, the one..."

Lourdes wouldn't let her speak the words. "It's alright. He's been... reprimanded."

"Really? By who?" She would have gone on and on if Lourdes didn't stop her and, although she didn't really want to, she knew she couldn't be late returning.

"I'm sorry, but I've got to go. If I'm late, I'll really end up in trouble. Don't be worried, ok?"

Her friend nodded, but didn't seem convinced. Unable to explain further, Lourdes hugged her tightly in return, kissed her cheeks, and turned away.

Unbearable pain spread through his body in an agonizingly slow progression. It felt like being immersed in scalding water, but slowly. Oh, so terribly slowly. Every inch of his body burned. The pain tore at his sanity. It clutched greedily at his will to live. Why now? Why again? Confusion twisted into a knot of frustration and misery so intense it strangled him. He didn't want to cry, but he couldn't control the tears that stung his eyes any more than he could stop the pain. It enveloped him so slowly, horrifically slowly. He couldn't breathe, couldn't cry out, couldn't think! The sensation was far worse than ever before. It pierced into him like a thousand knives, slowly. Terribly, terribly slowly. It was beyond bearing.

His scream echoed through every room in The Tower.

It shattered the quiet calm that had settled on the ancient stonework of the blood-stained table and reverberated from the iron bars that blocked the full radiance of the morning sun. It startled Lévesque so completely he leapt up from his desk where he'd been writing his report. He drew his sword and rushed to the door, searching the chamber with agitated confusion and frightening Lourdes nearly to death. She was only just returning from the kitchen pushing a squeaking cart that was laden with enough food and drink for five people, but at the sound of his scream she stopped abruptly, abandoning the cart as she raced into the main chamber with Lévesque right behind her.

He was sitting up on the bedroll where he'd fallen asleep, gasping for breath. Shaking prodigiously, he searched the room with blatant fear, unconcerned about the tears that wet his cheeks as he tried to understand what had just happened. Looking up at Lourdes when she drew closer and knelt down beside him, his expressive features were strained with fear and confusion.

"Are you alright? Did you have a nightmare?"

His stare locked with hers. Had it been merely a

dream? Could a dream feel so agonizingly real? He shook his head, unconvinced, but there was no evidence either on his body or in the room that he had endured the torture he had just felt. Bewildered, he continued to look around him, searching the corners of the room for Phillippe, for demons, or for any sign that he was not losing his mind, but he could find nothing. There were no dark shadows writhing in the corners and Phillippe was dead.

"Nightmare," Lévesque scoffed, turning aside as Lourdes leaned closer and put her arms around Tzadkiel's shoulders to hug him gently. The comfort of her embrace was incomprehensible. Sweeter than anything he'd experienced since taking human form, he closed his eyes and leaned close to her. Wrapping his arms around her, he held onto her as he fought to calm his erratic breathing and the tremors racing through his body and she held him for several moments without saying anything. Finally, she leaned back to look at him worriedly and asked once more if he was alright, but he didn't know how to answer her. He'd never experienced anything like this dream before. He'd rarely slept long enough or well enough to dream since being brought to The Tower and before that time he didn't require sleep. Taking a deep breath, he wiped the back of his hand across his cheeks to dry them.

"I hardly know. It felt so real."

"They do, I know," her voice trailed off tellingly as their gazes locked. He could see in the depths of her distinctively hued eyes that she was not yet capable of talking about what had happened to her. The pain of it was clearly still too close. Comprehending this, he nodded without saying anything and didn't press the issue. In the silence that stretched between them, her gaze wandered over his body. Drawing back to look at him more extensively, her mouth fell agape as she shook her head, but she could find no words to articulate her disbelief at his incredible rate of healing. He smiled.

"I told you I'd heal." His confirmation brought a dim smile to her face, which brightened when his stomach growled voraciously. Looking down at himself with absolute bewilderment, as if his stomach had never growled before in his life, he was equally puzzled when the sound prompted her to get up from the floor and return to the cart she had left at the entrance of the chamber. He had not even noticed the cart until that moment, but as she began pushing it towards him, its wheels squeaking and rattling ridiculously, he stared at it unable to believe what he saw.

The cart held more food than they could have both eaten in a week's time. There was another large bowl of sumptuous oatmeal laden with berries and nuts, and drizzled so liberally with honey that it dripped down the sides of the bowl. There were also four loaves of bread stuffed with cooked vegetables and cheese that were stacked neatly within an open burlap sack. Several unsliced loaves were tucked into a similar sack. A generous wheel of cheese was presented in an open box. An overstuffed flour sack contained apples and pears aplenty, while a large bunch of carrots lay beside it tied together with twine. A small pouch held an assortment of nuts and a square of linen enfolded a hearty provision of jerky. On the lower shelf of the cart was a box of assorted implements such as knives, linen napkins, a tin of matches, and other sundries. This shelf also contained a large pitcher of water, two metal tumblers, a short barrel marked 'Cider-Apple' and another marked 'Cider-Pear".

As they investigated, trying to make sense of the absurdly disproportionate provision, Lévesque, who had stood watching them silently for several moments after sheathing his sword, disappeared back into his office. Moments later, he reappeared carrying a folded officer's uniform, undergarments, and a pair of highly polished leather boots that laced to the knee. He approached them with a guarded expression, nodding at the food cart with approval before he looked down at Tzadkiel. Handing the clothing and boots to Lourdes, he spoke with a distinctly surreptitious tone. "This should be sufficient provisions to last a few days, at least."

They looked at each other, entirely confused.

"I realize now it was a mistake to bring you here. My mistake, made worse each day I allowed it to continue. I can't change that." His stare locked with Tzadkiel's as he continued. "I can't apologize or expect to be forgiven for something so heinous, but I can't allow such a situation to continue, either, and be made worse through continuing to condone it. All I can do is try to correct it."

Tzadkiel stared at him doubtingly. Taking hold of the sheet that covered him, he wrapped it around his hips as he stood up to face the man responsible for the torture and abuse he'd suffered for so long. "You're letting me go?" His question was as suspicious as his stare, but Lévesque looked down at Lourdes instead.

"I'm letting you both go. She can't stay here." He thought a moment and reiterated. "She *shouldn't* stay here. With you gone, there'll be no one to protect her from Sauvage and I can't order him not to harass her. We both know he will...and worse."

Tzadkiel looked down at her as well, his lavender gaze penetrating hers as he considered. She said nothing, watching them in silence as her freedom and safety were discussed without any input from her at all, but before he could ask her thoughts on the matter, Lévesque continued.

"Understand me," he said firmly, stepping closer to speak in an even more hushed tone, "the Marshal will not sanction your release. I cannot sanction it, not officially."

Again, their gazes locked and, although Tzadkiel understood what Lévesque was telling him, he asked for an explanation anyway. "Clarify."

"I can make it happen. I can give you food, clothing, even transport." He gestured at the clothing he'd given Lourdes. "Disguise you as an officer so you can leave The Bastion unhindered with your servant at your side." Glancing down at Lourdes, he spread his hands wide, palms down, in a negating gesture. "But that's all I can do. After that, once your 'escape' is reported, which I'll have to do promptly, we both know I'll be ordered to hunt you down."

Tzadkiel pondered the situation; then looked down at Lourdes who still said nothing. Crouching beside her, he looked into her eyes. "Please, tell me what you're thinking."

Predictably, Lévesque sighed sharply. "We don't have time for what she's thinking."

Glaring up at him with undisguised annoyance, Tzadkiel silenced him without a word. Returning his gaze to her, he spoke softly. "It's so dangerous. Either way; whether you stay here or come with me." She clearly had no idea what to say or how to decide, but he knew he could not make such a decision for her. Choosing to give her time to consider, he got up to ask further questions. "When do you think it best to go? Do you have a route in mind?"

Lévesque looked toward the window, judging the time as he answered. "I'd set off this afternoon. Officers don't travel at night. They don't travel unused roads either, so stay close to the Byland road until you're well past the watch tower. That's several miles outside The Bastion."

Tzadkiel nodded, looking down once again at Lourdes, who sat with a perplexed expression, watching and listening much like a child might. Fixing an intense stare on Lévesque, he spoke with a tone of authority and confidence he had not used since the day on the beach so long ago. "Tell me your plan, in detail. I don't want to risk anything going wrong."

11

Year 2135.
The 2nd Era of the Great Cataclysm
Regional countryside outside Chambon, France- Le Lieu
de la Miséricorde

L ourdes and Jordan brought their third child into
the world just as it nearly shattered apart. The
second Horseman, War, rode hard across countries and
continents. Hate and intolerance drove communities
apart. Disputes over borders, cultural differences, and
religious ideology spawned battles that killed tens of
thousands. Suspicion and fear festered in the hearts
and minds of so many that brothers fought against
brothers. Violence thrived.

Sheltered from the calamity the Horseman poured
upon the lost by remaining on the protected lands of
the Place of Mercy, Lourdes and Jordan brought up
their children amid the lush groves and purified
streams of the family farmstead. It never grew weary of
producing its bounty. It never failed to support them,
and, somehow, while war devastated and destroyed, the
land upon which they lived protected them entirely.

It was the blessing The Rider had spoken, that they would live unhindered and unharmed, and they never forgot it. Teaching their children the simple philosophy of grace she had learned from her parents and that she had shared not only with most of the surrounding villages, but more importantly, with Jordan, they instilled a message of kindness and hope the world could not provide.

Those who lived on the periphery of *Le Lieu de la Miséricorde* shared in its bounty as well. Though they had once been hostile, greedy neighbors who tried to steal what they would have been given freely, those who lived outside the borders of the farmstead eventually became grateful tenants and the blessing expanded to renew their lives equally. As years passed and the world outside the thick woodlands that formed the boundaries of the farmstead grew more distant and fell into famine, the sheltered village became a world unto itself and the philosophy of kindness and generosity, begun so long ago by its founders Gabrielle and Annabella, prospered.

Year 2446
The 96th Year of the 4th Era after the Great Cataclysm
Day One - Le Bastion de la Résolution, - Marçais, New France

As Tzadkiel and Lévesque discussed their plan, Lourdes sat staring at them. Her thoughts were a jumble of emotion and uncertainty. She had only ever needed to make a decision once that would change her life and since that time the opportunity to choose for herself was never given. Since coming to The Bastion, Madam

Ornaly made all decisions of consequence and Lourdes had become accustomed to having little or no say. Now, however, faced with such a significant choice, she found she was bewildered, not to mention overwhelmed. Watching without listening very closely to what they were saying, she concentrated, instead, on the one who had become more important to her than any person had been since her parents were alive. She wasn't sure what it was about him that compelled her or why she had risked so much for him. She could barely rationalize, even to herself, the reasons why she had put her own safety at risk and endured the brutal consequences without turning away from him.

Captain Lévesque was right. With Tzadkiel gone, Sauvage would have no one to stand in his way. She couldn't bring herself to think about the horrible things he would do or how she would suffer at his hands if she decided to stay. Her life would become a living Hell and she'd be lucky to survive. If she decided to go with Tzadkiel, she had no idea what would happen. She'd never lived anywhere other than the small farmstead where she was raised and The Bastion where she had come after her parents had been taken from her. Life on the run didn't sound appealing and she didn't have the skills she presumed necessary, such as being able to ride a horse or live off the land. Still, the thought of staying in a place where she would be easy prey to a man as unthinkably sadistic as Sauvage was more than enough motivation. The uncertainties facing her were daunting, but it was not fear of the unknown that returned her gaze, again and again, to Tzadkiel.

It was something else altogether. Something she could not quite name. Something that felt familiar and comfortable. Something that felt right. As she watched him preparing to leave, she realized the thought of him not being there was unbearable. It was as unbearable as his screams had been for the past year while she was forced to listen, helplessly. As unbearable as his tears had been when he cried in pain after Phillippe had done such unspeakable things to him. She had done so much to help him, sacrificed more than she ever meant to, but watching him leave and knowing she would never see him again was something she suddenly realized she was entirely incapable of doing.

Getting up from the floor where she was sitting as they discussed their plan, she approached quietly, not wishing to distract him from studying the map they had laid on the stone table that was still stained with his blood. He was committing the route they had chosen to memory while Lévesque returned to his office to arrange the paperwork that would grant passage off Bastion grounds. Standing and watching him quietly, she waited for him to notice her and, as he studied the map, she studied him.

It was truly remarkable how quickly most of his wounds had mended. Although not entirely healed, they looked as if they had already seen several days of good care and it was equally apparent that his strength had returned, at least, more sufficiently than she'd seen before. His eyes no longer closed involuntarily out of fatigue and he no longer spoke in breathless, broken whispers. As he stood in the late morning sunlight, the glimmering around him seemed to penetrate his body and radiant from it. It turned in spiraling eddies as if caressing his body and sparkled luminously from the crystal he wore around his neck. When she looked down at herself, at the hand she raised into the same light that streamed over her, there was no comparison. It was just sunlight.

"Have you decided?" Noticing her as she stood

staring at the sunlight in which they both stood, he moved away from the table he clearly wished to never see again and drew close to her, his features warmed by hopeful curiosity. His voice was soft and he watched her with an expression she could not quite distinguish, which left her unexpectedly uncertain. She bit her lower lip fretfully.

"May I ...c-c-come with you?" The softness of her stammering query brought a gentle smile to his lips and he stepped closer, returning her anxious gaze as he took her hands in his own.

"You needn't ask me. It's entirely your decision." He paused, closing his eyes as he seemed to search for the right words and her heart hammered, worried he might try to dissuade her. "It will not be easy. It'll be dangerous and, no doubt, frightening." He paused again to look at her with a portentous expression, as if to ensure she comprehended the risks of such a decision, but she nodded. She'd taken risks before. He had been a risk, and she'd paid dearly. She understood only too well.

"I understand."

He looked down at her small hands that he held gently in his own. "If you come with me, I will do everything in my power to protect you." His words were a promise she understood with her heart more than her head and a rush of poignant emotion swelled within her. Unprepared for such a response, she smiled shyly, feeling both relieved and nervous beyond description, but he smiled as well and stepped back from her. Wincing sharply, he looked down at his leg. Where the sheet rested against his thigh, bright spots of scarlet betrayed the unanticipated fact that the wound on his thigh was still bleeding. "I need to bandage this. It's simply not healing."

Staring apprehensively at the stained sheet, Lourdes turned without a word and moved to the place where he'd been lying earlier, collecting the basin of medical supplies for him, as well as the suture kit he'd chosen not to use. Returning hurriedly, she held them out for him as a mute question, but he shook his head.

"I know it seems contradictory, but sutures will only impede the healing process. I just need to bandage it tightly and spend more time in the sun."

She wasn't convinced, but decided not to argue. How could she argue something she didn't comprehend?

Looking down at himself more critically, he continued with a perceivably disgusted tone. "I ought to get dressed, but I'm covered with blood." He certainly was. Phillippe...or whatever had possessed him...had taken obscene pleasure in running his hands through his blood, spreading across his entire body what he didn't lick with sloven delight from his fingers and the result left Tzadkiel crimson nearly head to toe. She'd tried to wash some of it away, but hadn't been successful. Spinning on her heel to return again to the same place as before, she picked up the bucket of water and hauled it closer so he could wash up if he chose to, however, when she set it down, she couldn't keep from grimacing in pain. Crossing one arm over her abdomen with a muffled whimper, she didn't notice his expression immediately fall into concerned shadow.

"What's the matter?" He moved closer, looking into her downcast face anxiously, but she shook her head.

"Nothing. Just," she drew a breath, nearly incapable of speaking the word poised on her tongue. "S-s-sore." Her voice broke and she gulped back the wave of ponderous emotion threatening to rush in on her. Shaking her head to dispel her feelings as she intentionally re-directed the conversation away from herself and back to him, she ignored his concerned stare. "You should be spotless if you're supposed to be an officer." Her ineffective quip only

caused him to stare at her even more intensely, but she
turned away, unable, or perhaps just unwilling, to revisit
the horrible memory. Pointing in the direction of the well
room, she offered another alternative. "You could wash up
in the well room. There's plenty of water and you," her
gaze flickered down his body before she continued with
an apologetic tone, "you'll need more than a bucketful."

Staring at her wordlessly for a protracted moment,
it seemed he might insist on discussing her situation
further, but he relented and looked down at himself instead. "You're right; I'm atrocious." Picking up the
bucket she'd brought him, he walked in the direction of
the well, stopped abruptly, and turned back with a dry
chuckle. "Probably ought to bring the uniform, huh?"

Bobbing a swift curtsy, she hurried to collect the
garments Lévesque had given to her, which she'd
placed on the corner of the food cart. Tzadkiel hadn't
asked her to get them and it wasn't terribly difficult,
but when she trotted back with them, she found him
staring at her with even greater consternation than before. She stared back and shrugged, perplexed.

"What?"

"You're not my servant, Lourdes."

She cocked her head in confusion.

"You curtsied to me." His dismayed pronouncement
made her gape and blush awkwardly.

"I, I'm sorry, it's…just a habit."

He considered her explanation and nodded indistinctly. "I understand. I just don't want you to think you
have some obligation to serve me. You don't. You are a
servant no longer."

Flummoxed, she stared at him blankly. She hadn't
even thought about the fact that she would no longer
live to serve others. It simply hadn't occurred to her.
She'd served so long it felt almost normal, but, despite

the revelation of his words, she wasn't given time to wonder about them. Coming back from his office, Lévesque interposed a characteristically acerbic remark. "Until you're out of sight of the watch tower, she's your servant and you need to treat her as such. Don't forget that."

Tzadkiel turned his gaze on him with evident irritation, but said nothing. Handing him the folded orders he'd written, Lévesque noticed the blood-stained sheet and paused.

"You alright?"

Tzadkiel nodded only once. "Well enough."

"Well enough to ride?"

"Yes," he agreed again and looked sideways at Lourdes. "What about Lourdes?"

"What about her? She's your servant. She doesn't get a horse."

Tzadkiel shook his head. "I can't travel at speed with a walking servant." His tone reflected his frustration, as if pointing out the obvious shouldn't have been necessary, but before Lévesque could reply, he flinched. Closing his eyes to conceal the pain he still very clearly felt, he reflexively covered the wound on his thigh and groaned.

"I can suture that." Atypically, Lévesque repeated his previous offer, but Tzadkiel shook his head.

"It will heal."

"If you were lying on your back all day, I might agree, but you'll be riding."

Fixing a surprisingly annoyed glare on him, Tzadkiel refused to discuss the matter further and Lévesque cursed under his breath.

"Stubborn...." Not willing to argue over something he realized was pointless, Lévesque turned to Lourdes and pointed in the direction of the medical supply closet. "Go collect additional supplies. You're bound to need them."

Hesitating awkwardly, Lourdes looked between them uncertainly before she haltingly curtsied and went. She might not be a servant once they left The Bastion, but until they did, she dared not disobey anyone, particularly Captain Lévesque. Particularly since he was going out of his way to help them escape. Particularly because she hadn't forgotten how he'd threatened her just the night before. Why he had suddenly decided to let them go, she couldn't imagine, but it didn't matter, not really. All that mattered was that somehow the impossible had become possible. Now all they needed to do was to get away without being captured.

The Tower was oddly quiet with no guards on duty save those she'd seen outside the doors when she returned from the kitchen. Perhaps Lévesque had dismissed them so he could arrange their escape? Whether he did or not, the medical supply closet was open and there were no guards to harass her. Relieved, she went inside and tried to take her time. She wasn't entirely adept at wasting time. It wasn't something she'd ever had the occasion to do, either before coming to The Bastion or after, but she had the liberty now. More importantly, it was necessary now. Tzadkiel would need time to draw enough water from the well to wash away the blood that covered his body and stained his hair. He would need time to clean the wound on his leg and bandage it. He would need time to dress.

She filled a pillowcase with the things she thought they might need; rolls of bandages, tubes of medicinal ointment, a small shears to trim excess wrappings. She paused when she came to the shelf containing assorted linens. Lévesque might think it impertinent, but a blanket would certainly be useful and he hadn't actually specified she should take only medical supplies. Tucking a woolen regimental blanket under her arm, she smiled suddenly and pulled a towel from the shelf as well.

Tzadkiel would need one.

Which meant she needed to get it to him in time for him to use it.

Which meant…. she blushed and shook her head.

Which meant she needed to stop wasting time.

Hastening her footsteps in the direction of the well room, she didn't pause until she heard the sound of splashing water coming from the dimly lit alcove. Loitering in the hallway, she tried to give him a few more moments of privacy. Not because she would have been embarrassed to return too quickly and catch him mid bath, but because she realized she might not. The realization astonished her. Given everything that had just happened and the way she'd been treated, she wondered why she thought she'd be safe with him.

Would he try to take from her what Ghislain and Sauvage had taken? Would his demeanor change once he was free? Could she truly trust him?

Perhaps. She wasn't entirely sure, but something inside her seemed to shout that she could. Perhaps because they had already shared so much more than two people might ever share. Perhaps because she had felt drawn to him long before she ever actually met him. Perhaps because he was an angel.

She scoffed aloud. "No wings, no halo, no harp silly bird." Mocking herself using the same nickname her mother often used, she shook her head and walked slowly along the corridor until she reached the entryway to the well room. Turning her back, she cleared her throat and presented the towel she'd brought for him by extending it behind her. He chuckled softly at her shyly offered courtesy and moved to take it from her, thanking her quietly before she moved away. Returning to the narrow passage between the supply closet and the well room, she stood silently considering what the next few days might bring for several protracted moments. Fear certainly, adventure possibly, and danger probably, but more than likely all of them and, of course, him.

Him.

Her thoughts tumbled. The idea of being with him day and night was suddenly as compelling as it was unsettling. She felt comfortable with him; she thought she could trust him, but what would those days and nights bring? Might she regret presuming she could trust him? Her musings roiled in conflicting directions for several moments until she finally shook her head in frustration and decided she'd wasted enough time wasting time.

As she moved back towards the main chamber that had been a chamber of horrors beyond description just one day before, she could not contain the sudden smile that curved her lips. Stopping in her tracks, her smile slowly transformed into an admiring gape. No longer covered in blood, Tzadkiel stood beside the table in the radiant sunlight, a vision of masculine beauty. His towel-dried blond hair, tinted a reddish hue as a result of being long covered in blood, shimmered in the sun's bright glow as water sparkled over his still wet body. He had not gotten dressed, but was concentrating on wrapping the only wound on his body that remained unclosed; the one on his upper thigh. He didn't notice her watching him and she hesitated before turning around, her inquisitive gaze lingering over him as her cheeks warmed to a rose-hued blush.

The uniform Lévesque had given him was that of a high ranking, regimental officer made of a combination of black cotton and black leather. It didn't immediately impress, particularly when lying folded upon a blood-stained table, but when put on the snug fitting black trousers were undeniably flattering. The tailored leather coat was worn over a dark, cotton undershirt and was embroidered along its edge with golden trim. Set off smartly along each outer panel of the coat and the standing collar by a row of gold buttons embossed with the Eminent Protectorate's seal, it was closed with individual straps of black leather that crossed the front of the coat from one button to the other. Epaulettes bearing the EP seal and looping golden fringes accentuated Tzadkiel's broad shoulders and the entire ensemble was embellished by two braided gold cords ornamentally draping the neckline.

Black leather boots with lacings to the knee took several minutes to don before he cinched a wide leather belt across his hips. After putting everything on, he walked with a purposeful stride to the small dais above which Jshunamir was still hovering on guard. Taking up a baldric of soft gray leather and an over-the-shoulder sword harness, the only things remaining from what he'd been wearing on the day he encountered Lévesque, he took his sword in hand. Unstained and untarnished, though it had not been cleaned, it glittered as beautifully as it had on the day it was forged countless ages before. Its inlaid archaic runes glimmered with a silvery light all their own. Sheathing the sword in the harness created to allow him to carry the weapon across his back, he put the harness on and strapped it across his chest. Slinging the baldric over his shoulder and adjusting the empty scabbard at his hip, he turned to face the table and only then noticed

Lourdes who stood watching him with an unguarded stare.

She'd given him a towel and had made herself scarce while he dressed, but had returned with a bundle she carried in front of her. How long she'd been watching him he wasn't sure, but she was clearly unable to express herself. Crossing the floor with an unhurried stride, he looked down at himself and then back at her with an openly curious expression. "Does it suit me? I think it's a bit," he hesitated, seeking the right word, but she finished his sentence with an openly approving tone.

"Magnificent?"

Her compliment caused him to laugh self-deprecatingly, but his smile broadened. Placing his hand over his heart, he closed his eyes appreciatively before turning to gesture at the food cart. "We should eat that oatmeal, don't you think? Can't pack it and we don't want it to go to waste."

Her delighted agreement was over-shadowed by a remark from Lévesque who returned from his office and prompted them to hurry. "I've arranged for your horse to be saddled and ready within the hour. She should take the goods requiring transport to the stables as soon as possible."

Tzadkiel returned his stare from across the room, his expression hardening. "She does not need to serve me. I'm more than capable,"

Lévesque scoffed impatiently. "Do you want this plan to fail before you start? She is supposed to be your servant. She would be expected to see to the provisions and details of your departure. It's her duty, not yours. You will only go to the stables when you're ready to leave, getting neither of your hands nor your feet dirty."

Recognizing he was right in what he said, even if he didn't like it, Tzadkiel sighed with resignation and nodded, but looked down at Lourdes and directed his next words to her. "One final duty to perform."

She nodded and stepped back to depart, but he caught her hand and pulled her back.

"There's time. Eat first." His consideration of her needs and feelings obviously annoyed Lévesque, who shook his head and returned to his office muttering under his breath, but Tzadkiel paid him little heed. Their first meal together had been one of gentle ministration with her caring for him and ignoring herself. Now, he could put her needs first and he would not overlook them simply for time's sake.

Raising the sticky bowl from the cart, he handed her one of two spoons provided and offered the bowl so she could take the first spoonful. Not much of a gesture, perhaps; not much in comparison to what she'd done for him, but it was what he could do in that moment. As he watched her, as they shared the sumptuous simple meal, he began to understand there was much he wished to do for her. He had so much to repay, yet, even more than that. When he looked at her and when he thought about her, he felt a compelling emotion he'd never experienced before.

Unexpectedly, she closed her eyes as if she might cry.

"What is it?" His concerned query drew her back from the precipice, but, although she shook her head, he knew well enough something distressed her. He reached to touch her shoulder gently, watching her with mounting anxiety. "Are you afraid? Unsure?"

She looked up at him blankly, nodded and then shook her head. Her response perplexed him into silence, but after a moment she sighed and offered a better explanation. "I just realized I won't be able to say goodbye to Brigyda."

"Brigyda?" he repeated softly.

"She's my friend. A very good friend. She took care of me when…." her voice trailed off and he began to understand that she simply could not force herself to speak about what had happened. "She's so young and on her own. I know she'll worry." Looking away from him, she fought to suppress her emotions and he found himself unable to think of anything useful to say. Frustrated by his ineptness, he looked across the chamber toward Lévesque's office.

"Is she the young servant who was here before you came?"

Stifling her emotion and wiping her eyes hastily, Lourdes agreed. "I offered to take her place. She was so frightened by," she didn't need to say the words. He understood.

"I know. I tried to speak to her. Tried to tell her I was alright, but I think I only frightened her more." Handing the bowl of oatmeal to her, Tzadkiel set his spoon down. "I'll be right back. Please, eat." Not waiting for her to argue, which he felt certain she would try to do, he walked determinedly to Lévesque's office and stopped in the doorway to look around the small room with a critical gaze. Lévesque was standing with his back to the door, looking out the barred windows, but he knew he was there and spoke with predictable irascibility.

"You're burning daylight."

"I know."

"The guards will return soon. I only arranged for them to be gone long enough for you to prepare."

"We'll be ready shortly. Lourdes didn't eat today and barely had anything yesterday. You wouldn't want her to draw attention by fainting, would you?"

Lévesque grumbled, but agreed with a silent shake of his head before changing the subject back to something he could control. "What do you want?" he asked without turning around and Tzadkiel glared at him for a protracted moment, his thoughts careening from their intended course in an unanticipated tempest of anger and hatred.

What did he want?

He wanted to draw his sword! He wanted to not feel guilty when he considered allowing himself the liberty of pouring out his wrath on this despicable man. He wanted to find Sauvage and make him pay for what he'd done to Lourdes, but wasn't he the Archangel of Mercy? Shouldn't he forgive them, rather than despise? Shouldn't he choose compassion over retribution?

Shaking his head, he refocused. "The young servant who served here before Lourdes, will she return?"

Seeming confounded by such a bizarre inquiry, Lévesque finally twisted to look over his shoulder incredulously. "I have no idea."

Tzadkiel drew a deep breath, endeavoring to control his mounting annoyance, but it was difficult when faced with so exasperating a man. He attempted to make his request as straightforward as possible.

"She's Lourdes' friend. After we've gone, if you see her, might you tell her Lourdes escaped unharmed?"

Scowling, Lévesque turned fully around to stare at him with a mixture of disbelief and vexation clearly evident in his gaze, but before he could refuse, Tzadkiel met his stare, strengthening his request with irrefutable logic. "It would do no harm to tell her, nor would it implicate you in any way."

Lévesque considered without replying and Tzadkiel returned his silent glare, unmoving. His non-confrontational insistence was inescapable. At last, Lévesque sighed sharply. "If it means you'll get the hell out of here, then I agree. *If* I see her again. I will not go looking for her." Closing his eyes, Tzadkiel inclined his head with unspoken appreciation, then turned away, returning to Lourdes with a reassuring smile.

"Do not worry about your friend."

She had never been to the stables. She'd never had reason or permission to go there, so she walked slowly as she pushed the rattling cart laden with food and supplies, unsure where to go or who she should speak to. Lévesque had given her the name of the officer on duty, a Lieutenant Chevalier, who should already have received his orders to saddle a fine steed and ready a packhorse in preparation for their departure. Moving uncertainly along the narrow footpath leading from The Bastion, she watched the guards who milled about off duty and those who practiced in the training yard with the vigilance of a wild animal. They could do whatever they liked as long as their commanding officer didn't catch them and the last thing she wanted was to become another man's amusement. Again.

Her uneasiness didn't go unnoticed.

"You there. Where do you think you're going?" An older guard with a grizzled beard stepped from the barn's open doorway to block her way. Instinctively, she dipped in a curtsy and, without meeting his gaze, offered the folded paper she carried.

"If you please, Sir, Captain Lévesque has sent me to find Lieutenant Chevalier." She hoped by using Lévesque's name she might avoid any unpleasantness. He raised a skeptical brow and reached for the orders, grunting in an unconvinced manner as he scanned the handwriting on the paper.

"Captain Lévesque, eh?" he repeated noncommittally.

"Yes, Sir."

"What do you want with Lieutenant Chevalier?"

She bobbed another curtsy. "My master is preparing to depart, Sir. Captain Lévesque said a horse would be ready for him on the hour and a pack horse for provisions." Her soft reply warbled with nervousness and her hand trembled when she gestured at the cart laden with supplies. He looked at her suspiciously. Turning without speaking to her, he moved back into the stables, taking the orders with him and her heart hammered with apprehension. Where was he going? Should she follow him? What would she do if he didn't return the orders to her? Several moments dragged on like an eternity until he came back out, motioning for her to follow him as if she ought to know better.

"Well, come on then. What you doing? I haven't got all day." Hurrying to fall in step behind him, she pushed the cart before her and looked around with cautious wonder at the massive barn that housed several dozen horses and their tack. The animals peered out at her curiously, some nickering in welcome, others tossing their heads with agitation, and her pace slowed the further in they went. Bales of hay lined the stables. The walls were hung with assorted riding equipment and several buckets of water were scattered about, all neatly organized, but seeming haphazard to her unaccustomed gaze. As they walked, a dark colored, powerfully built dog trotted into the interior and barked at her assertively, causing her to shrink away and slow her pace even more.

"Keep up!" Shouting to her from half a barn away, the guard stopped to wait for her. His expression hardened and she gasped in surprise and hurried to catch up with him, the cart squeaking and clattering in protest and the dog trailing after her barking persistently. "Leave that contraption there. You're spookin' the horses."

Hesitating to leave behind their provisions, she stepped away from the cart reluctantly, then paused to look back. "But, Sir?"

"Leave it. We'll bring the mule to it. Goliath!" Shouting at the dog, his exclamation seemed to satisfy, or perhaps intimidate, the animal who grumbled and ceased his barking, but continued to follow her even as the guard pointed to the far end of the barn. A mule was tethered to the rear wall, its head drooping in a bored doze and he gestured at it impatiently.

"Untie that animal there. I've been on my feet all morning. Don't need to be wandering about after pack mules." Motioning for her to hurry as she walked by him uncertainly, he continued to mutter as she went towards the back of the barn, his grumbling mingling with the dog's whining and the heavy sound of her own footsteps upon the wooden boards of the barn floor. Approaching the animal cautiously, she spoke to it in a reassuring tone as she untied its tether and led it back to the place where the guard waited. When she reached him, he turned towards the outer wall, taking from it the tack necessary for their journey. He outfitted the mule appropriately and affixed two sacks of grain to the pack saddle before moving closer to her and studying her skeptically. "You know what all this equipment is for?"

Opening her mouth as if to agree, she couldn't force the words from her lips any more than she could manage to look convincing and though she nodded, he didn't believe her for a moment.

"Haven't a clue, have you?"

Biting her lower lip uncertainly, she shook her head. "I'm sorry, Sir, I haven't. The servant who usually accompanies my master when he travels fell ill and it was left to me," she tried to explain, the words tumbling from her mouth in a far more rational explanation than she expected, but he only shook his head begrudgingly.

"Just my luck. Nothin' but a kitchen maid, aren'tcha?" He shook his head another time. "Look, see these bags on the sides of the beast? You fill 'em. Simple. Just keep the load even, that's all. You haven't got all that much, but it's got to be distributed evenly, understand?"

She nodded mutely.

"The pack saddle contains a leather tarp to cover your goods, 'case it rains, and there are a few tools if any of the horses throw a shoe."

She stared at him blankly, not needing to say she didn't have the first idea how to shoe a horse and he shook his head another time.

"Can't be traveling too far with so little?" His questioning gaze betrayed his curiosity.

"Only enough provisions, Sir, to reach the next city." She bobbed a curtsy and stepped forward to begin packing, mindful that Tzadkiel would be coming to meet her and acquire the horses in less than an hour. The guard stepped back and watched for a moment as she began loading the bags of food into the soft panniers on either side of the mule, but when he noticed the short barrels of cider on the lower shelf of the cart, he grumbled and moved away. Unsure what he was doing, she watched him with a sideward gaze while she continued to pack, her curiosity mounting when he collected two rope slings and returned, mumbling still.

"They didn't tell me you'd have barrels of ale. If I'd have known, I would have done this early. Can't just tie them to 'is tail, you know." Complaining incessantly, he attached the rope slings to the pack saddle near the rear of the animal before he turned to pick up one of the short barrels.

"Hold that open," he told her brusquely, assisting

her with slinging the barrels to each side of the mule before he ensured everything was secure. Satisfied that it was, he patted the animal's rump firmly. "Might offer 'im an apple or three when you get where you're going." It was the first kind thing he'd said and Lourdes turned to look at him with a surprised smile. Dipping a curtsy, she nodded.

"I will, Sir. Thank you." Her genuinely appreciative tone made him stare at her with an unreadable expression before he shook his head yet another time and turned away.

"Pretty thing like you has no business traveling with an officer. Just asking for trouble, if you ask me." Muttering, he returned to his post at the stable entryway and she followed him with an astonished stare. Perhaps he wasn't such a bad sort after all. Looking at the mule, she wondered if she should remain where she was or follow the guard outside? Would he indicate to her when or if she should follow him? She waited several uncertain moments, then jumped as a man's voice rang from beyond her line of sight.

"Bailey, that animal ready?"

The guard straightened from his lounging stance abruptly "Yes, Sir. Right here, Lieutenant." Waving his arm in a frantic gesture for her to come out to the entryway, he stopped and saluted as a younger man dressed in an officer's uniform came into view. Holding out the orders she'd given him without another word, the guard waited for his instructions, just as she did. Watching them closely, Lourdes noticed the name on officer's uniform above an impressive display of medals. Chevalier. He was the one she'd been sent to find. He didn't appear much older than she was and his green eyes were the color of a misty morning. His short-cropped chestnut brown hair escaped his cap near his temples and his high cheekbones and clean-shaven chin accentuated his handsome, youthful features. He was lithe, broad of shoulder, and tall, though not as tall as Tzadkiel. Without looking at her, he spoke with an official tone that betrayed nothing. "You're the servant traveling with Admiral Kiel?"

Admiral Kiel? Her thoughts scrambled for a moment before she dipped in a swift curtsy and agreed quietly. "Yes, Sir."

The soft femininity of her voice caused him to look up at her sharply and he stammered out an additional question with clear astonishment. "You...you've got your supplies loaded?"

"Yes, thank you, Sir."

One brow raised incredulously as he inspected her from head to toe. "You're traveling with him?" he repeated hesitantly. Nodding, she noticed the older guard shaking his head with obvious disapproval though he didn't grumble this time or even mutter under his breath. Stepping closer to her, the Lieutenant studied her with a critical gaze, his scrutiny sending a tremor through her. Though he seemed barely older than she, his serious bearing lent him an air of authority that commanded respect. "Can you shoe a horse?"

His doubtful inquiry sent her thoughts tumbling. Why would he ask such a thing? If she said yes, would he require a demonstration? Uncertain if she should be truthful or lie, she stared back at him dumbly.

"Do you know how to saddle a horse?" He looked her up and down once more and reiterated. "Can you even lift a saddle?" His stare grew more critical and he shook his head when she didn't answer. Turning back to the guard he'd called Bailey, he spoke under his breath. "I'll warrant she's not traveling with him to shoe or saddle."

Bailey grunted and shook his head, glancing back at Lourdes with an expression of concern he seemed unable to disguise and her astonishment doubled, but even as he did this, Lieutenant Chevalier snapped to attention and the older guard hastily followed suit.

Walking casually along the footpath leading to the stables wearing a uniform that accentuated his tall, powerful physique and carrying a pair of gloves in his hand absently, Admiral Kiel approached with an air of confidence and authority that was undeniable.

He was greeted by three stares.

12

L évesque watched the Archangel from the corridor between his office and the main chamber of The Tower where he stood unobserved. He'd spent the last year in this place, overseeing the torture of someone he should never have met and he couldn't deny how angry he felt about it. Angry because he was forced into a situation he was entirely unprepared for; angry because he'd let that anger dictate his actions which were, invariably, angry.

Now, at least, he was doing something to change all that.

Hopefully.

Dressed in an admiral's uniform, the Archangel stood next to the barred windows, his eyes closed as he basked in the midday sunlight. It sparkled around him in a spectral dance, like smoke curling upward from an extinguished candle, and Lévesque couldn't help wondering about it, but there was no time for musings. Shaking himself from overthinking the matter, he looked down at the richly embroidered peaked cap and black leather gloves he held, squared his shoulders, and moved out into the chamber.

Tzadkiel turned his head as he approached, fixing

an intense stare on him that made Lévesque distinctly uncomfortable. Looking down once again at the finishing touches to the uniform he'd already provided, he held them out while looking past the confrontational glare of the Archangel. "It's time."

Tzadkiel glanced down at the offering, reaching to take it without otherwise breaking his stare. "I know."

"Thought you'd better thoroughly look the part," Lévesque explained, gesturing at the cap and gloves. Again, Tzadkiel glanced at them, but didn't reply. Lévesque shifted uneasily, meeting his gaze at last.

"I truly hope we never meet again. I wouldn't want to repeat," he didn't finish his thought, but Tzadkiel nodded, comprehending what he left unspoken. Straightening, Lévesque braced his stance.

"Best get on with it then."

Perplexed, Tzadkiel cocked his head and Lévesque elaborated without further prompting. "I don't want to even think about trying to explain your escape without so much as a hair out of place. I'll need bruises to substantiate such an occurrence and we both know you've been wanting to provide some since the day we met. Now's your chance. Make it good."

They considered each other for a protracted moment and it was obvious the Archangel struggled with his desire to oblige him. It seemed far more difficult for him to allow himself such a liberty than Lévesque anticipated and the Archangel stared at him for several moments before he seemed to decide. Reaching out, Tzadkiel offered his hand, his lavender gaze locking with Lévesque's.

"Know this. It was within my power to oppose you at any time. Your actions served a greater purpose."

Unsettled by this unexpected absolution, Lévesque stared at him before taking his hand to shake it, once. Then he braced himself as the expression on Tzadkiel's features darkened to one that betrayed the rage, indignation and loathing created by the torture he had been forced to endure. He dropped the peaked cap and gloves to the floor and, in spite of being the personification of mercy and compassion, the force of his fists and the power behind the multiple kicks he delivered after Lévesque fell were as inescapable as they were unforgettable.

Walking along the footpath he'd been directed to during their planning conversation, Tzadkiel relished the freedom that had been restored to him as the warm caress of the midday sun filled him with a sensation of vitality he hadn't felt in nearly a year. He could easily have stopped, closed his eyes and tilted his face up towards the sky, extending his arms while breathing in the sweet, fresh air again and again. After the staleness of The Tower that never felt the cool touch of a breeze or the freshening kiss of rain, even the scents from the stables of a bustling castle were refreshing.

He wanted to stop and drink in the moment, but, of course, he didn't. There would be time enough for relishing his freedom later. Now, he focused on the massive barn towards which he was walking and the difficult task that lay ahead. Treating Lourdes with the disdain an officer would customarily direct towards a servant would be far more challenging than maintaining an air of aloofness, yet both had been pointed out as vitally important if he didn't want to attract undue attention. The thought sent a pang through him, but he didn't have any options, not if he wanted to ensure they both made it safely beyond the walls of Le Bastion de la Résolution and its watch tower several miles away. Coming to the entrance of the barn, he slowed and returned the silent stares that were focused on him by the officer on duty, an older guard, and Lourdes who stood quietly to one side seemingly desperate not to gape at him in awe.

"Admiral." The youthful officer addressed him respectfully and saluted. "Sorry for the delay, we were just bringing your horse around, Sir." Lieutenant Chevalier apologized politely and looked with an urgent stare at the guard beside him who snapped his head once in acknowledgment, turned sharply and strode off. Admiral Kiel slowed his pace, studying the young lieutenant for a moment before silently inclining his head.

"Everything's in order, Sir," Chevalier continued, turning to motion for Lourdes to bring the pack mule out of the barn. She obeyed with quiet hesitation and Admiral Kiel barely glanced at her as his gaze swept over the stables. He relaxed his stance, clasping his hands behind his back as he waited, inwardly uncertain while outwardly composed. He knew enough not to engage in idle conversation with lesser ranking officers, but Chevalier seemed determined.

"Is there anything additional you require, Sir? The orders from Captain Lévesque indicated you're traveling light and fast, but if you need any supplemental armaments, tack, or," Admiral Kiel raised his hand and Chevalier fell silent as he studied the embroidery adorning the visor of the Admiral's cap that irrefutably declared his distinguished rank. His gaze also took in the intricately embossed leather harness that supported the large sword he carried across his back. Its exquisite silver handle glimmered in the bright day's light, as did the lengths of his unusual, strawberry-blond hair that he'd not quite managed to entirely tuck beneath the impressive peaked cap he wore.

"Nothing additional." His succinct response cut the

lieutenant's inspection short and he turned his gaze once again to Lourdes, his brow twitching upward before he smiled respectfully and stepped backward. The sound of hooves on gravel approached.

"Captain Lévesque wanted to ensure I selected the fastest horse we have, Sir, which I've done, but he's a high-spirited beast. Requires a strong hand, if you take my meaning, Sir?" Admiral Kiel looked at the officer without indicating whether he understood or not, but when Bailey came around the side of the barn with as fine a steed as he'd ever laid eyes on, it was difficult for him to remain impassive.

The stallion was a magnificent blue roan with a black mane, tail and striking banding on his legs. He stood easily seventeen hands and tossed his head defiantly against the bridle as Bailey handed him over to the Admiral and backed away. Moving closer, Tzadkiel laid a hand on the beast's powerful shoulder, running it up along his neck and across his broad cheek while he looked the horse directly in the eye. Bailey and Lieutenant Chevalier watched with amazement. The stallion was notoriously difficult to control, but within mere moments he looked back at the Admiral with a calm gaze, lowered his head, and nickered companionably. Admiral Kiel nodded with approval, a crooked grin turning his lips as he turned back to Chevalier. "He's splendid. Andalusian?"

Chevalier nodded, mutely offering a riding crop, which was dismissed by a scoff and shake of the head.

"I'll not need that."

Chevalier responded to the disdainful remark professionally, although a blaze of irritation glinted in his eyes. "His name is Garrenbale, Sir. He's been trained to know and respond to it."

Admiral Kiel nodded offhandedly as he turned an unexpectedly cold glare towards Lourdes, giving the first outward indication that he even knew she was there. "Everything ready?" Speaking to her with as firm and dismissive a tone as he could produce, he cringed inwardly when she flinched at the harshness of his tone. Bobbing a curtsy, she answered timorously without looking up at him.

"Yes, Sir."

"Good. We're burning daylight." Looking back at Lieutenant Chevalier, he nodded only once in acknowledgment, then swung up into the saddle in one powerful, fluid movement. The stallion danced sideways, familiarizing himself with the weight and bearing of his rider, tossing his head repeatedly against the pull of the bridle even as the Admiral acquainted himself with the steed's robust energy. After several moments, he looked down at Lourdes, his satisfied grin fading abruptly into a fierce scowl. "Where's her horse?"

The silence that answered him prompted a glower that even Lévesque might have evaded. "How do you expect me to travel at speed with a walking servant?" The curt severity of his tone was both shocking and intimidating, causing Bailey and Chevalier to look at each other in surprise before the lieutenant checked the orders he still held in his hand. Clearly discovering that no additional horse had been pre-arranged, he shook his head and shot a disgruntled look at Bailey, gesturing back into the stables with a sideward nod. "My oversight, Sir. We'll have one ready in less than five."

Fixing his stare on the youthful officer, Admiral Kiel didn't speak a word, nor did he need to; his annoyance was unmistakable and it prompted the lieutenant to follow the guard he'd sent to collect an additional horse. Bailey selected a smaller animal, more suited to Lourdes' diminutive stature, and Chevalier helped to fit it with the appropriate tack before hurrying to deliver it to the Admiral with a respectful bow. "My commanding officer is Captain Rousseau, if you care to," he provided in a tight voice, anticipating some form of reprimand, but his offer was met with a silent shake of the head and subtle raising of the Admiral's hand.

Inspecting the less impressive horse with a critical a gaze, Admiral Kiel nodded only once to indicate he was satisfied, his stallion turning unexpectedly in an agitated circle, anxious to be off, but the beast's angst didn't distract the Admiral's intense stare. He allowed the steed the liberty of dancing impatiently, fully in control of him, while he watched Chevalier hand the second horse back to Bailey.

The guard led the reddish-dun-colored mare to a mounting block and offered Lourdes his hand, which she accepted as her expression faltered between shyness and trepidation. Openly unsure how best to climb onto the waiting mare, she stood uneasily as the Admiral's stallion continued to skitter restlessly. The leather of the saddle and harness creaked in the awkward hush that fell and Tzadkiel noticed Lourdes' apprehension, realizing with an inward cringe that he had never bothered to ask if she knew how to ride. Obviously, she didn't and her discernable uneasiness cut at him like a blade. Observing the interaction between the guard and Lourdes, he noticed how Bailey spoke quietly to her, instructing her how to position herself in the saddle and how to use the reins and her heels to guide the mare.

"She's gentle. Be gentle with her and all will go well." Looking up at the Admiral as he spoke these words, the guard's intimation was unmistakable, but before he could decide how to respond, Lourdes raised her gaze to him with unconcealed timidity. Her misinterpretation of his aloof performance wounded him deeply and he stared back at her, wishing he could communicate to her in some unspoken manner that his petulance was merely an act, but there was no time to pull her aside to explain. Moreover, the reasons that spawned his behavior remained. If they were to make it beyond the watch tower without being apprehended, he needed to maintain the assumption that she was his servant. So, he forced himself to speak with the harshness he'd heard in Lévesque's voice more than once and directed an annoyed query at her that made his stomach twist when her nervousness distorted into observable fear.

"Are you quite ready now?"

She nodded timorously, even as Bailey tied the pack mule's lead rein to her saddle, patted the animal one last time, and stepped back. Tzadkiel's gaze fleetingly locked with Chevalier's as the flustered lieutenant watched them depart and he didn't miss the shake of his head or the words he and Bailey muttered between themselves as they rode away from the barn.

"She's in for a hell of a time with him."

"Irascible prick."

They were quite right. Feeling positively dreadful about the way he'd treated them and, most particularly, the way he'd treated Lourdes, he fought with himself. He wanted to explain, but knew he shouldn't speak with her while they were still within the castle's walls. It would only raise suspicion. With so many guards watching them, it felt imperative he continued the act, even in spite of how difficult it was to treat her so unkindly. Until they were beyond the watch tower, he had to keep up the ruse lest one of the many guards stationed along the street detain them and start asking questions.

With each passing moment, however, her fearful stare on him felt like a dagger sinking deeper and deeper into his back and it finally became unbearable. He had to do something. Anything. Hoping to alleviate her fears even a little, he circled back and brought his stallion beside her small mare. Leaning down to speak to her as confidentially as possible while they clattered along the cobbled avenue, he was horrified when she cringed away from him, lowering her head in an unmistakable gesture of apprehension that communicated her mistrust as loudly as if she had screamed in terror. For appearances sake it was perfect, but her sudden fear of him nearly made him ill.

"It's alright, Lourdes," he spoke gently, but she would not look at him. Thoroughly unsettled, he realized there wasn't much he could do. He certainly couldn't stop in the middle of the street to try to reassure her. He tried again. "You're my servant, remember?"

Glancing up at him hesitantly, she nodded, uncertainty filling her gaze. Unsatisfied, he watched her with a disconcerted stare, recognizing after a moment that he was only making her more uncomfortable. Without stopping to discuss the situation there was nothing more he could do. Instead, he set a goal to pass the watch tower as quickly as possible so they could stop, and to that end, he pressed his heels against his steed's flanks, urging him forward into a ground-devouring canter that soon left her some distance behind him.

Watching as he left her behind, Lourdes felt the knot in her stomach tighten. Could she have been so wrong about him? Could she have misinterpreted his behavior so dreadfully that she believed she was safe with him when she truly was not? Why was he behaving the way he was, treating everyone so contemptuously? Was he merely putting on an act or had the gentleness he'd shown her in The Tower been the act? She had no idea, but the doubt churning in her stomach combined with her nervousness about riding a horse for the first time in her life was enough to make her sick.

It would not do.

Certainly, she'd misunderstood. Certainly, it was all an act.

Unable to make sense of him, she decided to concentrate on the moment. It was far more important not to fall off her horse than worry about a man she clearly didn't understand. She didn't understand the horse she was sitting on either, but Bailey's surprising instructions helped her in this regard, at least. She quickly discovered the horse would shy and pull away if she held the reins too tightly, but if she relaxed and allowed the animal the freedom to simply follow the steed ahead of them, she plodded along at a comfortable pace. She also discovered if she pressed her heels against the horse's sides in an attempt to nervously hang on, the animal would slow and stop. It would then take quite a bit of urging to get her going again, which resulted in her falling even farther behind. If she clenched her knees against the saddle, however, and allowed the horse's rhythm to become her own, she and the mare both felt secure.

By the time she figured this out, Tzadkiel had reached the main gate of the castle and was waiting for her to catch up. Sitting astride his magnificent horse with his face turned up to the radiant afternoon sun, he didn't seem to realize how the guards posted at the gate watched him with askance glances, visibly unsure what he was doing or why. However, when he heard her horse and the pack mule coming up behind him, he twisted around to look back at her and the guards uncertainly looked at each other again. Finally, one of them decided to approach him.

"Admiral, Sir."

Looking down at the guard with a critical expression, Tzadkiel handed him a rolled piece of paper and looked away, not bothering to watch as he read it. The young guard, appearing little older than twenty, looked at it before he stepped aside to show it to one of his fellow sentries. They seemed slightly confused and looked repeatedly from the order he had given them, to the Admiral waiting for them to open the gates, and back again, discussing something of concern between themselves. One shook his head and pointed towards the gatehouse and it was enough to provoke the Admiral to speak.

"Is there an issue?" His curt tone brought the guard back to his horse immediately, shaking his head.

"No, Sir. Well, it's just," he looked back at Lourdes and the pack mule, visibly confused by their presence since they were not mentioned in the order Lévesque had written. "The order specifies passage for one Admiral Kiel," the guard explained with observable hesitation. The Admiral sighed with profound exasperation.

"Does an Admiral typically travel alone, with no supplies of any kind and no servant to fetch and carry?"

Discernibly flummoxed, the guard shook his head. "Uh, no, Sir."

"Do I need to waste Captain Lévesque's time by bringing him here to explain his order to you?"

The young guard snapped his head up. "No, Sir."

"Would you like to question his order further?" The Admiral's tone was growing even more terse, causing the young guard to shake his head insistently.

"Course not, Sir." He motioned to those guarding the gate. "Let them pass." Stepping back, the shaken guard watched with an unmistakably indecisive gaze as they rode by him, returning to his fellow guards after they passed to examine the order again. Lourdes watched until the gates closed behind them, certain that at any moment she would see them open the gates and a full contingent of guards would race after them, but to her relief they remained closed. Turning to face forward at last, she patted the mare she rode and spoke softly to her.

"I think we may have both just escaped Le Bastion, though I'm not sure if it's a good thing or not." As if in response, the mare nickered softly and Lourdes smiled, her gaze finding Tzadkiel who rode a short distance ahead. In spite of his odd behavior and how nervous he made her, she couldn't help watching him with an admiring gaze. Surely, she had misunderstood him. Hadn't Lévesque been adamant that he should treat her like a servant so their departure would not raise any suspicions? Surely, he was doing just that.

They continued along the Byland Road for what felt like several miles, her mare and the pack mule plodding along at a steady pace while Tzadkiel urged his extraordinary stallion to gallop ahead and fall back repeatedly, circling leisurely each time to wait for her to catch up. He also rode to the nearby hilltops to visually survey the surrounding countryside, lingering sometimes so long that he would need to gallop after them. He clearly loved riding and his skill was impressive. He rode as if one with the stallion; his body rocked in a smooth, easy rhythm with the horse that made it look effortless. Lourdes knew it wasn't; at least, it wasn't for her, but it was for him and he obviously relished each moment. As she watched him, she realized he was probably ecstatic to be free after spending so many long months caged like a neglected animal inside a tiny prison cell.

When they came upon an unremarkable graying tower with several EP Guards milling about at its perimeter, he brought his horse in close and rode just ahead of her once more. The fierce scowl that had

turned his otherwise handsome features brooding before they left the castle returned and the guards nodded
to acknowledge him or froze in rigid attention when
they noticed his rank. None of them stepped out onto
the roadway to impede their progress and, although
she glanced behind several times as they rode on, none
pursued.

They rode throughout the afternoon, putting as
much distance between themselves and the watch
tower as they could. Tzadkiel continued riding ahead
to explore the countryside and falling back to wait for
her while her horse and the pack mule walked at a
steady, gentle pace. Only after they had gone many
miles and the late afternoon sun began to glimmer in
lengthening rays did he return to ride beside her,
speaking to her, at last, in the deep, gentle voice she had
come to recognize. "There's a stand of oak trees near a
stream not far ahead if you'd like to stop?"

Gazing up at him, she smiled dimly and nodded, inwardly fighting the twinge of uncertainty that stabbed
at her when she met his penetrating gaze. She hated not
feeling sure about him when she had thought herself
entirely certain, but her few experiences with men left
her apprehensive, whether she wanted to be or not. He
watched her for a moment longer, the deep lavender of
his unusual eyes reflecting unmistakable concern, but
he said nothing. Instead, he urged his horse forward,
leading the way and she willingly followed.

It was at least another mile, perhaps two, before
they reached the small grove of oaks he had found.
Nestled along the banks of a burbling stream a short
distance from the road, the tall trees provided inviting
green shade from the glare of the late afternoon
summer sunshine. Turning her horse from the road,
she followed through the tall grass that filled the
meadow stretching from the road into the distance.

Several times, her horse dropped her head, anxious to crop the inviting forage and it took some convincing to keep her moving forward, but at last they stopped beneath the boughs of an expansive, ancient oak and she relaxed her grip on the reins so the horse could eat. Tzadkiel swung his leg over the withers of his stallion and leapt to the ground, wincing with unexpected discomfort when he landed. Bending forward to rub his thigh with a grimace and soft groan, he took the reins of his steed and tossed them across the saddle.

Moving to take the horse by his bridle, he stepped closer and spoke quietly to him, his words either too soft for Lourdes to make out or in some other language. She couldn't be sure, but was unable to understand what he said. Intrigued, she watched as the two seemed to communicate, the horse nickering and bobbing his head several times before Tzadkiel released him to forage and, to her surprise, the high-spirited animal didn't charge off at a full gallop, but meandered happily amidst the oaks, grazing as he went.

Utterly at a loss to explain his actions, she looked down at her own horse and wondered if she could ask her not to wander off as well. The thought immediately made her scoff at herself. Perhaps she should worry about out how she was supposed to dismount and leave talking to animals for another time. Fortunately, when they had set off, Bailey had been there to help her climb onto the mare and she'd had a mounting block to stand on, but there was no such luxury amid the oaks. She was glad her dress was full enough so she could sit astride the horse without needing to hike her skirt up to her waist, but she had no idea how to dismount, so she decided to wait for help.

"Are you alright?"

The question they had come to ask each other so often brought a timid smile to her lips. "Yes. I…I'm just not sure how to," looking down at the mare, she shrugged uncertainly and his expression brightened with sudden understanding. Striding closer with an unhurried pace the brooding glower with which he had masked his face during his interactions with the EP Guards transformed into something far more attractive and charming and she couldn't keep herself from staring at him. How could he have been so intolerable just a short while ago, yet now...her thoughts tumbled.

"I can help, if you will allow me. Can you swing your leg over the saddle to sit sideways?" His softly spoken question sent a flutter through her even as he turned his head away to permit her a moment to resituate herself and she was thankful for his unanticipated gallantry. She didn't consider herself bashful, but it wasn't exactly a dainty maneuver. She managed to turn without falling off the patiently standing mare and, when she sat in a side-saddle position looking at him with a confusion of emotions tumbling through her she could barely fathom, he turned back to her and raised his hands. "May I?"

She nodded even as another flutter danced in her stomach. Placing her hands upon his broad shoulders, she allowed him to lift her from the saddle and set her gently on the ground. She looked up at him falteringly. Standing so close to him, she realized just how tall and strong he was and how easily he could overpower her, if he chose. Her caramel gaze locked fleetingly with his and a shiver serrated through her that she could not contain. She frowned. How could she admire him one moment and fear him the next? Perplexed by her unpredictable emotions, she stood in awkward silence while he stepped back and turned to whisper something indiscernible in the mare's ear. Just as his stallion had done, the mare nickered softly and seemed to nod her head before she was set at liberty to crop the lush grass. Lourdes watched in confused wonder as he untied the lead rein for the pack mule and spoke quietly to it as well. The animals roamed the grove beneath the oaks and headed in the direction of the gurgling stream, but didn't go beyond the stream or venture back towards the road. After watching them for several moments, her curiosity got the best of her.

"Did you speak to them?" The incredulous question slipped from her lips before she could contain it and she cringed at its absurdity. Biting her lip nervously, she expected him to mock such a ridiculous notion, but he smiled and nodded as if nothing could be more natural.

"I merely asked them to stay close. Are you hungry?"

Standing unmoving, she stared at him with astonishment while he trailed after the pack mule to collect one of the loaves stuffed with cooked vegetables and cheese, as well as two apples. When he turned and noticed how she was staring at him, he stopped and shook his head. "Not hungry?"

Not hungry? Was he serious? She shook her head; then nodded and shook her head again, attempting to put her bewilderment into words, but her indecisive response only made him laugh.

"I'm sorry, I have no idea what that means, but I think you should eat something." Coming back to her, he gazed at her briefly before he sat down and looked up at her as if she were the one behaving oddly. Sitting down beside him after an awkward pause, she tried, but couldn't manage to get his answer out of her head.

"You spoke to them?"

Tearing the loaf in two, one portion ending up larger than the other, he held them out for her to choose which one she wanted as he answered softly. "Do I not speak to you?" His answer confounded her even more. Taking the smaller portion absently, she shook her head.

"Well, of course, but,"

"But, what?"

"I'm not an animal," she answered, as if he ought to realize the simple logic of her argument, but he cocked his head slightly to one side and seemed entirely lost.

"Does that make a difference?"

Her eyes grew wide. "Well, of course it does."

"Why?"

"Because.... animals don't understand language." Her matter-of-fact tone made his smile broaden.

"Course they do. You just saw me speak with them, didn't you?"

Entirely baffled, she stared at him, unable to verbalize her confusion, though it was entirely evident in her expression. He took a bite of the sandwich he held and chewed thoughtfully.

"I know. There is much I need to explain to you."

She nodded mutely, images of enchanted swords, blood-thirsty demons, and glimmering light that healed even the most horrifying injuries spinning through her mind. She glanced down at the sandwich in her hands, prepared to wait on his explanation, but looked up at him once more. "Why did they call you an Archangel?"

He looked at her for several protracted moments as if considering whether or not he should answer the question. His hesitancy confused her even more, but she didn't press him. His piercing stare seemed to look straight into her, seeking something. Reassurance? Lowering his portion of their small meal, he drew a profound breath and the expression of concern that so often worried his features returned.

"Because I am."

Tzadkiel knew the question would eventually come.

He had a great deal to explain to her and he knew it would be difficult for her to believe what he told her. There was even the chance she would decide her trust in him had been misplaced and she would return to The Bastion or set out on her own. Losing her was the last thing he wanted, for many reasons. After everything he'd gone through, everything he'd suffered, he couldn't face the thought of losing her. Somehow, he had to explain himself in a way she would understand, and moreover, in a way she would accept. Though it might be easier, he wouldn't lie to her. Lying was as abhorrent to him as violence, although, upon reflection he realized he'd utilized violence on more than one occasion when necessity dictated, but lying to her was not an option. Not merely because it contradicted everything he understood about himself, but because he truly desired honesty to be the foundation of his relationship with her, whatever that relationship might be.

At the moment, it wasn't much of a relationship. The manner in which she stared at him clearly indicated she thought he may have sustained greater injury than she'd initially suspected and he didn't doubt that any further elucidation on his part would only intensify her misgivings, but there was nothing else to be done. He was an Archangel. He could no more deny it than he could make himself something he wasn't. Contemplating all these things in the space of a few moments while she stared at him with a skeptical expression, he lowered his gaze and forced the words from his lips.

"I'm an Archangel, Lourdes. I realize that sounds a bit," he paused to find the right word. "Ludicrous."

She didn't deny it.

"I only ask that you listen to what I have to tell you with an open mind before drawing any conclusions. I am the Archangel of Mercy. I have come to earth to learn if mercy still exists among the human population. There are many who live in the shadow of darkness. My purpose is to find mercy in a human before the final Horseman, Death, is unleashed."

"Death?" The confusion in her eyes began to transform into fear and the sight of it twisted his stomach into a knot. It was the last thing he wished to see, but he couldn't really blame her. The Horsemen were the world's greatest nightmare and he understood why she would fear him if he had anything whatsoever to do with them. Raising his hands in a placating gesture, he continued as gently as he could.

"It's a terrifying thing, I know, but I'm not a Horseman. I'm a servant, a messenger of hope, whose hope was fading. I couldn't force myself to believe the heart of humanity had been lost. So, I asked to be allowed to search, even for just one human who might still comprehend the true meaning of mercy, and 100 years was given." He paused, allowing her a moment to process the magnitude of what he had just said. Noticeably unnerved, she sat staring at him for several moments before she stammered uneasily.

"You're an... an angel?" She was attempting to comprehend something that was, justifiably, incomprehensible. He understood her confusion, but he didn't want her to be afraid of him because she misunderstood so he tried to offer a better explanation.

"I'm an angel who has taken human form. I'm very much the same as you are as you have seen. I feel. I need. I suffer."

She blinked at him vacantly before her eyes took on a light of vexation. "How could you let them torture you?" The sharp edge of her question cut him like a blade and he closed his eyes. Her anger was reasonable. Because of his decision to endure the unthinkable, she had suffered just as much as he had and, in many ways, her suffering was more significant than his own. She hadn't chosen it.

Overcome by a sudden rush of guilt, he considered carefully. Was there any way he could help her understand something he could barely rationalize to himself? "I didn't simply allow them. Not initially. I'd searched for nearly 100 years and found little evidence to support my hope. Then, I encountered Lévesque, who injured me so severely I couldn't oppose him. He took me as his hostage and kept me from healing through the torture you witnessed. It kept me in a perpetual state of weakness that left me with few options."

Shaking her head, she interrupted with a bewildered tone. "But your sword?"

He nodded. "Yes, I could have put a stop to it by calling Jshunamir, but I hoped if I waited," he faltered, stammering to explain something that eluded even him. He tried again. "I hoped, through my suffering, I might," again he paused, unable to put his motivations into words. How could he justify a decision that allowed such unbearable torments? Could she understand a hope so strong it had led him to make such inconceivable choices?

Setting aside his food, he offered his hand to her without speaking. She looked at it with visible uncertainty, but he waited, neither rushing nor compelling her into any action and when she placed her small, trembling hand in his he covered it with his other. The warmth of their gentle clasp was more poignant than he anticipated. He suddenly realized how small her hands were, how small she was, and recognized the responsibility he'd accepted when he'd promised to protect her. He also felt the shiver that ran through her when he slowly raised his gaze to hers. "I was reaching out, Lourdes, in the only way I had available. I didn't want to give up. I hoped if I waited, if I endured, someone would reach back."

Her gaze fell to study their hands and the gentle way he touched her. He hoped it might be enough. He hoped she would understand what he could not clearly articulate. He hoped she would understand his hope. Looking up at him again, her expressive features betrayed her uncertainty, but she answered him softly. "I reached back."

"Yes." He smiled briefly, but his expression shifted back to intense concern and he continued with a tone that was hushed by honest emotion. "I do know what you suffered for reaching back."

His words struck her like a fist.

The intrigued expression that had momentarily brightened her features twisted into misery and she struggled to suppress the harrowing memories his words provoked. They seemed to easily overpower her. Squeezing her eyes tightly closed, she whimpered and pulled against his grasp to cover her face with her hands, but he wouldn't let her go. He'd seen her ignore her pain and emotions on more than one occasion. He knew the dangers of such avoidance. She needed so much more.

Drawing her closer, he released her hand only so he could surround her with a tender embrace and she didn't resist the warmth of his strong arms. Sobbing as she struggled to contain her reaction, she pressed her face to his chest and fought the inevitable, but it was too much. The fear and anguish she'd been suppressing seemed to crash in on her and she wailed desolately. He recognized the sound. He'd heard it on many other occasions and he understood her need to be comforted.

It was what he was. Compassion. Gentleness. Empathy. The warmth of his embrace and the softness of his whispered reassurances, however, seemed like grains of sand beneath a tempestuous sea. They felt monumentally inconsequential. Placing one hand behind her head, he cradled her in an embrace that drew even greater spasms of emotion from her, as if now that the gate had opened the flood of pain she had kept stringently contained surged over her in an irrepressible torrent.

Her bitter crying brought tears to his eyes and he longed to soothe her misery in some better way, but holding her and gently reassuring her was all he could do. Pressing his cheek to the crown of her head, he closed his eyes. He wished with every ounce of strength he possessed he could enwrap her in the lavish consolation of his wings and soothe her with the lush balm of peace that was native to his realm, but he could not. All he could do was rock her tenderly and speak comfortingly as all the empathy within him poured out like velvet rain.

Her tears cut him like Phillippe's daggers. The sound of her sobs stole his breath. Not because he had never heard such pain before; he had on many occasions. As the Archangel of Mercy, he'd witnessed the cruelty of mankind more times than he wished to remember. He'd stood beside the lost and the lonely, the neglected and the shunned, but her crying was different. Her suffering pierced him in a way no other's ever had and he drew her closer against him in a desperate attempt to calm her.

As the embodiment of mercy, he felt emotion on a different level than most. The strength of his empathy connected him on a far more profound level than most humans. Because of her gentleness, her depth of mercy and compassion, she too felt this intense connection. She wept for herself, for the pain and violation she'd endured, but she wept out of an inability to fathom such cruelty, as well. It was beyond her comprehension, which is what made her so beautifully unique, so invaluable, and so vulnerable.

Opening his eyes, he looked down at her with the realization that the horrors yet to come, all that the final Horseman would unleash, could devastate her utterly. He knew the Horseman would try to claim her, if he could, in whatever way he could. Whether that meant harming her physically or mentally, he would try to destroy her because the Horseman was the embodiment of destruction. He was Death. It was his purpose.

Tzadkiel drew her close to him, crossing his arms behind her and closing his eyes with resolve that made the determination he'd needed to survive the last year seem insubstantial. Focusing his thoughts, he directed a message to the one who stood behind him, waiting, pacing like a cage beast.

"I am her sanctuary. I will not allow you to harm her."

Resonant laughter echoed in his mind. *"Release me or you shall know my wrath!"*

EPILOGUE

Traces of luminous light brightened the darkening sky as the stars in the distant heavens winked into sight. Cerulean sky transformed to indigo and the droning cadence of daytime insects was replaced with the harmonious serenade of crickets and katydids; their repeating lullaby irresistible. Weary from a day unlike any she'd passed in many years, Lourdes curled up on the blanket spread beneath the overarching boughs of the ancient oak and slipped into sleep, leaving Tzadkiel to watch the hours turn.

After the captivity and isolation he'd suffered, the freedom of breathing the sweet, night air and liberty to enjoy the music of the earth were blessings that could easily have overwhelmed him. Sitting back against the oak beneath which Lourdes slept, he gazed up at the expansive cosmos stretching overhead and sighed. The reconnection he felt to his native realm was far more significant than he anticipated, yet he was left with an awareness of singularity he never experienced in his former state. As perfected energy, he was part of everything and everything was part of him. Now, he was distinctive, set apart, and felt very much alone.

He'd felt a similar loneliness during the interminably long months of his captivity, but he truly had been alone then. Now, he was not. Lourdes was with him. She was right beside him, sleeping peacefully in his company, trusting him absolutely, but for reasons he could not comprehend he still felt alone. Looking down at her, he watched her sleep, noticing details he hadn't seen, or hadn't permitted himself to see, during the day.

She had unbraided her hair. The lengths of its gentle waves spilled over her shoulders and caressed her cheek in the whispers of the night breeze. The subtle light from the rising moon illuminated the oak grove in silvery shimmers that played across the rosy blush of her cheeks and lips. His gaze lingered over the softness of her ivory complexion and he struggled against the unexpected urge to touch her.

His thoughts spiraled.

The moment stretched out like a candle's flame and he lost track of time as he watched and considered. Considered what he had never considered before. Ever. He considered what it meant to be human. What it meant to be flesh and blood; singular, yet driven to find union with another. He considered how he would relate to her in a relationship where he had already promised to protect her from harm and be mindful of her needs. He considered what those needs would be and if he was capable of truly understanding them...

Here ends book one of the Mercy Series.
Tzadkiel and Lourdes' story continues:

Book Two of the Mercy Series- Clandestine
Book Three of the Mercy Series – Sanctuaire
Book Four of the Mercy Series – Precieux

Dear reader,

We hope you enjoyed reading *Misericorde*. Please take a moment to leave a review, even if it's a short one. Your opinion is important to us.

Discover more books by Cynthia A. Morgan at
https://www.nextchapter.pub/authors/cynthia-morgan-fantasy-author

Want to know when one of our books is free or discounted? Join the newsletter at
http://eepurl.com/bqqB3H

Best regards,

Cynthia A. Morgan and the Next Chapter Team

The story continues in:
Clandestine by Cynthia A. Morgan

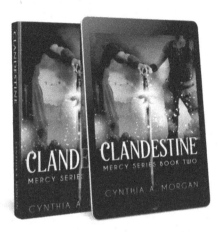

To read the first chapter for free, please head to:
https://www.nextchapter.pub/books/clandestine

The story continues in:

Claudestine by Gwilfer A. Morgan

To read the first chapter for free, please head to:
https://www.nickharter.pub/books/claudestine

ABOUT THE AUTHOR

Cynthia A. Morgan is an award-winning author; freelance writer and a member of the *Poetry Society of America* and *Artists for Peace*. Creator of the mythical realm of Jyndari and author of the epic fantasy *Dark Fey Trilogy*, Morgan's powerful story relates how the power of hope, acceptance and forgiveness can change the world, when positive action is taken to create change. The only way to achieve peace is to become peace.

Morgan is also the author of the popular blog *Booknvolume* where over 18K followers can explore Morgan's own brand of poetry, English Sonnets, musings about life, personal recipes, photography, book reviews and more.

Upcoming projects include a fictional drama in Regency Period England, a non-fiction exploration of the supernatural/paranormal and beliefs around the world, and a return to the realms of Dark Fey in a prequel/sequel.

Some of her other interests includes a deep love for animals and the environment. She is passionate about music and theatre, is frequently heard laughing and finds the mysteries of ancient times, spirituality, and the possibilities of life elsewhere in the cosmos intriguing. Morgan believes in the power of love, hope and forgiveness, all of which is reflected in her lyrically elegant writing style.

You can find Morgan through social media in the following places:

The Dark Fey Trilogy on Amazon: My Book
Blog / website: www.booknvolume.com
Author's Website: www.cynthiaamorganauthor.com
Amazon Author Page: Author.to/CAMorganAuthor
Twitter: https://www.twitter.com/MorganBC728
Facebook https://www.facebook.com/booknvolume
Pinterest: https://www.pinterest.com/creativiapub/
author-board-cynthia-a-morgan/
GoodReads: https://www.goodreads.com/author/
show/14174277.Cynthia_A_Morgan
Publisher's Author Page : https://www.creativia.org/
cynthia-morgan-fantasy-author.html

Misericorde
ISBN: 978-4-86745-765-8

Published by
Next Chapter
1-60-20 Minami-Otsuka
170-0005 Toshima-Ku, Tokyo
+818035793528

14th April 2021

CPSIA information can be obtained
at www.ICGtesting.com
Printed in the USA
LVHW041010060521
686676LV00006B/771

9 784867 457658